A WHISPER IN THE DARK

ELIZABETH S. DEVECCHI

Come find us!

a amazon.com/stores/author/B0BKQP8Z1Q
f facebook.com/WickedHousePublishing
X x.com/WickedHousePub
o instagram.com/wicked_house_publishing

For my husband and kids,
whose antics never fail to inspire my creativity.

"Dogs do speak,
but only to those who know how to listen."

- Orhan Pamuk

ONE

"Dammit, Alvis! You're going to get us both killed."

The large, cream-colored dog stood in the middle of the road, paws planted, refusing to move forward. Sarah, who was at the other end of the thick, braided, green-and-white leash gave a tug, but the dog countered by shifting his weight back until he was almost sitting, his collar threatening to slide up and over his head. She pulled a deep breath through her nose, then walked back toward him, brows furrowed. Raising a hand toward the driver of the minivan they were blocking, Sarah mouthed the word "sorry." With each step, the dog scooted backward toward the curb they had just left. When both dog and owner were back up on the sidewalk, the minivan continued on its way.

"What the heck, Alvis? Seriously, what the heck?" She sighed and stared down at the eighty-pound hound mix.

His head hung low, and his tail swayed from side to side as if directed by a soft, shifting breeze. He turned his dark, expressive eyes upward. They darted here and there, only occasionally locking on Sarah's, but never for more than a second or two.

"Oh, Alvis, I'm sorry. I know you have your reasons. Come here." She pointed to the ground in front of her and lightened the tone of her voice. "Come here. Come on. It's okay. I'm not mad."

Alvis hesitated. His tail lifted higher and wagged more decisively. He moved closer, looking up at Sarah as if in search of a sign she had truly forgiven him. When she reached down to pat him, his whole body wiggled and he sprung up like a jack-in-the-box to assail her with apology kisses. She caught his front paws with one arm and stroked the top of his head with her other hand.

"Okay, Alvis. Down. Let's not make another scene." She pulled her arm back, letting his front paws drop, and brushed soft beige hairs from her jeans. "We have to cross to get back home. Let's go!"

The second attempt to cross the street was even less successful than the first. This time Alvis thwarted the effort by laying down before they had even stepped off the curb, causing Sarah to lurch backward when the leash went taut.

"What the..." She walked back to the dog, who stood as soon as the leash went slack. "What is up with you?"

Alvis whimpered while she looked around trying to figure out what was spooking him. He was a quirky dog for sure, rescues often were, but she didn't see any of his usual triggers in the area. There weren't any plastic bags blowing about, or inflatable lawn decorations. They were on a quiet suburban street lined with mature shade trees and flanked along the way by neighborhoods and parks. It was about mid-morning, so the daily rush off to work and school had died down and only the occasional car went by. They had seen a few other people out walking, some with and some without dogs. Alvis had not shown the slightest hint of anxiety at any of these encounters. So far, the only other interruptions to their walk had been thanks to the occasional squirrel skittering by just out of the dog's reach and taunting from the trees above.

Sarah gave Alvis a pat on the head and took a step toward the road, this time focusing on his reaction. He looked across the street and once again braced his paws. Frustration knotted her shoulders, coiling them up her neck. She followed his gaze and rolled her eyes, letting her shoulders drop.

"Really? *That's* your problem? A storm drain? Since when?" They had walked that same route dozens of times since moving to the area and the dog had never so much as flinched at the sight of a storm drain before, at least not that she'd noticed. "Did someone show you the movie *It*?" She chuckled, making a mental note to include the reference later on, when she told her husband and the kids about Alvis's new fear.

It had required months of coaxing and training for the dog to master his fear of trash bins and kids on bicycles or skateboards, and now he was afraid of storm drains. Two steps forward, one step back was the story of their lives with Alvis since they had adopted him the year before. But they all adored him and he showered his family with total devotion.

"Okay, Alvis. I get it," she said, leading the dog down the sidewalk until he no longer resisted crossing the road.

For the rest of the four-mile walk, she was keenly aware of his efforts to avoid any and all storm drains. Each time they encountered one, he swung wide into the grass on the far side of the sidewalk. And he refused to cross the road anywhere near one of the gaping openings. It wasn't too much trouble now that she knew what to look for, but an annoyance for sure. She hadn't realized just how many drains there were in the neighborhood until then.

"I suppose you expect a thank you for drastically increasing my step count," she said when they snaked around what seemed like the millionth storm drain along their path.

Alvis looked up at her, ears flapping in the wind and tongue dangling and bouncing to the rhythm of his rapid panting. She smiled. He was an easy dog to read, at least. Nobody could ever say that they were unsure of Alvis's mood at any given time. All you had to do was look at his tail. When he was happy it curled into a tight coil up on his back, unfurling a bit with each degree of anxiety, and dropping straight down between his hocks when he was sad or overwhelmed. At the moment, he was sporting a tight curl.

When they turned onto the final stretch of road to the house, Alvis picked up his pace and the last of Sarah's tension slid away like leaves off autumn trees. She sighed. Only a couple more storm drains stood between her and a fresh cup of hot coffee. She was planning out the rest of the morning in her head when the neighbor, Ben Thomas, who lived on the opposite side of the street, stepped out his front door. He was holding a trowel in one hand and what looked like a handful of tulip bulbs in the other.

"Hey there, Sarah," he called out when he saw her.

She raised her hand and waved. "Kind of early to plant tulips. Sure you don't want to wait a bit?"

Ben paused for a moment, seeming to think this over. Then shrugged and set the bulbs and trowel down next to the front steps. "Mary used to take care of all that. Had them shipped in from overseas every year. These were in the garage. I guess she never got the chance to plant them, or maybe she just forgot about them when she got sick. I figured I would give it a shot."

Sarah pursed her lips, forcing them into a tight awkward smile. Her hand twisted around Alvis's leash. She never knew quite what to say when talking to someone who had lost a loved one. "Well, I'm sure they'll be lovely."

"Hope you guys had a nice walk. That wind has a bit of a chill to it."

She nodded, took a step, and opened her mouth to follow up on his welcome transition to a conversation about the weather, when the leash squeezed her hand like a boa constrictor. She looked back. Alvis stood frozen, his muscles taut and hackles up from the back of his neck all the way down to his tail, which had completely unfurled. Sarah scanned her surroundings, then walked back to him.

"What's up, Alvis?" She reached down to pat his head, but he dodged. He was staring at the neighbor, a low growl rumbling in his throat.

"Alvis. Knock it off. You know Mr. Thomas." She tried to get his attention, but the dog was laser focused on Mr. Thomas, his growl now clearly audible.

"I am so sorry. He's been acting quirky all morning. I'm not sure what's up with him." Sarah raised her free hand and hunched her shoulders, shaking her head.

Ben inched back toward his front door. He looked a bit unsure, but was smiling. "You never know what these shelter dogs have been through. No big deal."

Sarah clapped her hands and kissed at the dog. "Come on, Alvis! The house is right there. Want some snacks?"

At the word "snacks," Alvis shifted his gaze and his tail curl tightened, but a thick line of hair down the center of his back remained at attention. Before he could refocus on the neighbor, Sarah moved her body to block his view and held up a closed hand, as if something were clenched inside her fist.

"Let's get snacks, Alvis. Come on," she repeated several times until the dog walked with her in the direction of the house.

When she looked back across the street, Ben was nowhere to be seen.

"Good job, Alvis. Let's alienate the neighbors before we have the chance to really get to know them, why don't we?"

The dog, tail once again curled up against the soft, smooth fur on his back, looked up and tilted his head to the side.

LATER THAT EVENING, Alvis sat at attention by the table watching the family eat dinner.

"That's crazy," said Sarah's husband, Greg, after she recounted the story of her morning walk.

"That's Alvis!" Christina, their thirteen-year-old, reached out to pat the dog, grinning.

Alvis scooted closer to her, hoping for a handout.

"The storm drain thing is very Alvis. But I am a little concerned about the way he acted when he saw Mr. Thomas. We haven't lived here that long. I don't want to be known as the family with the vicious dog." Sarah shooed the dog back away from the table. "No table food for you, sir."

"Maybe Mr. Thomas is an enemy spy," said a voice from the other side of the table.

Christina looked over at her little brother. "You think everyone is a spy." She rolled her eyes.

"Well, Alvis hates that kid from the bus, and he's a total jerk. So, obviously, he has good judging."

Christina snorted. "Judgment, not judging, doofus."

Eleven-year-old Sam stuck his tongue out.

"That's enough, guys." Sarah glared at her daughter, then looked over at her husband. "Good judgment or not, Greg, maybe we should get him some more training."

"Alvis, the world's most expensive *free* dog." Her husband shook his head.

"Training is less expensive than a lawsuit, honey."

"This is true. See if you can find someone in the area. I'll ask around at work, too. I think I remember one of the guys in IT talking about having a Doberman or Rottweiler, or something."

Attention shifted away from Alvis, and the conversation turned to work, school, and other events of the day. And at the end of the meal, Greg got up and poured a couple cordial glasses of limoncello. Sarah directed the kids to clear the table.

"It's Sam's turn. I cleared by myself yesterday." The young girl folded her arms across her chest.

"That's because I had homework." Sam started chewing on the end of his thumbnail, a nervous habit that had evolved from his earlier days of thumb sucking.

"Enough. Sam, get your hand away from your mouth. You're going to ruin the nail. Christina, help your brother clear the table. Then, I want you both to load the dishwasher. If you hurry, you'll have time to watch TV before bedtime."

This last statement resulted in immediate cooperation from both kids, which she guessed would probably last right up to the moment they had to agree on something to watch. But, it was working for now.

"I need to talk to Dad. I don't want to hear any more fighting, or you'll have to surrender all electronics and go straight to bed when you finish clearing."

Sarah walked into the office at the front of the house, and Greg handed her a cordial glass.

"Did the driver's licenses come today?" he asked between sips of limoncello.

"Oh shoot. I forgot to grab the mail. Wait here and I'll go see."

She finished the contents of her glass and handed it to him. "I'll be right back for a refill."

When she walked to the front door, Alvis came bounding over and sat under a peg on the wall that held his leash. He looked up at her with clear expectations.

"Sorry, buddy. Not this time." She gave him a quick tap on the head. "This is a solo trip." She slipped out the door, making sure to pull it closed behind her before the dog could attempt to join her.

The night air was crisp and cool. A gorgeous harvest moon illuminated the sky. Sarah thought about ducking back into the house to grab her coat but knew that Alvis would be right there waiting. Besides, the mailbox was only a block and a half away, near the entrance to the neighborhood, and her sweatshirt was doing a good enough job at taking the edge off the cold. She pushed her hands into her pant pockets and continued down the driveway to the sidewalk.

A pleasant calm had taken hold in the neighborhood. She turned her arm and glanced down at her watch. It was 8:30 pm on a weekday. People were likely at home digesting, spending some family time together, or getting ready for the next work and school day.

She was a few steps away from the cluster of mailboxes when a sound caught her attention. It had not rained much the past month, yet the sound of rushing water was coming from a storm drain inlet a few steps away.

It was more of a feeling, really, thanks to an inner-ear condition called SCDS. Not only was she privy to an array of inner sounds most people could not hear, such as her eyes moving in their sockets or her tongue gently gliding across the backs of her teeth, but there were certain outside noises that hummed through her like a warm wind on bare skin. She'd had it since birth, so it was her *normal*. Sarah felt that the people who suddenly found themselves in this world were much less fortunate. Aside from the occasional vertigo, she got by.

She closed her eyes, the hypnotic echoes traveling just under her skin, winding through her muscles, deep into her ears. Without the background hum of traffic on the nearby interstate, new sounds emerged. She stood still, taking in the night chorus. A bat squeaked above her, and leaves rustled where squirrels cozied into their nests high in the trees for the night. Under all this, the caressing whispers of motion rising from the opening in the curb rushed up to meet her, washed through her, bumping up goose pimples along the way.

Ok, Alvis, she thought. *I can see how that might creep you out. It almost sounds like a secret conversation, a convention of dark hidden creatures. Sewer Dogs, perhaps?*

Her grandfather's bogeymen of choice. The ones whose lust for blood and anger kept her from sneaking out at night and inspired a knack for keeping her emotions under control. *Watch your sass and keep those hateful eyes to yourself, little lady. There are creatures out there that'll suck the rage from you like sweet tea through a straw.*

Sarah pushed down the memory and opened her eyes, laughter puffing from her nose. *Perhaps I have been reading a few too many Koontz books,* she thought.

Still, she knew the dog's hearing was much better than her own and if for some reason the drains were carrying more water than usual, it might explain Alvis's new fear. Which didn't mean she had any clue as to how to address it. She would bring it up to the trainer once they found one. Her left hand fumbled around in her pocket until she found the mailbox key and inserted it into box 2A.

TWO

The elderly man sat in his family room, an imposing figure nested deep into his favorite recliner. In his lap, he cradled a framed photograph. Exhaustion hung on him like a weighted blanket. He longed to find a way back to the day the photo was taken. Back to a time when Mary was by his side. She smiled up at him from the checkered picnic blanket he'd spread for her many years ago. A blue silk scarf held her wavy, often unruly, auburn hair in place despite the wind, which had succeeded in turning up a corner of the blanket in front of her. She was holding her skirt down with one hand and trying to push the corner back with the other, tickled by the fruitless-ness of her efforts to keep things in place. They were happy. And now she was gone.

"The neighbor's dog doesn't seem to like me, love. Seems I don't have your knack for creatures."

It was his habit to talk to Mary through this particular photo. He had hundreds more, but this one was so *real*. It was taken in a moment of bliss, and there was motion to it. His thumb brushed the glass, and he imagined reaching in to help her tame the blanket, to participate once more in that magical, innocent day. It was taken before their first move, before things became complicated, before the break-in and the horror that ensued. It was taken before he fully understood their responsibilities, *his* responsibilities.

"Maybe he senses something. Maybe he knows I'm tainted. You always said that animals can read us better than we know. He seemed okay with me the last time we met... before." He shook his head, smoothing his eyebrows with his index finger and thumb, the way one might rub a lucky rabbit's paw.

"I'm sorry. You know I am. But, if you were here... just you... you would understand that I did what I had to do. Without you, without Princess, I wouldn't know what to do if they'd refused to leave, if I was unable to chase them away. I'm too tired to pick up and move again and it wouldn't be the same without you. They won't follow me. Besides, I like it here. We have nice neighbors. You should have seen all the sweets and casseroles they brought when you had to leave me. They still make sure my pantry is stocked and help with the yard, too." He smiled, his index finger circling her face, caressing the glass above her cheek. "You always did know how to choose the best places."

The corners of his mouth quivered, then surrendered to a frown. "I couldn't just leave them with our problems. It wouldn't be fair. It needed to stop."

Ben stood and walked toward the picture window, its sill dulled by dust. He moved the shade just enough to peek outside, before directing his attention back to the photograph.

"There's a new family across the street, you know. You would love them. Their kids are always outside catching critters, snakes and toads and things. Not attached to the phones and the games like little zombies. You would love them, and I know they would love you... if you were here." He brought the frame up to his chest and embraced it. Gentle sobs bubbled up from his core until his eyes were wet with tears.

He'd felt such anger when she passed, she and her Princess. And, going through the boxes in their attic, stumbling through memories of their time together, had been like a match to kindling. He wasn't an inherently angry person, even in the most frustrating of times. It was one of the things Mary had loved most about him. She told him so, often. After a child-hood rife with horror, she'd needed her "big, gentle Ben." But the thought of having had to share her, together with the shame of feeling relief, however slight that feeling was, had pushed him to do something he hadn't thought possible. He had betrayed her trust... gone back on his word.

He settled back into his chair, memories rolling through his mind like Super 8 film projected onto a wall, then drifted off thinking of their days together. His mind wandering from dreams of the good times he'd had with Mary down somber paths, thick with fear. Paths fraught with gruesome scenes of sacrifice, dark bargains struck to insure their continued journey together, a lonesome trio.

THREE

Sarah cracked her eyelids open and lay still, wondering what had pulled her out of a pleasant dream involving beaches, margaritas, and dolphins. Her mom-hearing kicked into high gear, dragging her the rest of the way to reality. She stilled her eyes to silence their whooshing only to have another faint whooshing replace it. This one she recognized to be the refrigerator water dispenser. She breathed in through her nose, blew the last of her slumber out through her lips, and slid out of bed, taking care not to wake her husband. On the way to the door, she slipped a terrycloth robe from the bedpost and put it on. Alvis, forever her shadow, rose from his dog bed in the corner of the room and followed close behind.

"Can't sleep?" She walked over and sat next to Sam at the kitchen counter.

He was seated on one of the stools, nursing a glass of water. The microwave clock cast an eerie blue beam onto his cheek. It was just after three o'clock in the morning. Sarah sat, and Sam leaned his head against her arm, reaching down with his free hand to pat the dog.

"Can I stay home from school? Can you homeschool me?"

Sarah caressed the top of his head, sculpting his wavy chestnut hair with the tips of her fingers, as if prepping him for a family portrait.

"Why, buddy? Are you having trouble at school? We haven't been here very long. If you stop going to school, you might miss out on meeting a new best friend."

He sniffled and nestled closer.

"I don't think that's gonna happen," he said, his voice just above a whisper.

"Of course it is. You are one of the coolest kids I know. There is nobody on earth who knows more about creepy crawly creatures than you do."

He pulled back his head and looked up at her. "Nobody cares about that stuff, Mom. The other kids think I'm weird... and stupid."

"Who thinks you're weird and stupid? Is someone bothering you at school? If someone is bothering you, you need to tell us." Sarah cupped a hand under Sam's chin.

"It's nothing," he said, pulling back. "Mostly the kid up the street. Mostly just on the bus. Please don't say anything. It'll get worse if you do. He just says mean things sometimes. I can ignore him."

"If he's bothering you, then we need to tell someone, sweetie."

"No. I can wear my headphones and listen to music. Please, Mom."

The mama bear in her was rising up, trying to take over, but she knew Sam was right. If she stepped in too soon or in the wrong way, it could make things worse. She'd been a kid once, had her own bullies. She pushed her bear back into hibernation.

"Well, you try the headphones thing, but promise me you will let me know if he keeps bothering you."

He nodded.

"And remember, there are a whole lot of kids in your school that are looking for friends, same as you. You just have to meet each other. Give it some time. Now, we'd better both get back to sleep if we want to be able to function tomorrow, or today, rather."

Sam yawned. He took a sip of water, slid down from the stool, and placed his glass in the sink. When he walked past his mother, she reached out and pulled him in for a bear hug and a kiss on the forehead before standing up and directing him back to his room.

"Hang in there, buddy. Things will get better."

Sam nodded without turning his head and trudged away.

Before heading back to bed, Sarah warmed a cup of water in the microwave and grabbed a chamomile teabag from the pantry. She plopped it in and let it steep, warming her hands on the outside of her mug. A few drops of honey, and her best hope for getting back to sleep was complete. She wandered down the hall toward the office, guided by the soft green glow of the outlet nightlights, which stretched out before her like runway lights. The faint sound of an ambulance drifted in. Their house was just a few miles from the local fire station, so it wasn't unusual to hear a siren or two during the night. Sarah reached out and tilted the top slats of the plantation shutters to peek out the window.

A shadow slid across the front lawn close enough to send her heart flip-flopping into her ribs. She ducked to the side, sending a wave of chamomile over the top of the mug and onto her hand. Alvis growled.

"Shit!" She set the mug on the sill and wiped her hand on the front of her robe. It hurt, but the burn didn't look serious. "It's fine, Alvis. Sit."

After scolding herself for being so jumpy, she leaned forward to take another look, shushing the dog and taking care to stay just to the side of the window. Despite clear skies and a glorious full moon illuminating the neighborhood with the tint of an old black-and-white film, she saw no sign of the shadow or anything that could have caused it. The world lay still. Sarah was sliding the shutters back down when a light went on across the street, in Ben Thomas's house.

She tilted the slats until only the slightest opening remained, enough to peer out but not enough to be seen, or at least she hoped not. After the incident earlier that day with Alvis, she had no desire to have the label "nosey neighbor" added to "vicious dog owner." Though, at the moment, the overwhelming urge was to be just that, a nosey neighbor. The Thomas home had roller shades on the front windows. With the light on in the home, Sarah could see forms shifting on the other side of the ivory-colored vinyl, though it was impossible to make out what they were.

Ben Thomas, she thought. *Ben Thomas is what they are, stupid. He is probably up for a drink or a snack. Poor guy said he has trouble sleeping since his wife passed.*

The thought of Ben's wife jogged a sense of embarrassment, which heated her cheeks.

Spying on an old man in the middle of the night. You have reached a new low, Sarah. A new and humiliating low.

She was about to close the shutter the rest of the way when

the front door of the Thomas house opened. Ben stood in the doorway. He looked around, pausing to stare directly at the window where Sarah stood frozen, her breath trapped in her throat. There was no way he could see her. The lights in her home were off and the plantation shutters were almost completely closed. Still, she did not dare move. Maybe he was just looking in her general direction. Even with the moon as bright as it was, there were details she couldn't make out. Maybe it just seemed like he was staring right at her.

Don't be an idiot. There is no way he can see through wooden shutters.

Sarah willed him to move, to do something, all the while allowing herself only shallow, sparse breaths. Her hand was clenched around Alvis's collar so tightly her fingers were numb.

"Please don't bark, buddy," she whispered.

A few moments later, which seemed an eternity to Sarah, Ben stepped out onto the front stoop wearing a bathrobe and large, oddly-shaped, oversized slippers. Once he was down the steps, he looked around at the ground, then reached down to pick up the trowel he had set down earlier. He knelt on the walk that led down to the sidewalk and began to dig. Sarah watched him dig five shallow holes, then go back to the front steps and fetch the bulbs which she had commented on that afternoon. He placed one in each hole, giving each a gentle pat after filling the earth in around them. When he was done planting, he sat on his front stoop and admired his work. It looked like he was talking to someone, gesticulating as if in an animated discussion, though there was nobody with him.

Poor guy. He's probably talking to his wife.

Another pang of guilt about spying shot through her, but

she was afraid if she finished closing the shutters now, he might notice the movement. She had decided to leave things as they were and to slink back away down the hall with the dog, when Ben stood and turned toward his front door. On the way inside, he pulled something from his pocket and tossed it behind the bushes that lined the front of his house, concealing the foundation.

Maybe he's feeding the rabbits to keep them away from the bulbs, she thought on her way down the hall toward the bedroom, wiggling the pins and needles from her fingers.

"And maybe it's none of my goddamn business," she said to Alvis, who answered with a whine and a head tilt.

FOUR

The sounds of children on the sidewalk out front woke Ben from the deep sleep that had finally welcomed him after hours of restlessness the night before. He opened his eyes, ran his palms over his beard-stubbled face, and stretched. A faint thud sounded on the carpet below. He had fallen asleep in his chair again, and after a moment of confusion, he realized both where he was and the source of the thud. He sat up and leaned over the side of the chair, running his hand along the carpet until he found the framed photograph of his beloved Mary.

"Sorry, sweetie," he said, checking for damage, relieved to find none.

The first beams of the rising sun peeked around the sides of the family room window shades. Ben climbed out of his recliner and walked over to place the frame on the bookshelf where he kept it with four other photos of his wife, arranged in a half-circle. He had completed the make-shift shrine by centering her favorite scented candle in front of the images.

Directly behind the candle, the darkest of the group, was the only picture he had of Princess. He picked it up and examined it. He hadn't meant to include Princess. In fact, he had only noticed that Princess was there after Mary's passing when he was going through their photos, reminiscing. It was a picture of Mary in front of their new house—this house. They'd had some car trouble on move-in day and ended up arriving well after the realty agent's office had closed. The agent had left the key hidden in the bushes near the front stoop so they could let themselves in.

The move, ten years ago, was yet another attempt at a new beginning. Another chance to tweak their habits so they could try to put down some long-desired roots, this time successfully. Now, looking at the picture, the day rushed back to his mind, the slightest details occupying his thoughts as if only a few days had passed. He closed his eyes and relived their arrival.

"Ben, hurry. I want to get inside to set up the air mattress and find a place for Princess to settle. It's getting late and she's disoriented." Mary was holding the suitcase containing some bedding and a couple changes of clothes each. The moving truck would arrive the next day with the rest of their belongings.

"Not before I take your picture," said Ben, waving the camera. *"It's a tradition. New town, new start."*

"It's so dark. It's not going to come out. We can take it tomorrow. Besides, we're all tired and you know I don't like it when you aren't in pictures with me."

"Humor me, honey. I don't want pictures of myself. I want to fawn over the gorgeous photos I take of you."

She giggled and swatted at him with her free hand.

"Well, I need pictures to fawn over, as well."

"You don't have time to fawn. You never stay still enough to even look at any of our pictures. When was the last time you took two seconds to indulge in some relaxation?"

He reached out and took hold of her hand, then raised the camera once more, holding it directly in front of his pleading eyes.

Mary sighed and set the suitcase on the stoop.

"My big, gentle Ben. You do those sweet eyes and you know I can't say no. Make it quick."

She straightened out the beige peacoat she always wore for travel in cooler months, and positioned herself at the top of the steps.

Neither one of them had noticed Princess creep closer to the stoop through the bushes, blood-matted hair still clinging to the skin at the edges of her jaw. A bad tire on their old VW camper-van had made them vulnerable. Princess had assured their arrival.

BEN SHUDDERED, opened his eyes, and examined the resulting snapshot. There was Mary in her peacoat, suitcase set beside her, smiling that radiant smile she claimed to reserve only for him. And, if you knew where to look, and what you were looking for... there was Princess.

That day had been rough on Princess. Moving to unfamiliar environments always was. He wasn't sure if Princess was capable of feeling guilt or anything similar, but liked to imagine that she at least understood she was the reason for their frequent moves. He would never know for certain, though, because she did not communicate with him like she did with Mary. Maybe what Mary had claimed was true, and she wasn't able. But Ben suspected it was more a matter of Princess not wishing to do so. From the very beginning he understood that theirs was a relationship of mutual tolerance centered around their shared adoration of Mary.

When Mary grew ill, Princess suffered, too. Mary had assured him that Princess would not outlive her, could not. But that had its own consequences. In all honesty, Ben didn't want to outlive Mary either, and he wanted no part of the bargain with Princess, but he had made Mary a promise. And she knew him to be a man of his word.

Voices from outside drew his attention once more. Now that he was fully awake, he noticed a tone of distress in one. He walked over and opened the shade on one of the front windows. Two boys stood on the sidewalk just a few steps away from his yard. They both wore backpacks and were most likely headed for the bus stop. The smaller boy, who was visibly upset, was the youngest member of the new family across the street, Stan, or Sam, he couldn't remember which. The other one, Tyler, lived a ways up the road, in the direction of the stop. His mother liked to drop by to chat and often brought Ben groceries. He observed the two to get a better idea of what was happening.

"What's wrong, weirdo? Didn't you hear me talking to you? It's rude not to answer when someone is talking to you, dumbass." Tyler was standing very close to the smaller boy, raising his hands in a menacing way, inches from the boy's face.

"Knock it off, Tyler. I just want to go to the bus stop. I'm not bothering you. Why can't you just leave me alone?" said the smaller boy, taking a step back and putting in some earphones in an attempt to deescalate the situation.

From behind the window, Ben could see tears welling in his eyes.

Tyler let him take a few steps past, then grabbed the earphones by the cord and pulled. They popped out of Sam's ears and detached from whatever they had been connected to in the boy's pocket when he spun around.

"Maybe you'll listen to me now," said Tyler, holding the earphones up and swinging them around.

"Give them back!"

Despite an obvious disadvantage, the owner of the earphones reached out to grab them. In doing so, his hand brushed the side of Tyler's head, sending the larger boy into a rage. He was forming his hand into a fist when Ben burst out onto the front stoop.

"Anything I can help you boys with?" Ben was a large, imposing man, and must have seemed even more so from the top of the steps.

Tyler swung the earphones and flung them into one of the trees at the edge of the yard. Then he took off up the road toward the bus stop. The other boy stood with his head tipped skyward, staring at the branches that now held his earphones captive.

"You okay?" asked Ben. The boy nodded.

"Is it Stan or Sam? I'm sorry, but I am absolutely horrible with names." His gentle voice distracted the boy's attention away from the tree.

"Sam, sir. I'm sorry, Mr. Thomas, sir."

"Sorry for what?"

Sam pointed at the earphones.

"Nothing to be sorry for. You didn't put them there. Would you like me to get them for you?"

The boy pulled a phone from his pocket and looked at the time.

"I'm gonna miss the bus if I don't hurry."

"What if I give you a ride to the stop?" Ben pointed to the little Chevy parked in his driveway. "Then, I'll come back home, fish those doohickies out of my tree, and have them waiting here for you when you get home."

Sam looked at his feet, brows furrowed.

"I'm not supposed to ride with strangers," he said.

"You could run and ask your mom if it's okay."

By the look on the boy's face, Ben gathered he had no desire to let his mom in on what had happened a few moments prior.

"Well, how about you run and try to catch the bus. In the meantime, I'll change out of my jammies, pull out my ladder, and shimmy up to retrieve your headphones. If you miss the bus, you can knock on my door and I'll give you a ride to school. If you want, we can type 911 in on your phone and you can hold it so you can push the call button if I try to kidnap you."

A reluctant grin crept across the boy's face.

"In any case, you can swing by my place after school and I will hand over your property. Sound good?"

Sam looked him over, then nodded.

"Sounds good."

He took off running up the street toward the stop. The boy had already turned the corner when Ben heard the unmistakable hiss of school bus brakes.

He went back into his house to change out of his pajamas, happy he wouldn't have to drive the kid, Sam, to school. Word on the street was that the school carpool line was an absolute nightmare. He heard about it every time Evelyn Whistler,

Tyler's mom, came by to ask if he needed anything from the store.

Fait accompli, he headed into the garage to get the ladder. It had been quite a while since he'd needed a ladder. He would have to shift a few things to get to it. So, Ben set to work moving boxes and repositioning yard tools, inching closer to the wall where the ladder hung, draped in cobwebs. He lifted a bag of potting soil Mary used for her starter plants, and a shadow scurried to the back of the garage into an area still dense with boxes.

The bag dropped out of his hands and the soil spilled out onto the floor.

"Dammit!"

The lone garage light flickered for a moment like it was considering going out, but it held fast. Ben looked in the direction the shadow had gone. He told himself it was certainly a mouse, a rat even, but a part of him was afraid it might be something else.

"Get out of here. Shoo," he hissed, spittle misting the air and catching the light. There was a faint scratching noise from behind a stack of boxes.

He chided himself for being so jumpy and paranoid, then closed his eyes and took a few deep breaths through his nose, letting each one leave through his mouth as if he were blowing out candles. It was a trick he'd learned from a neighbor after the funeral.

The scratching came again, sounding almost like a whisper. Mary used to talk to him about whispers.

"They sound like nothing you've ever heard," she'd said. "They soothe me, Ben. They make me feel safe and powerful."

"I thought I was the one who made you feel safe," he

always retorted, lifting his arms to make whatever muscles he could muster, and turning the conversation away from things he preferred not to discuss. Things he feared would make him see her in a different light.

Ben covered his ears and walked over to the opener switch near the door to the house. He pressed the button with his elbow and the door went up, letting in the morning light.

"There is nothing for you here." His voice intertwined with the creaking and grinding of the rising door.

"Mary is gone and there is nothing for you here," he said, feeling silly, like a child rubbing a rabbit's foot... or whatever they did nowadays for luck.

He decided to leave the door open for the rest of the day, porch pirates be damned. Hopefully, the bright sunlight would convince whatever it was to leave. He walked back to the bag of spilt soil and cleaned the mess he had made. When he moved the last box between himself and the ladder, a beam of light showed through a hole in the wall where it met the floor. After fishing the boy's headphones from the tree, his next task would be to patch the wall.

Ben carried the ladder over to the tree and set it up. A movement from across the street caught his eye. There in the window of Sam's house, he could see the dog staring at him, hackles raised.

FIVE

Sam could admit when he was wrong, at least to himself. Alvis must have had his wires crossed, as Dad liked to say. The old guy across the street actually seemed pretty nice. If he hadn't come bursting outside, bathrobe flapping in the wind, Tyler would have flattened him. Grabbing for the earbuds was a stupid move. But thanks to Mr. Thomas, he was going to get them back when he got home.

The ride to school was tense. All the other kids from the stop were already on the bus when Sam got there. Apparently, Tyler had not expected him to have the guts to ride after what had happened. What Tyler didn't know was that Sam found the thought of having to tell his mother why he missed the bus and risking her escalating the situation much scarier. He sat at the very front of the bus, where nobody dared cause trouble, thanks to Ms. Liz, their ex-marine driver.

The moment the door swung open at the school, he hopped off and disappeared into a sea of fellow middle schoolers, ducking around a corner when Tyler called out, "See you on the bus ride home, weirdo!"

Thankfully, that turned out to be an empty threat. Tyler had gotten himself into trouble during school and had to stay after. When Sam saw his nemesis walk into the principal's office after the last bell rang, he did a subtle fist pump and turned to head toward the bus ramp, knocking into a girl wearing a dark green denim coat and carrying a small stack of books. The book at the top slipped off the pile and fell to the ground.

"Hey, be careful," she said, pushing the fallen book against the wall with her foot before it could get trampled by the herd of kids rushing down the hallway toward freedom.

"Sorry," said Sam. He reached down, picked up the book, and brushed it off. "*Snakes of Australia*. Cool book. Most of the snakes there are venomous, you know." He handed it to her.

"Yeah, there are tons of deadly creatures over there." She balanced the book back on top of the stack. "I wrote a paper about them. I have to give a presentation tomorrow."

"Cool."

He looked at the spines of the other books she was carrying. They were all books about snakes. Other than his older sister, Sam didn't know any girls who had any kind of interest in snakes. The girls in his classes were usually talking about clothes and TV shows he had never heard of.

"You ride my bus," she stated, her tone matter-of-fact.

His face smoothed into a blank stare. He had not noticed her on the bus, though in his defense, he spent most of his time on the bus looking out the window, trying not to get noticed himself.

"Oh. Hi," he mumbled, not sure what else to say about that.

"Your name is Sam, right? I remember because my name is Sam, too, but I'll bet yours doesn't stand for Samantha."

He shook his head.

"Okay, well, we should probably get to the bus before it leaves without us."

He nodded.

"You don't talk much, do you?"

He chewed his bottom lip like a piece of Red Vine licorice.

"Never mind. Let's go. My mom will kill me if I miss the bus again."

They took off toward the bus ramp, slowing to a speed-walk when a teacher told them not to run, and hopped onto the bus just as Ms. Liz was grabbing the lever to close the doors.

"I've got to sit with my little brother and his friend. See you later." She sat in one of the seats toward the front. Sam nodded and walked back further until he found an empty seat.

At each stop, he peeked over the top of the seat in front of him to see if his new friend got off the bus. If he could call her that, a *friend*, that is. But as it turned out, his stop came before hers. When he passed her seat, he gave a subtle glance to the side. She waved, setting off fireworks that buzzed from his toes to the top of his head.

"SAM, IS THAT YOU?"

"Yeah, Mom." He tossed his book bag onto the mudroom floor and wandered into the kitchen where his mother was seated at the table in front of her laptop.

Her right hand was resting on the keyboard, while the left

gripped and massaged the back of her neck. She cocked her head; a loud pop followed.

"How was school, sweetie? Any trouble with anyone?" She closed the computer and motioned for him to come sit.

"Nope. Everything was fine." His mom leaned forward, eyes squinted, as if he were an insect under a magnifying glass.

"Really, Mom. It was fine," he said, trying to convert the stupid grin that had been glued to his face since the wave, to something a little more neutral.

"Come, sit, and I'll get some cookies from the pantry." She patted the seat of the chair next to her and stood.

"Actually, can I run across the street for a minute? I was tossing my earphones around and they got stuck in a tree. Mr. Thomas said he'd get them for me."

"Mr. Thomas, the enemy spy?" She smirked and tussled his hair. He shrugged, then patted down the cowlick on the top of his head.

"Okay, maybe I was wrong about him being an enemy spy. Can I go? And after, can I go down to the stream to see if the turtles are out?"

He tilted his head down and to the side, raised his eyebrows, and pulled the bottom right corner of his lip between his teeth. He thought about bringing his hands up together in begging position, but didn't want to seem too desperate. For now, stage one puppy dog eyes should suffice.

"Do you have any homework?"

He was ready for this, and his face shifted to a more confident expression.

"Nope. I finished it at school."

"Make sure you put your phone in a plastic baggie, so it doesn't get wet. And if I call or text, you need to answer right away." The squinty eyes were back but seemed softer now that they were most likely only searching for acknowledgment.

"Yes, ma'am." Sam held his hand to his forehead in an exaggerated military salute. Then he spun around on one heel, almost falling as he took off toward the door.

"Okay, wise guy. Just don't be too long. You still have some chores to do around the house."

SIX

Sam walked across to Mr. Thomas's front door. He reached toward the doorbell, hesitating at the sound of rustling in the bushes. He was bending down to see if there was a rabbit, or better yet a snake, when the door opened. He straightened.

"Hey there, Sam. Perfect timing. I was just coming out to check on the bulbs I planted. Hang on. I'll grab your headphones."

Mr. Thomas disappeared into his house, returning a few minutes later with Sam's earphones. He opened the storm door, stepped out, and handed them to the boy.

"Where are my manners?" he said, raising a palm to his forehead. "Would you like some cookies or something? I have those ones with the chocolate stripes on top in the pantry. Mrs. Thomas was the one with the manners and social awareness for the both of us, I'm afraid."

"That's okay," said Sam. "I'm not really hungry. I'm going down to the stream to see if the turtles are out."

"Oh. That sounds exciting. Maybe you can stop by and show me one if you find any?"

Sam scanned the neighbor's face, trying to determine if Mr. Thomas was really interested. He looked sincere, but you never knew with adults.

"Well, I don't usually catch them, but I guess I could bring one by if I do."

"I would appreciate that. It's been a long time since I've seen a turtle up close. Mrs. Thomas and I used to do a lot of camping. She loved turtles." He sighed and looked at the ground.

"She did? Did she like frogs, too? How about snakes? Not a lot of ladies like snakes."

The old man grinned. "Oh, Mary loved all kinds of critters. We even had a pet snake for a while."

Sam's eyes widened and his jaw dropped. "Really? What kind? What happened to it?"

"It was a king snake named Larry, and it escaped from its terrarium right before we moved away from that house. Try as we might, we could not find him anywhere. Who knows, Larry may still be roaming that basement." He laughed.

"They can live to be thirty, you know."

"Well, shoot. Maybe I should call those people up and let them know."

At this, the boy snorted a laugh through his nose.

"He probably got out of the house just as soon as he could. They aren't very aggressive anyways."

"You sure do know a lot about snakes," said Mr. Thomas.

Sam decided his neighbor sounded impressed, not patronizing. He nodded.

"Hey, are you having trouble with Tyler, from up the street? I know his mom. I could have a word with her."

The boy's smile evaporated.

"No, sir. It's fine. Please don't say anything."

"I won't if you don't want me to. But don't let him bother you. He may be bigger than you, but it wasn't too long ago he was sucking his thumb and dragging around a little blue stuffed bunny. He's not so tough." Half a smile crept back. "Oh, and he is terrified of snakes. I've seen him skedaddle pretty darn fast when a garden snake slithered in front of him. And that wasn't even that long ago."

"Really?"

"My point being, sometimes people just put on an act because deep down they're afraid. Remember that."

Sam nodded.

"Happy hunting and feel free to ring my doorbell anytime, especially if you have creatures you want to show off."

"I will."

The stream was about three blocks away from his home. Sam could have walked it blindfolded. From the very first day they moved into the neighborhood, it had become his favorite place. There were plenty of fish, turtles, snakes, and frogs. He'd even caught a few crawfish.

Sometimes he could still convince Christina to come with him. She used to love catching creatures just as much as he did. But lately, she had made some new friends, and there was this boy she liked, Steve. Anyhow, the more time she spent with them, the less she had for adventures... and for Sam.

Maybe I can come here with Samantha, if she doesn't live too far away, he thought while flipping some rocks to see what he could find underneath. He found himself grinning at the thought of finally having a friend of his own.

"Samantha," he said, trying out the name. "Sam."

"What did you say? Do you have a *girlfriend*, weirdo? Or is your real name Samantha?" The voice came from behind him.

Before Sam could turn around, something slammed against his back and shoved him forward. He stumbled into the stream, extending both hands to stop his fall. Two threads of blood appeared under the clear cold water where his hands had come to rest against the rocks at the bottom of the stream. He stood and examined the gashes on his palms. When he looked down, he noticed a good-sized cut on his left knee as well. The frigid water or his anger, or maybe both, dulled any sensations of pain.

"Careful. It's really slippery here, weirdo. Oh no. Did you fall down? Should I go get your mommy? Or maybe your girl-friend, *Samantha*, can come kiss it and make it better." Tyler was making kissing sounds and laughing. Then his face turned serious. "Come on out. We're not done."

Sam stood still and silent, hands clasped together to slow the bleeding. He glared at Tyler from the water, his shoes suctioned into the silty muck of the stream bed. Anger, fear, and frustration jabbed at his heart as if it were a piñata, and he felt the back of his throat closing, trapping them all inside.

"I said come out, loser."

A small snake slithered by at the edge of the bank between them, most likely disturbed by Sam's fall. Tyler took a step back, fear flashing across his face before he could force it back into a scowl.

"That was for hitting me in the face this morning." Tyler's pocket buzzed and he reached in to pull out his phone. He glanced at the screen and back at Sam, who was starting to feel a little woozy. "I have more important things to do. Enjoy your bath, weirdo."

Tyler walked up the street toward his house. It wasn't terribly cold out, but wet clothes and a cool breeze started Sam shivering. He looked at his palms. The right one was bleeding steadily, while the left had all but stopped. He reached his left hand into his right pocket and pulled out his phone, still sealed in its plastic baggie. It didn't look broken, no cracks on the screen.

When Tyler was finally out of sight, Sam worked his way out of the water, taking care not to step on any of the rocks with a green algae sheen. He did not want to fall again. He reached his hands back into the stream to wash away the dirt and sand, then pulled the sleeves of his shirt over his palms as bandages. He blotted at his left knee and saw that the bleeding there had slowed to a tiny, firm bubble of red that should soon harden into a scab.

Once he had checked himself over, tears began to warm his cheeks. He tried but couldn't stop the cascade. The wounds on his hands and knee didn't even hurt that much, but he was so angry. Why wouldn't Tyler just leave him alone? The more he thought about it, the faster the tears streaked down both cheeks and the more helpless he felt.

I understand.

His breath caught in his throat for a moment. He turned his head, aiming an ear in what he thought was the direction from which the whisper had come.

I understand.

He tried to pinpoint the source of the whispering, but nobody else was there.

I know how you feel. I am alone.

There it was again, from behind him. He spun around and saw only the culvert that channeled the stream into a pond across the road. He had walked a short way into it once with Christina after each had dared the other. It smelled horrible and they had both run back out when Christina's flashlight revealed a water moccasin floating in the shallow water.

He approached the opening and peered inside. "Hello? Is someone in there?" he asked, his voice barely audible. "Careful. There are snakes in there, the venomous kind."

I understand, it said again.

Only, now Sam wasn't actually sure if he was hearing the words or feeling them. They sounded like a cool breeze shaped into soft words, a sourceless breath entering his head and echoing through his mind. Was it coming from the culvert? It had to be.

"Who are you? Are you stuck in there?"

I am alone. I have no friends. I am afraid.

This time the voice had direction, a source... the culvert.

"Do you need me to get help for you? I can go get my mom."

No. Please. You cannot tell anyone I am here. They won't understand. They'll be afraid. The voice paused. *Are you afraid?*

Sam thought about it. He knew he probably should be afraid. He hadn't actually seen any horror films. His parents said he was too young. But Christina had told him about some pretty scary ones. And he'd heard other kids talking about them at school. This seemed like the perfect setup for some murderous creature to snatch him. Still, his instincts told him that whatever was in there did not want to hurt him, that it wanted to be friends. It sounded, no, it felt like it was afraid and in need.

"I'm not afraid of you," he answered, honestly.

"Sam! Where are you?" Christina appeared near the stream where Sam had been originally, his usual spot. "Mom has been calling you. You need to come home. It's time for dinner." She looked upset. "Why didn't you answer?"

Sam looked at the culvert and back at his sister. The whispers had ceased. She probably scared whatever it was away. He thought about telling her.

"You didn't go in there, did you?" She came closer, examining her little brother and pointing to the culvert. "What the hell happened to you? Did you fall into the stream? Mom is going to freak out."

"Please, don't tell her or Dad. They won't let me come by myself anymore, and you're always busy. Please?"

She looked him up and down, shaking her head.

"You don't think they're going to notice? You're a mess."

"You can sneak me in," he pleaded. "I'll change upstairs and put on some Band-Aids."

He showed her his hands.

"Jesus, Sam! What the hell?" Her eyebrows leapt up toward her hairline.

"Can you help me clean up?"

Christina took a deep breath and exhaled loudly. Then she placed her hand on Sam's shoulder, looking down at him with an air of older sister wisdom.

"Fine. I'll sneak you in and help you clean up. But, when your hands are better you have to help with my chores on top of doing your own for two weeks. Deal?"

He smiled and gave her a hug, taking care not to touch her with his bloody hands.

"Thank you."

"Whatever. Gimme a sec to text Mom that I found you."

After she hit *send*, they started toward the house.

"Did you find any interesting creatures?"

It was obvious to him that the question was an attempt to distract him, but its effect was the opposite and he struggled over how much he should say about his little adventure.

He bit his bottom lip and decided maybe he would tell her about the culvert another time. "Oh, just a little water snake and a couple of frogs."

SEVEN

Christina never stayed mad at him for very long. She smiled and chatted, keeping his mind off of his wounds while they walked home from the stream.

"Hey, guess what?" she said. "I got a callback for the school play. Know what that means?"

Most of Sam's interests lay squarely in the world of nature and its creepy crawlies, leaving his theatre lingo lacking. He shrugged.

"It means they liked my audition and I get to go back. It means I have a good chance at getting a part in *Charlotte's Web*."

"Cool," he said. "I hope you get it. That's the one with the pig and the talking spider, right?"

"Yeah. All the animals talk."

"Doesn't the spider die?"

"Well, sure... yeah, but it's kind of a circle of life thing. It's a good play. I'm trying to get the part of Fern, the farm girl."

He thought this over for a moment.

"You should try for the spider."

"Right, because she dies? Ha ha."

He sighed. She must have thought he was trying to be a wiseass.

"No. The spider is way more interesting than the girl. The spider knows what's going on. She's the one that saves the day. Even though people don't notice her, she's important."

Christina slowed, her brows furrowed. They fought a lot lately, but he wanted her to know that he could be serious too, and not just a little kid. He missed hanging out with her. Since she started high school, she was always busy with her new friends. At times it felt like he didn't even know her anymore.

She was the one who had taught him how to properly wrangle a snake. And now she was hanging out with a group of girls that made squeamish faces if he even talked about snakes, frogs, or anything other than kittens and bunny rabbits around them. And they always shooed him away. All they wanted to do while they were at the house was put on make-up, look in the mirror, and talk about boys.

"Well, maybe I will get the part of the spider. They had us reading for a couple different parts."

"That would be really cool. Can I come watch it if you do? I mean, if you get a part, any part?"

"Of course," she said. "Now, wait out here while I look to see if the coast is clear for you to run up the stairs. You can run, right? And you aren't dripping blood from anywhere? Oh, and take off your shoes."

He looked down at his wounds. The stiff, cool breeze brushing against them on the walk home had helped to dry his clothes and he didn't seem to be dripping anything from anywhere. He raised both thumbs, then removed his shoes while she ducked into the house, leaving the door open. Alvis poked his head out. He sniffed at the hole in Sam's pants.

"Christina? Did you find him?" their mom's voice asked from the kitchen. Then, her voice lowered and he heard snippets about Alvis and some dog trainer they wanted to try.

"Yeah. I found him," Christina called out. "He just went upstairs. I told him he has to wash up before dinner."

She leaned back out and waved him in, pointing to the stairs when he entered.

"Good call, sweetie. Who knows what he was handling at the stream. Go see if you can hurry him up. Dinner is ready."

The two ran up the stairs and into the bathroom with Alvis on their heels.

"Okay, I'll get you some clean clothes. You start washing up." She looked at the sink and then back at him. "Just get into the bathtub. I'll bring your clothes and you can undress and wash in there." He nodded. "Hurry up. Dinner is ready."

Christina disappeared, then came back with some sweatpants, underwear, socks, and his Spiderman hoodie.

"Here you go," she whispered, setting the clothes near the sink. "Do you need help with your hands or your knee?"

"Nah. I got it. There are Band-Aids in the drawer."

"Okay, but remember to disinfect. I'll take a look at them after dinner. For now, just hurry."

His sister shut the bathroom door and he heard her go down the stairs, followed by the clicking of Alvis's claws.

"He's coming," she said, her voice elevated for his benefit, to relay the message that he should hurry.

He smiled at their mom's response. "So's Christmas."

It was the same line she always used when she was in a

hurry and was told someone was coming or on their way. Now, it was oddly comforting.

Sam washed up and carefully placed a skin-colored Band-Aid on each hand. He'd slapped the first one he found in the drawer on his knee because it would be covered up by his sweatpants, but Star Wars bandages on his hands might draw attention. He looked over at the bathtub where his damp, muddy clothes sat in a heap, then drew the curtain. He'd have to remember to grab a trash bag from the pantry so he could stash it all in his closet after dinner.

"I heard you talking about a trainer for Alvis," he said when he finally went down and turned the corner into the kitchen. They were all seated at the table waiting to start dinner.

Alvis, who was sitting in his usual I-hope-someone-drops-food-while-they-eat spot, perked up when he heard his name.

"Yes. I was telling your mom that there's a guy at work who gave me a number. He used this trainer for his Dobie, says the guy's amazing. His dog sits and stays until given a command, even if the guy leaves the room for a while. He showed me a video. The dog also does the usual down and shake stuff, and fetches."

"Maybe he can teach Alvis to do my chores," said Christina.

Both parents grinned. "Fat chance," said Mom.

Sam approached his place at the table. "Sorry it took me a while, Mom. I got some mud on my shoes and I wanted to try to rinse them in the bathtub. Don't worry. I took them off and carried them upstairs."

Christina looked him over, pinching her lips and giving a subtle nod. They both turned their attention to their mom,

Listen to the dog
NOT the whispers!

Elizabeth S Dowch.

Dante
(the real Alvis)

who was doing her mom scan, eyes shifting up and down, leaving Sam feeling like he'd been under one of those broad sci-fi laser beams that see through anything.

He was passably clean. His sweatpants hid the cut on his knee and he had done a reasonable job positioning the Band-Aids on his palms so they weren't noticeable, unless you knew they were there.

"Okay. Let's eat. I want to give the trainer a call before it gets too late, and I have an article I have to finish up before bedtime." She passed a large bowl of bowtie pasta to Christina. "Sam, did you get your earphones back from Mr. Thomas?"

Sam, a mouthful of bread puffing his cheeks like a chipmunk prepping for winter, nodded.

"He is such a nice man. We should have him over for dinner. It must be lonely eating all by himself."

"I think that is a wonderful idea, honey." Their father smiled. "Let's see if he can come tomorrow. I'll be home a little early if you need me to pick anything up at the market."

"You can make your homemade pizza," said Christina. "I can help when I get back from callbacks."

"You got a callback, sweetie? That's awesome," said Dad, eyes crinkled at the corners. He reached over and gave her a pat on the shoulder.

"It's *Charlotte's Web*, right?" asked Mom. "Which part are you up for?"

Christina smiled over at Sam. "I am hoping to get the part of Charlotte, you know, the spider."

EIGHT

Sarah waited until both kids were off to school before she walked over and knocked on Mr. Thomas's door. She thought about bringing Alvis along since it was time for his daily walk but decided that after the growling event the other day, it would be better to reintroduce them when both had fair warning. It would just take a few minutes to extend the invitation, and then she would run back and leash Alvis up for his walk.

While she waited for her neighbor to answer the door, she looked back over her shoulder at the office window of her house. There was Alvis at attention, looking confused and perhaps a little betrayed. Sarah waved at him.

I'll be right back, buddy. You'll get your walk. Don't worry, she thought, and laughed when she saw him bark, then sit, as if he'd heard her thoughts and answered.

The sound of a deadbolt sliding turned her attention back to the door in front of her, which opened to reveal Ben Thomas. He was dressed in pajamas and a terrycloth bathrobe and held a coffee mug in his left hand.

"I'm so sorry if I woke you," she said when he opened the

storm door. She glanced down at his feet. He was wearing oversized dinosaur foot slippers, complete with claws. The corners of her mouth quivered, threatening to reveal the grin she politely suppressed.

"Nonsense. I already have a half-empty cup of coffee in my hand. I've been up long enough to brew a pot, and then some. Oh, and these," he lifted one foot, then the other, "were a gift from my wife. Inside joke."

Sarah's cheeks warmed into solid blush.

"Give me a moment to get presentable."

Before she could tell him not to bother, that she was just extending an invitation to dinner, he disappeared back into the house. She turned and shrugged her shoulders at Alvis, who was still at the window. He barked and tilted his head.

When Ben returned, he was fully dressed and holding two coffee cups, steam drifting up over their rims.

"Come on in for a moment. I insist. If I drink the whole pot by myself, and I know I will if it's just sitting there, I'll be jumping out of my skin."

"Just for a few minutes," she said. "Alvis still needs his walk."

As if to punctuate her statement, barking and frantic clicking sounded from across the street, where Alvis was now tapping the glass with his claws. Sarah, brows knit, eyes glaring, held her hand in the air, palm down, and lowered it quickly. The command for "lie down." The dog stopped scratching at the window but stood up instead. She shook her head and turned back to her neighbor, exasperation painted on the canvas of her face.

"Like I said, I can only stay for a few minutes. Otherwise, he'll come right out through the window." She smiled.

"So be it." He held the door open with his elbow and handed her a cup of coffee on her way in. "Next time, bring him on over. I love dogs."

"I thought about it," she said. "But he wasn't very well-behaved last time he saw you. He can be kind of quirky. Poor guy came from a kill shelter and has all kinds of fears. He used to be terrified of the trash bins when their lids were hanging open, and lately, he's convinced that the clown from *It* has moved into our neighborhood."

Ben's forehead crinkled.

"I'm afraid I don't know that clown."

"Oh. It's a movie. Well, actually, first it was a book by Stephen King. Anyhow, Alvis thinks there are monsters in the storm drains. He won't let me walk anywhere near them."

"Ah, well dogs are intelligent and perceptive creatures. I'd stay away from the storm drains."

Sarah laughed and they made their way to the kitchen, where Ben had put out a plate of muffins along with some cream and sugar for the coffee.

He pointed to the muffins. "Evelyn Whistler is trying to fatten me up. Please take some home with you when you leave. There are too many for just me. They'll go stale."

"Thank you. You didn't have to lay out a spread for me."

"No trouble, really. Now, what brings you over my way?"

Sarah put a spoonful of sugar into her coffee and gave it a stir.

"We were wondering if you would like to join us for dinner tonight, or another night if that's too soon for you to plan." She took a sip from her cup.

"Hmm. I will have to check my social schedule." He

paused, shifted his eyes up and back, then grinned. "Oh, wait. I have no social schedule. I'm in. What should I bring?"

"Just yourself. We were thinking of making some home-made pizzas. Is there anything, in particular, you like on your pizza?"

"I'll eat just about anything on a pizza, even the little fishies. Are you sure I can't contribute with a salad or dessert or something?"

"No need. Really. Just bring your shining personality over at around 6:30." She took one last sip from her cup and stood. "I really need to get going now or Alvis might have an accident in the house. Should I set this in the sink?" She held up her hand and wiggled the cup.

"Just leave it on the table and make sure to bring some muffins home with you. I look forward to dining with you and your family tonight. Maybe give one of those muffins to Alvis and tell him it's from me." He winked.

"We should probably do a quick meet and greet to get you two reacquainted, when you arrive."

"I'll bring some treats, perhaps a steak." A kind and mischievous grin graced the elderly man's face.

He walked her to the front door and saw her out. When she exited the house, she saw Alvis pressed up against the office window across the street. There would be quite a few nose prints to wipe off after their walk. She turned and thanked Ben for the coffee and muffins and walked back to the house.

When she opened the door, Alvis almost knocked her over. At first, she thought he was going for the muffins, but he didn't seem to notice them at all. He backed up a couple steps and looked her up and down, then approached and sniffed at her as if he'd not seen her in days.

"What the heck, buddy? I was just across the street. Want a piece of muffin?"

She broke off a small part of one of the oversized muffins and lowered it to his level on the palm of her hand. He sniffed at it and looked up at her.

"Go on. Take it. It's not gonna bite you, silly dog."

Alvis sniffed it again and removed it from her hand with a slow deliberate movement, watching her the whole time.

"This is from Mr. Thomas," she said. "You'd better be a good boy when he comes over tonight." The dog cocked his head to the side.

Sarah walked to the kitchen and set the muffins on the counter. When she went back to the front door, Alvis was poking the leash with his nose. She took it off its hook and clipped it onto his collar.

"Okay, Alvis. Let's see what else you decide to be afraid of today." She reached down and gave him a pat on the head before opening the door and heading out with him for their walk.

When they approached the first storm drain on their path, Alvis jumped back and lowered his head. His hackles leapt up and she heard him working up a growl. She tried to coax him closer to show him that there was nothing there, but he refused. The rushing whispers of running water rose up to meet them. A faint low hum rumbled under it all, resonating through her head. And when she closed her eyes, she could feel the sound merging with the beating of her heart. It was a pleasant inviting sensation, akin to the primordial sounds used to achieve states of deep meditation. She'd written an article about the meditative practices in ancient India at her last job, in her previous life.

Alvis jerked on the leash, snapping her back from the clutches of the relaxing white noise, and reinforcing his unwillingness to get any closer to the drain. She took a deep breath, her mouth drawn in a thin, tight line, and looked into his deep, frightened, stubborn eyes. He quickly looked away.

"Here we go again," she said, shrugging, and let him lead her well away from and around the drain.

NINE

The wait at the bus stop was peaceful that morning. Tyler wasn't there and the other kids at the stop were gazing down at their phones, eyes glazed. Sam said good morning to Ms. Liz on his way by and took a seat near the front, tensing when he saw Tyler walk down his driveway and turn in the direction of the stop. Sam looked around. His fellow riders stared droopy-eyed at their screens. Had they noticed Tyler pick up a trot and wave his hand when the door closed?

Apparently, the bus driver had not. She drove off before he could reach the stop. Guilt tickled Sam's conscience, with a side of fear at the thought that his bully might have seen him. But it was all but forgotten when he caught movement out of the corner of his eye and realized Samantha was waving at him from across the aisle, at the back of the bus.

He lifted a hand to wave back, his pulse skipping when she patted the empty seat next to her. As soon as the bus stopped to gather another group of kids, he hooked his backpack with his arm and walked to where Samantha was sitting. She scooched over, widening the empty space.

"Sit down, silly. Ms. Liz already shut the door. My little brother's sick today."

Sam set his bag down between them, then sat and studied his feet, worrying the pull tab of a zipper on his backpack between his index finger and thumb. The bus jerked forward. He instinctively reached out to steady himself against the forest green seat back in front of them, inhaling through his teeth when his injured palms made contact.

"What happened to your hands?" asked Samantha, brows knit one over the other.

Sam's hands squeezed shut. His fingers curled over the bandages his sister had helped him change when they were getting ready for school. The left one had bled when they pulled off the old bandage, yanking the fresh scab with it. He unfurled it and saw the hint of a rust-colored shadow in the center of the dressing.

"Oh, this?" He feigned surprise, like he'd forgotten it was there. "Nothing. I slipped when I was catching frogs at the stream." It was mostly true. She didn't need to know that he'd had help falling.

"Oh. I hope it doesn't hurt too much. You disinfected it, right? What kinds of frogs did you end up catching? Were there any turtles out? I saw a snapping turtle at the stream the other day."

The barrage of words rushed at him like a swarm of bees, or maybe butterflies, given the enthusiasm of their source, who fluttered from one subject to the next at dizzying speeds. Sam watched her, his brows raised and lips parted into the shape of an oval, unsure of when and what to answer.

"Well?" she prodded. "We don't have all day. We're almost at school."

"There weren't any turtles out," he said, zeroing in on the most recent question... or at least he thought it had been. He licked his bottom lip, sliding the left side of it between his teeth.

"And the frogs?"

"Oh. Umm. Well, there were cricket frogs, and some toads."

She nodded, her face smoothing into a pleasant smile. One that proved contagious.

"Did you finish the presentation thing you were writing about venomous snakes?" he asked, after thinking to himself that he was glad they had met, then remembering how they had met.

She looked up to her left as if trying to find the answer to something on the ceiling of the bus, her mouth pinched. Then, her eyes widened.

"Oh, you mean the Australia thing. Yeah, I got an A on my paper. Most of the girls in my science class did their reports on *the Cuddly Koala* or *Majestic Kangaroos, with their adorable little jellybean joeys.* Mr. Peterson said mine was very original, and he can't wait to hear my presentation. One of the boys said it was weird that I like snakes, but I could tell that he was interested when I told him some snake facts. Want to read it?"

Jealousy had edged into his mind when she mentioned the boy in her class, and he'd almost missed the last bit.

"Read it? Yeah. Sure. I'd like that."

"You might think you know a lot about the snakes in Australia, but so did I, and there were some things that really surprised me," she said, digging through her book bag until she found a bedraggled-looking stack of papers held together by a staple.

Sam nodded and accepted the papers as if he were being entrusted with the final draft of a Nobel Prize-winning research project. He slid it into one of the folders in his backpack, careful not to wrinkle it any more than it already was.

"Keep it as long as you want," she said, grinning. "It's already graded, and I don't need it for my talk."

The bus pulled up to the ramp. Ms. Liz slid the door open and watched as the middle schoolers, most of them not yet fully awake, traipsed down the steps toward a day of learning. Sam and Samantha arrived at the front of the bus deep in conversation about the best way to hold a rattlesnake. They turned briefly to say thanks for the ride, as they always did, then continued their animated discussion. Ms. Liz grinned and shook her head.

Once they were off the bus and in the main lobby of the school, Samantha said goodbye and turned to the left.

"Wait, you're going that way?" asked Sam, confused.

"Yeah, I'm in B-wing," she quipped. "See you on the bus ride home. I'll save you a seat if I get there first. You do the same."

He nodded and made his way to his locker, half a dreamy smile pasted on his face. When he got there, he had to reach past the replay of the bus ride looping in his mind to retrieve his combination. He turned to the last number, lifted the handle, and pulled the door open. A hand slammed it shut before he could put anything inside, snapping him out of his reverie.

"Did you see me trying to catch the bus, weirdo?" Tyler glared at him. "Did you see me and *not* say anything?"

Sam stared, teeth clenched behind pursed lips. He shook his head.

"I saw you look out the window. You think it's funny that I missed the bus, weirdo?" Tyler's face was inches away from his now, and he was poking his index finger into Sam's chest. Sam shook his head again, faster this time.

"You're lucky I caught a ride. If I'm late again, I have to stay after. If I have to stay after, I miss tryouts. Then, I guess I'll just have to play football with your head." He pushed his hand against Sam's head, knocking it against the lockers.

"Everything okay here?" Sam had never been so happy to hear Coach Z's voice.

Tyler backed up a few steps and faced the PE teacher. He put an arm around Sam's shoulder and pulled him sideways, smiling. "Oh, hey there, Coach Z. Yeah, everything's great. My neighbor Sam and I were just kidding around, right Sam?"

They both looked at Sam. The teacher raised an eyebrow. Tyler squeezed his fingers into Sam's arm and smiled his biggest fake smile.

"Umm. Yeah, Coach Z. We live down the street from each other. We always kid around like this," said Sam. His mouth curved into a tight lipless smile, and he put an arm up on Tyler's shoulder, which had the added benefit of loosening Tyler's grip.

Coach Z scrutinized the two a bit more, then nodded. "Fine, but maybe bring it down a notch or two."

Both boys nodded. The coach walked away, distracted by a small commotion by the water fountain.

"Good choice, weirdo," said Tyler, smacking him on the back before leaving.

Sam's lips parted, letting out a long hard breath he'd been holding in during most of the exchange. Then he focused in on something Tyler had said and smiled. Football tryouts started this afternoon. They'd announced it over the loudspeaker pretty much every morning since last week. That meant no Tyler on the bus ride home... for the whole week. His smile widened.

Sam spent the rest of the school day floating from class to class and wishing time would speed up. During third period, his science teacher asked if everything was alright... twice, because he had not heard her the first time, despite the fact that she was standing over his desk. He'd forgotten to eat his lunch, too. He went through the line and bought his lunch. Then he sat down to eat it. Then, somehow twenty minutes slipped by in the space of a second, a bell rang, and he'd found himself sitting in front of a full lunch tray, a cold French fry grasped between his fingers.

When the final bell rang, Sam practically bounced out the door of his history class, apologizing to the teacher when he came close to knocking into him.

"Whoa there, Sam. Why the big hurry? Can't wait to get started on that paper, eh?" said Mr. Tate, laughing, after he stepped to the side to avoid impact.

"Sorry, sir." Sam grinned sheepishly, then rushed down the hallway toward the bus ramp.

Samantha had beat him onto the bus, which didn't surprise him since B-wing was closer to the bus ramp. She waved when she saw him and motioned for him to come sit next to her. Sam drummed the tops of the seats with his fingers as he inched his way down the aisle. The kids walking in front of him seemed to be walking in slow motion.

"Thanks for saving me a seat," said Sam, sitting and setting his backpack on the floor between his feet.

"Of course," said Samantha, launching right into a story

about seeing an assassin bug in math class and being the only one who knew what it was and what to do about it.

"Have you seen any at the stream?" she asked.

"Assassin bugs?"

She nodded.

"Maybe. I haven't really paid attention. I mostly go there to find reptiles and fish. There are some decent-sized wolf spiders, though."

Samantha nodded at this vigorously. "Yes. We have those in our yard, too. They are marvelous."

A faint smile lifted half his mouth. A girl that liked spiders. He hoped she wouldn't *grow out of it* like Christina said she had.

"I've also seen some crawfish," he said, sitting up a little straighter. "They were pretty big." He held up his index fingers, spacing them about ten inches apart.

"Seriously?" Samantha's eyes widened. "Did you get any pics?"

He cinched one side of his mouth and shook his head. He hadn't thought of it at the time. "Well, you can take some next time you see them. Are you going after school today?"

That had not been the plan, given the amount of homework he had, but didn't his dad always say the best plans were flexible?

"Sure. After I drop my stuff off at home. Maybe I can get some pics to show you."

She scrunched up her face and scratched the side of her head. "Or... I could meet you there."

"Yeah," he said, maybe a little too quickly, then bit down on his lip.

"Cool. What's your cell number? I'll text it and you'll have mine."

Sam looked around. His sister had told him horror stories of kids overhearing cell numbers and tormenting the owner to no end.

"Can I write it down for you?"

Samantha shrugged and nodded. "Sure. That'll work."

She reached into the top pocket of her book bag, pulled out a sticky note and the last inch of a Number 2 pencil, and handed them to him. He jotted down his number, trying to hide his difficulty gripping the tiny pencil stub with his bandaged hand. When he finished, he folded the sticky note and passed it and the pencil back to her.

Samantha took them, then touched the edge of his closest hand with her own, sending a tingle of static up his arm, into his core.

"Do they hurt?"

He shook his head.

"Good."

They spent the rest of the ride talking about the frogs and how if the stream were a little less polluted there would maybe be more species. Well, Samantha did most of the talking. Sam mostly added "uh-huhs," some head nodding, and glassy-eyed grins.

"Oh, hey. Isn't this your stop?" she asked, breaking the spell.

Sam spun his head to the side and saw that it was, in fact, his stop. Then he looked to the front of the bus and realized that most of the other kids from his stop were already off the bus. He jumped up and sped down the aisle.

"Bye," she called after him.

He turned and broke into a wide warm smile, then started down the stairs.

"Pay attention, Romeo. You almost missed your stop," said Ms. Liz in a soft, knowing voice.

He hopped off the last step, guessing that bus drivers saw a hell of a lot more than the kids thought they did.

NOBODY BUT ALVIS was home when Sam burst through the front door, panting, but the dog greeted him with enough energy to make up for the silence in the rest of the house. He picked up on the boy's happiness the moment the door opened and bounded over to participate in the festivities, whatever the cause.

"She asked for my number," Sam said to Alvis, after verifying that nobody else was there. There were no cars in the garage and Christina was supposed to be in school. Still, he'd looked in the office and peeked into the kitchen before daring to utter those words, which would have been irresistible fodder for relentless, well-intentioned, but still intolerable, teasing.

Alvis huffed and cocked his head to the side.

"She asked for my number," Sam said, a little louder and with more confidence this time. Then he plopped his backpack down in the mudroom and skipped back out to the kitchen with the intention to raid the pantry in search of sugar.

"Samantha. Asked. For. My. Number," he announced when he reached the pantry door, raising his brows and tapping Alvis's nose after each word.

The dog launched himself up at the boy, tongue outstretched to meet his face with wet slobbery kisses. Sam crumbled under the weight of the joyous assault and both boy and dog rolled backward onto the floor in a heap of yips and giggles.

"Okay. Okay, Alvis. If you knock me out, I won't be able to meet her at the stream, will I?" Sam held Alvis back with one hand while using the other to push himself up, wincing only slightly when his palm touched the floor.

He opened the pantry door and disappeared inside. Alvis waited for the boy to reappear, whimpering after each crinkle of a bag or rattle of a box. When Sam popped back out carrying an assortment of treats, including Alvis's beef jerky snacks, the dog broke into a whine, followed by some excited, high-pitched barks. Sam set his bounty on the kitchen island, sat on the closest stool, and tossed a snack to Alvis, who snatched it out of the air seconds after it had left the boy's hand.

A buzz sounded from Sam's pocket. He scrambled to pull out his phone, knocking a small stack of cookies onto the floor, which Alvis promptly addressed, drool dripping from the side of his mouth. After he read the message, Sam set the phone on the counter, his body slumping like a deflated lawn decoration.

"She can't go to the stream," he muttered.

Alvis snuffled, crumbs riding the lines of drool down from his jowls. He studied the boy with his large soulful eyes, trying to decipher the reason for such a drastic change in mood. Then another buzz. Sam glanced at the screen, bolting upright again. Alvis tilted his head, his attention riveted on his boy, ready to reflect whatever mood might result.

"She wants me to meet her at the playground later with pictures of anything I find at the stream!" He hopped off the stool, leaned down, and put a hand on either side of Alvis's face, smooshing it with the dog's loose folds of skin, and rubbing up behind his ears, which set the dog's back paw tapping.

Sam popped the last few remaining cookies into his mouth and tossed a bag of chips and Alvis's jerky back into the pantry. He let the dog out to the fenced part of their yard and watched until he was sure Alvis was done remarking his territory. Then he called him back in, secured the back door, and jogged toward the front. Alvis ran past him and sat at the entrance, his snout pointing up at his leash.

Sam ran his hand through his hair, then knelt down in front of the dog, frowning.

"I'm sorry, buddy. I want to take you with me. Really. But I can't catch crawfish, take pictures of them, *and* hold onto your leash. Not with these hands." He held his bandaged hands up in front of the dog. Alvis sniffed at them and huffed.

"Maybe next time." He ruffled the fur on the dog's head, and slipped out the front door, locking it behind him.

Before heading down the street, Sam made a quick stop to the side of the house, where he kept an old fishing net he often used at the stream and the pond. His waders, which he'd forgotten to put away, were sitting in the grass next to it. He grabbed the net, slipped on his waders, and took off toward the stream.

"Well, you must have had a good day at school today."

The voice startled him. He pivoted on the balls of his feet and saw Mr. Thomas walking behind him, in the direction of the stream. Maybe he really was a spy.

"It was okay," he said, shrugging a shoulder.

"Oh. Well, you were walking in more of an it-was-a-super-awesome-day way. So, I made an assumption." He smiled an easy neighborly smile. "Mind if I walk with you? I'm going to the mailboxes. I assume you're heading to the stream?" He pointed at the net.

Sam nodded. "I'm going to catch some crawfish."

Mr. Thomas's eyebrows popped up. "There are crawfish in our stream?"

Sam widened his eyes, aiming an intense stare at his elderly neighbor. "Yes. Huge ones, the size of small lobsters. I caught some with this net." He waved the net as if brandishing a sword.

"That's quite impressive," said Mr. Thomas, nodding. "May I watch you catch one before I get the mail?"

"Sure," said Sam, enthusiasm driving his voice up an octave. "Maybe you can help scare one out for me to net. I'll get you a stick."

The elderly man stopped, his eyes softening. "Are you sure I won't get in the way?"

"No way, Mr. Thomas. You can help me take some pics, too. I mean... if you want to."

"I would very much like that."

TEN

They caught three crawfish, two frogs, and a painted turtle. Sam also spotted a water moccasin about mid-stream and reached his net out to gently nudge the snake on its way. Despite the boy's obvious confidence in the matter, Ben's spine stiffened. He hoped he would be able to intervene in time, if necessary.

You're such a worrier, Ben. Not every creature is out to get us, looking for a fight. Some just ignore us, others even protect us.

Mary's voice floated in his head like a thick mist. In his mind, he saw her, facing down scorpions and rattlesnakes on their hikes… caressing Princess's back as she fed.

They all have a purpose on God's green Earth, Ben. What right do we have to judge?

"Water moccasins aren't really as aggressive as people say," said Sam, his voice a gentle breeze through the mist, whooshing it away. "If you leave them alone, they'll leave you alone. They're actually pretty cool, as far as snakes go. Did you know that they hold their heads above the water when they swim?" Sam had apparently noticed his discomfort.

Ben shook his head. Maybe Mary had told him something similar at some point, but he couldn't recall.

"You can tell the difference between them and water snakes by that, and the shapes of their heads. Water snakes have more rounded heads, less blocky."

"You're a pretty smart kid," Ben said. *The kind of kid that Mary and I would have loved to raise.*

Sam looked down at his feet and fiddled with the net.

"Don't be embarrassed." Ben laid a hand on his shoulder. "You are a smart kid and probably the most interesting person I know, too. Mary would have loved to talk with you about nature. I wish you could have met her."

Sam tilted his head up. "I wish I could have met her, too. She sounds like she was a cool lady." His mouth turned up in a smile.

The corners of Ben's eyes crinkled, swallowing up the tears that were threatening to rise.

"She was definitely a cool lady," he said, grinning. "Now, let's see some of those pictures we took."

Sam set his net down and pulled out his phone. They scrolled through the pics, both oohing and aahing as the images flashed by. Ben listened intently to all of the facts that Sam could think to tell about each. When they finished, they nodded, satisfied grins gracing both their faces.

The flow of the back and forth between them had come naturally, as if they'd known each other for years, and Ben felt younger than he had in a long time. Sam had even confided that he was going to show the pictures to a new friend he'd made, of the female persuasion. He'd quickly followed up with a just-a-friend disclaimer, but Ben had seen a definite twinkle in the boy's eyes.

"Oh, shoot," said Ben, bringing a palm to his forehead. "I totally forgot to get my mail."

This set both of them laughing.

"Want me to go get it for you?" asked Sam.

"No, that's okay. You need to get to the park to show off your pictures. I'll go later. I'm in no hurry to look at flyers and open bills." He rubbed his jaw. "Could you do me a favor, though? Could you send me the picture of that beautiful crawfish we caught? The one with the red and orange swirls? I think I want to print and frame that one, if it's okay with you."

He already knew just where to hang it. Mary had decorated one of the walls of the hallway leading from the foyer to the kitchen with her photographs of animals and insects, both beautiful and curious. Maybe it was time to add some new ones.

"Sure. That would be cool," said Sam, his hazel eyes sparkling over a smile that beamed with pride.

The two walked back toward their homes, chatting back and forth about which catch they thought was the coolest, native species versus invasive, introduced species, and exotic ones. It almost felt like conversing with the ghost of Mary, or perhaps the ghost of the child they'd never had, but badly wanted.

Thanks to the cruelty she'd suffered as a child, Mary couldn't have children. They'd talked seriously about adopting, but each of those conversations ended with the harsh reality that it would be too dangerous with Princess around. Once, when they were alone in the bedroom, Ben had whispered something into Mary's ear about severing the tie, moving on. For a moment, he'd seen longing and hope, eyes that called out to his. *Rescue me.*

But, it had lasted less than the tic of a second hand.

How dare you? You promised to stay with me no matter what. With US. He heard the words now in his mind, searing, rage-filled words spit out like venom, followed by scratching at the door. It had taken only a few minutes to calm her down. That was *Gentle Ben's* greatest talent, after all.

"Thanks for letting me come along," said Ben, when they got to his house. "I had a wonderful time and learned some new things about the creatures Mary loved so much. I'll see you at dinner later on tonight."

"See you at dinner. Umm, Mr. Thomas?" Sam said, chewing on the inside of his cheek. "You know how I told you I was going to the park to show the pictures?"

"Yes."

"Could you not mention that part at dinner?" His eyes were wide and his forehead creased by brows that pushed in and up toward his mussy chestnut hair.

Ben put his hand up near his mouth, sealing his lips tightly together and turning an invisible key to lock them. Then he flung his hand out to the side and flicked his wrist, tossing the invisible key off into space.

Ben watched the boy head for his house. A feeling of loss and of yearning rose in his soul, like an ember revealed under the ashes of a long-forgotten fire. He suddenly felt old. And, though he knew there was no way to go back, no way to claim the life he felt they had missed, he vowed to live the life he had now honoring Mary.

ELEVEN

Sam said goodbye to Mr. Thomas and headed home in a combination of long strides, skips, and hops. When he arrived, he set his net and waders by the side of the house and tried the front door. It was unlocked, which meant that Christina was home. She never locked it when she got home from school, something which irked their mother, who had grown up in a city and was constantly telling the kids that thieves always went for the easiest mark. Whatever that meant.

"Hey there," said Christina when he walked past. "How are the wounds doing?" she whispered, nudging her head in the direction of the kitchen to let him know that Mom was in there.

He gave a thumbs up and a "hey there" back.

"Callbacks went awesome," she said, then held up a hand, fingers crossed. "The cast list goes up tomorrow. I put Charlotte as my first choice." She winked and reached over to ruffle his hair.

He tolerated this, despite having explained a million times in every type of tone that he did not like it. It was already annoying when Mom did it. And, *she* was Mom, most definitely higher in rank than he was in the family pack. Christina was his *sister*. But he was going to meet up with Samantha in a bit to show off the amazing pics Mr. Thomas helped him get. And his sister seemed excited about her chances at getting the part she wanted. So, tolerance prevailed.

He went into the kitchen, where his mother was rather frantically chopping onions. There were bowls of various sizes and colors spread across the kitchen island. Each contained a different ingredient, or pizza topping, as his mother soon explained. Sam glanced into the different containers, noting which ones contained his favorites for later.

"Mom, I'm going to run over to the park to meet a friend for a few minutes. Is that okay?" he asked, plucking a pepperoni slice from one of the bowls and dodging a smack from her outstretched hand to pop it into his mouth.

"A friend?" she asked, moving the pepperoni bowl away from him. "Do I know this friend?"

She swept the chopped onions off the board in front of her into a white ceramic bowl and covered it with plastic wrap. Then, she turned her mom-scanner on him, prompting a rosy blush from his cheeks. He turned to feign interest in a bowl of olives in a futile attempt to avoid scrutiny. Everyone in the house knew that Sam despised olives.

"What time do I need to be back? What time is Mr. Thomas coming?"

"I told him to come at 6:30, but I would like you here to help set the table by six."

He let out a quiet sigh. His distraction technique seemed to be working.

"But you didn't answer my question. Do I know this friend?"

He shook his head, his shoulders tensing.

"Does this friend have a name?" his mother asked, her expression bordering between curiosity and amusement. It was obvious by her wording that she suspected the friend might be a girl. He would need to tread carefully to avoid the inevitable wave of teasing the truth would bring. Christina peeked into the room, her gaze lifting from her phone screen to Sam, then their mom.

"Sam," he said. "My friend's name is Sam." He wasn't lying; she told him the first day they met that her nickname was Sam.

"That's funny," his mom said. "Sam and Sam." She grinned. "I'm glad you made a friend. Is he in your classes? That must be confusing for the teachers."

"No. We ride the same bus."

His sister's gaze floated back to her cell phone. She'd obviously lost interest in the conversation. Disaster averted.

Sam was turning to go when his mother cleared her throat to call his attention back.

"Please take Alvis with you."

Sam looked at his mom, his body curving into a slouch. He blew out a rush of air, puffing his cheeks, and pinched his eyelids in as if suddenly saddled with an unimaginably heavy burden.

"Mom," he said, stretching her name out by six or seven 'o's. "Alvis wants to sniff *every* tree when I walk him. And you know how he is with new people."

"I know how he is when he doesn't get his walk. And we have a guest coming over tonight. I'm getting things ready for the pizzas. If you want to go meet your friend, Sam, at the park, you have to take Alvis."

Sam's face puckered into an expression of anguish, and his eyes rolled up and back.

"Take his snacks with you. Have Sam give him one. They'll be best friends after that."

"He pulls when I walk him, Mom." Sam was already imagining Alvis yanking his arm while he was trying to show off his pics. Or worse yet, Samantha oohing and aahing over Alvis instead of his pics. Either way, taking Alvis was going to crimp his style.

"He has been acting a little skittish on his walks," said his mom, brushing a hand through her hair and holding it back.

Sam suppressed a smile. It seemed like he might win this one.

"Okay. Christina will go with you. She can hold the leash."

Christina popped back into the kitchen, the hand holding her phone dropping to her side.

"What?" said both siblings at the same time, mirroring annoyance.

"That is my final decision. Christina, leash up Alvis, please. You are walking with Sam to the park. Do a few laps around the park while Sam hangs out with his friend and then you can both walk Alvis home and help me finish things up for dinner with Mr. Thomas."

She went to the refrigerator, pulled out a large piece of mozzarella, and hummed as she sliced it. It was her subtle way of letting them know that the conversation was over.

Christina glared at her little brother, shoved her phone into her pocket, and called Alvis, who trotted over with such unabashed enthusiasm that the girl was unable to hold her scowl.

"Okay, Alvis. Let's get you a nice walk," she said, patting the top of his head as he wiggled around her.

Sam stepped over to give Alvis some love. Leave it to Alvis to lighten the mood. At least he would be by himself in the park. If they parted ways early enough, Christina might not see that Sam was a Samantha. He could see by his mother's expression that the matter was no longer up for discussion and knew that pressing his luck might result in not being able to leave the house at all.

"Okay," he said, pulling his phone out of his pocket and looking at the last text he had received from Samantha. "Can we hurry, though? Sam's going to be there soon."

"Whatever," said Christina, clicking the leash onto Alvis's collar.

"Don't forget to lock the door behind you," their mother added when they opened the door to leave.

TWELVE

The familiar ping of an arriving text jarred Ben from a daydream. He reached over from his armchair and picked his cell phone up off the coffee table. It was from Sam. The boy had sent the picture of the crawfish, as promised, and included a few more along with it. A smile lit the elderly man's face.

"Such a thoughtful boy," he said, turning to his favorite photograph of Mary. "He sent the picture I told you about." He turned the phone screen toward the frame, as if to show her. "I'm going to hang it next to the one of the jellyfish you took when we were in the Keys."

He leaned forward, pushed himself up to his feet, and headed toward the office. The printer in the office produced beautiful color photos. He'd bought it for Mary as a Christmas present years ago so that she could print out her nature photographs. Hopefully, it still had enough ink to print out this picture, and maybe a couple of the others the boy had sent. If not, maybe Evelyn could get some for him on her next trip to the store.

The doorbell rang just when he stepped into the office and

was trying to remember how to send the image from the phone to the printer. He had no kind words for modern phones and their constant updates. Just when you learned how to do something, they up and changed it all.

He set the phone on the printer and went to the front door to see who was there, hoping not to find somebody selling something. He hated saying 'no,' and all the neighborhood kids knew it. Whenever the band, or the football team, or the theatre department, or whatever, needed to raise money, Ben always ended up with new candles, cookies, or popcorn. The cookies and popcorn he could handle, but he definitely did not need any more scented candles.

He opened the door and smiled when he saw Evelyn Whistler standing on his stoop holding an open tin of cookies, almost as if he had summoned her with his thoughts.

"Hi, Ben," she said when he opened the door. She held up the cookies. "I come bearing goodies."

"Come on in," said Ben, holding the storm door for her and waving her in.

She walked past him, the heavenly smell of homemade chocolate chip cookies wafting up from the plate to meet his nose. Of all the treats Evelyn brought over, these were always his favorites. And when they were fresh from the oven like these, it took every ounce of self-control not to eat the whole plate in one sitting. Mary used to hide them from him. Her original spot had been in the oven, but she'd switched to the top shelf of the pantry, behind the canned goods, after that time he had preheated the oven. He laughed at the memory.

"You are certainly in a good mood," said Evelyn.

"I was just thinking about that time Mary hid your cookies

from me in the oven, and I preheated it for dinner, not knowing they were there."

Evelyn brought her free hand to her cheek, shook her head, and laughed.

"I remember that. The paper plate caught fire and set off your smoke detector. Frank and I saw the fire trucks go by and ran over to see what was wrong. Mary was explaining to the firemen when we got there. All you could think about were 'those poor cookies.' It's one of the reasons I switched to tins, by the way."

Evelyn's smile turned melancholy. "It seems like just yesterday," she said, her voice trailing off and her eyes shimmering.

"Well, these cookies are going right on the counter where I can see them, smell them, and gobble them up," said Ben, trying to shift back to the positive. "To what do I owe the pleasure?"

"Oh, you know me. I like to stress-bake. And, with things the way they are now, that makes for a lot of baking. Also, I wanted to thank you for giving Tyler a ride to school when he missed the bus." She handed him the tin, and he set it on the counter.

"No thanks necessary. Could I interest you in some tea?" he asked. "I have a dinner to attend a little later, but there's always time for tea. How is Tyler doing? He wasn't very talkative on the drive to school."

Perhaps he could use this opportunity to address the Tyler-Sam issue, without talking about it directly and breaking his promise to Sam.

"Oh, you have a dinner date?" asked Evelyn, adding on a wink at the end.

"Sort of. The new family, the Parkers, invited me over tonight. They seem like nice people. Anyway, I don't have to be there until 6:30. Have a seat and I'll set the kettle on. Unless you'd prefer coffee." He pointed toward the coffee maker.

"Tea sounds wonderful," she said, glancing at her watch. "If I have coffee after four, I'm up all night."

Ben pulled out a chair for her, then went over to light the stove and set the kettle heating. On his way back, he moved the plate of cookies from the counter to the kitchen table.

"I have the perfect tea to pair with your delicious cookies," he said, smiling. Then he took a cookie and brought it to his nose, smelling it, eyes closed. "If there are any left when the tea is ready," he added with a chuckle before popping it into his mouth.

He sat down at the table across from her, noticing how exhausted she looked. Her face had rested into her usual graceful smile, but the sparkle in her eyes had fizzled. And he didn't remember seeing the deep lines now striping her forehead and branching out from the corners of her eyes.

"How are you doing, Evelyn?" he asked, his voice gently prodding past common courtesy to the level of genuine concern they had always shown for each other. The Whistlers had been there for him when Mary passed. And Evelyn never failed to think of him when grocery shopping or heading to the post office. If there was a way to repay this kindness, he wouldn't hesitate.

"I'm alright. Thanks for asking," she said, her answer robotic, like it was preprogrammed to play for anyone who might ask how she was.

"Really? I'm glad. But let's say you were to change one thing in your life right now. What would that be?"

It was a game he used to play with Mary to get her to talk about things she wanted to avoid talking about. Sometimes framing it as a 'what if' exercise got her to open up.

"Only one?" she said, creasing her brows. "Oh, I don't know. I would probably use my one wish for Tyler. He's having a hard time, and I can't get him to talk to me. I was actually hoping maybe he'd talked to you on the ride to school. You know, guy to guy."

Ben shook his head. The kettle whistled. He stood and walked to the stove, turned off the burner, and poured the boiling water into a teapot with several strings hanging over its top, each connected to a bag of Earl Grey deep inside.

"I wish he had, Evelyn. He barely said a word the whole ride," he said, walking back to the table armed with the pot and a tray topped with teacups, spoons, and sugar.

"He did say 'thank you' when I dropped him off, though."

This elicited a hint of the smile he'd hoped for. He set the tray down and sat across from her.

"Well, I'm glad to hear that he was polite, at least. It seems his manners and his homework have been slipping at school. He almost didn't get to try out for football this year, and that's something he's been looking forward to since last season. He and Frank worked so hard on his skills this summer... until, you know, Frank moved out. Anyhow, I had a talk with the coach and the vice principal and they agreed to let him try out. But, he has to get his grades up by the first game if he doesn't want to be stuck on the bench. I told him and got the usual scowl. I wish I knew how to get my sweet boy back."

Ben reached over and placed a hand over hers.

"Middle school years are the worst," he said. "He's trying to figure out who he is and it sure doesn't help that Frank has decided to try to figure out who *he* is now, too. You are a great mom. I'm sure he'll come around."

"Yes. Frank is trying to figure out who he is. That's a nice way to put it." Evelyn smirked. "You are a kind and tactful man. Mary was a very lucky lady."

Ben grinned and poured tea into both of their cups. Evelyn added some sugar to hers, her spoon tinkering against the inside of the teacup while she stirred, lost in thought.

"Ben, do you think I could send him over to help you with some yard work? Or maybe he could help clean your garage or something? I saw you working on that the other day. It would be good for him and maybe he'd even talk... get stuff off his mind. Stuff he wouldn't say to me."

Ben picked up his cup and took a sip. He wanted to help. And maybe this was a way he could help the Whistlers and Sam at the same time. But having Tyler poking around in the garage would be a bad idea. He hadn't gone through the boxes in there, yet. He didn't know... didn't want to know what Princess had stashed in there. It was one of her favorite places to hide.

"There's actually some work I need done in the backyard," he said, smiling and taking another sip of tea. "I'll let you know when I'm ready to get started on it. And tell him not to worry. I'll make sure it doesn't interfere with football."

"Thank you," she said, her easy smile returning with a dash of what Ben imagined to be hope sparkling in her eyes.

She drank a few more sips, then looked at her watch.

"Well, I imagine you'll want to clean up and get ready for your dinner," she said, standing. "I'm glad you're getting out of the house to socialize. You stay closed in here way too much. The Parkers are the ones across the street, right? The ones who bought Marjory's house?"

He nodded.

"They have a boy Tyler's age, right? I've seen him walking to the stream in his waders. Maybe I should invite him over for cookies or something. Tyler could use a friend. I've just been so frazzled lately."

Ben walked with her to the door, retrieving his phone on the way by the office.

"Always trying to take care of everyone else," he said, thinking to himself that getting the boys together would probably not be a great idea. "You need to take care of yourself, too. I'll tell you what. I'll try to organize a day when both boys can come over here."

Evelyn stepped out the door and turned.

"Thank you, Ben," she said, her hands clasped at her chest. "You really are a wonderful neighbor. I'll be heading to the store tomorrow afternoon. Remember to text me if you need anything."

"I will Evelyn. Thank you. And don't worry. We'll get Tyler back on the right track. He's a good kid."

Ben went back into the kitchen to tidy up. He stepped on the pedal for the trashcan to dispose of the teabags, scrunching up his nose when the pungent odor of a mixture of food scraps from the last couple days wafted up from the bin. He cinched and tied the bag to contain the smell, and added "take out the trash" to his mental to-do-before-leaving list. He bumped it up to the top of the list when he caught another whiff of the salmon scraps he'd thrown away the other day.

"Out you go," he said, grabbing the bag and heading to the garage where he kept his more serious garbage bins.

After tossing the bag in and making sure he'd sealed the top properly, he glanced around the garage and sighed. There was still a lot of work to do organizing and patching the hole he'd discovered. It would be nice to have some help. The ceiling lights flickered, making the dim space even darker. He would need to change those bulbs if he wanted to work on the garage in private, with the doors closed against the prying eyes of neighbors. He and Mary had put in bulbs that shone no brighter than a child's nightlight so as not to harm Princess. She did okay with all but the brightest, daylight bulbs, but was most comfortable in the dark. He'd been replacing the bulbs in the house little by little since Mary died, but hadn't bothered with the garage, yet.

He contemplated just how much they'd had to fashion their lives together around the comfort of an interloper. How many times they'd had to leave places and people they'd grown fond of. How many times he'd felt like maybe he, Ben, was the actual interloper.

A chittering sound, followed by scratching from behind the shelves stacked with garden soil and supplies, yanked him back to the present. He passed the back of his hands across cheeks now warm with tears and creased his brows. These were not the easy-flowing tears of sadness he'd cried at Mary's bedside when she passed. They were the burning tears of anger and frustration at never having been able to free her.

I understand. His mind twisted the scratching into words.

"The hell you do!"

Mary had always insisted all creatures had a purpose, and

she loved them all, or at least did not judge them. A pang of guilt tapped at his heart. What had he done?

They must be so afraid, so confused. Mary's sweet voice rustled about in his head. *So lonely.*

Ben sat on the steps, overwhelmed by feelings of loss, of solitude, feelings for Mary. Nobody could understand the depth of his despair. No person... His head felt thick, as if it were stuffed with cotton. Guilt flooded his thoughts. He laced his fingers together and squeezed.

They ask for a name, a name to connect you. Then they can protect you. Mary's voice flittered about in his mind.

What name does grief have? What would you call loss, if it were a living thing? An image of Princess hovered just behind his eyes. She was smiling at him... or at least her version of it.

A ping echoed from somewhere across the universe, calling to him. A ping that meant something just beyond his grasp.

What would you name your very best friend, if you had the power to do so?

Another ping, followed by a rumble, a tickle against his thigh. He rubbed his palm against his forehead, pushed his fingernails against his scalp. Ping, rumble, rumble. A text? Yes, a text. His phone was in his pocket. The mist faded; his eyes focused on a bag of soil. Movement. He caught movement.

"Goddammit!" he yelled, popping to his feet. "Goddammit! Get out of my head. I did what I had to do."

He grabbed the doorknob and pulled the door open, stumbling into the house.

THIRTEEN

"So, who is this Sam kid you're meeting at the park?" asked Christina, in a voice more indicative of small talk than genuine interest.

"We ride the bus together," said Sam, choosing his words carefully. "Sam's into snakes and stuff, like I am."

"Cool."

"You don't have to walk with me the whole way," he said, reaching down to pat Alvis, who had stopped to smell a tree. "You could walk the path that goes toward the pool and hang out there for a while, then pick me up on the way back. If you want."

Steve, the boy Christina liked, lived down that way. Sam knew this because she had dragged him and the dog there on other walks. They'd run into Steve shooting baskets in front of his house on a few occasions. It had not taken Sam long to figure out that these meetings were not as coincidental as his sister claimed. But he never let on that he knew.

Christina looked at her watch, then fiddled with Alvis's leash. He could see she was tempted.

"I don't need a babysitter. Alvis does," he said, nudging her toward a yes. "Besides, Mom will never know. We'll walk back together."

She arched a brow and the corner of her mouth pushed up.

"You really don't want this friend to meet me, do you?" she said, placing a hand on her hip.

Alvis tugged the leash, pulling Christina a few steps ahead of Sam. Had he pushed a little too hard? He furrowed his brows and breathed out hard through his nose.

"It's not that," he said, jogging to catch up. "I just don't want Sam to think I'm a baby that needs his big sister to walk him to the park."

"Understandable," said Christina, pinching her mouth and nodding her head. "Why don't you run up ahead to meet Sam? Alvis and I can go to the far end of the park. She won't even know we came together. Then, we'll just happen to run into you on the way home."

"Or you could go the other way..." Sam stopped and closed his eyes in an exaggerated blink, his mouth drawn in a grimace.

"So, it *is* a girl."

Sam looked up to face his sister's triumphant grin.

"Samantha, I presume?" She tapped her index finger under her chin.

Alvis jerked forward, pulling her off balance.

"Knock it off, Alvis," she said, catching herself.

"You okay?" asked Sam.

"Don't change the subject. You are meeting a girl at the park. Is it a friend girl, or a girlfriend?" she asked, nudging him with her elbow.

"She's a friend who happens to be a girl. And this is

exactly why I didn't want you to know." Sam exhaled, deflating as the air escaped his mouth.

"Oh, come on," she said. "I'm your big sister. It's my job to tease you." She gave him another nudge. He studied his shoes.

Alvis gave another frantic tug.

"Fine," said Christina. "I'll stop for now. And, if you do my chores for an additional week, I won't tell Mom and Dad. *And* I'll walk the other path."

Alvis whimpered. Both kids turned their attention to him.

"What the heck, Alvis?" said Christina.

"It's the drain thingy," said Sam, pointing toward the storm sewer. "Remember? Mom says he's afraid of them now."

"Oh, for the love of..." The dog yanked away from the opening, knocking into Sam.

Sam caught himself, then reached down to pat Alvis.

"What's wrong, Alvis? There's nothing to be afraid of. Dad says the only thing down there is water, and maybe some rats and raccoons." He looked at Christina. "Maybe he's afraid of raccoons. They can be pretty scary. Did you know that raccoons have almost twice the bite force quotient of a cat? They have super sharp canines, and their top teeth are like blades."

"I did not." She shrugged, her brows lifting in tandem with her shoulders. "But why am I not surprised you do?"

Sam rolled his eyes and walked closer to the drain.

"Look, Alvis. Nothing is coming to eat me. It's okay."

A low continuous rumble rose from Alvis's throat, and his hackles popped up from the back of his neck down to the base of his tail. Sam sat on top of the drain, patting his hand on the concrete next to him.

"See, Alvis? It's okay."

Alvis was now baring his teeth and pulling toward the drain, as if ready to confront some imminent danger threatening his boy. Christina stood at an angle, bracing against him.

"Come on, Sam. You're freaking him out completely. Knock it off."

"I was just trying to show him that there's nothing there," said Sam. He got up and took a step back toward his sister. The hair on the back of his neck tingled. He turned and cocked his head to the side. Alvis barked.

"What is it?" asked Christina, her voice barely audible over Alvis's deep, threatening barks.

Sam leaned his head closer to the drain, then straightened and bunched up his shoulders.

"Nothing. Just water, I guess," he said, then pushed the side of his thumb against his teeth and nibbled on the skin.

He didn't want to mention the voice, the one that surfed the rushing waters, that told him it *understood*.

"Get your thumb out of your mouth. You don't want your girlfriend..." Christina held up her free hand and raised her brows when he glared, "... your *friend who happens to be a girl*, Sam. You don't want her to see you chewing your thumb."

He pulled his thumb away from his mouth, but not before giving it one more nervous nibble.

"Okay, you go ahead to the park and I'll walk the other way. It's 4:30. I'll walk back this way in an hour. Be ready."

He nodded and took off in a half-skip toward the park, the mingled sounds of Christina trying to wrangle Alvis and the dog's protests fading with each hop.

Sam approached the park, craning his neck and scanning

the area to see if Samantha had already arrived. He checked his phone to make sure he hadn't missed any texts. Nothing. Maybe she wasn't coming after all. He swallowed hard, trying to loosen the knot in his throat, and walked through the mulch toward the picnic tables.

Of course she's coming, he thought, re-reading the last text she'd sent.

"Can't wait to see the pics you got. The crawfish sounds beautiful." He read the words aloud to make them more real, to convince himself that she was coming.

"Who's *beautiful*? Your imaginary *girlfriend*?"

He was tackled before he could turn toward the voice; Tyler Whistler's voice. Sam went down hard, his face displacing the mulch. Bits of dirt entered his mouth, the earthy taste combining with the salty metallic flavor of blood. He struggled to flip himself over, but Tyler was straddling him, pinning him down.

"What brings you to my park, weirdo?" said Tyler, flicking the back of Sam's head. "Are you here to meet your girlfriend, or because you missed me?"

Sam slid his hands between his face and the ground and tried to push himself up. Tyler set both hands on the backs of his shoulders and shoved him back down.

"Just leave me alone. What did I do to you?" Sam panted, letting his body slump.

"Oh, I don't know, weirdo. You moved in and now I have to see your annoying ugly face every day. You ruined the view."

Tyler grabbed the back of Sam's shirt sleeve, lifted one of his knees off the ground, and flipped him with the ease of a master chef flipping a pancake. Then he pinned both of Sam's hands with his knees, while the much smaller boy wiggled to free himself.

"My sister is coming with our dog. If he sees you, he'll attack and we won't even be able to stop him," Sam stuttered, spitting dirt and blood from his mouth.

Tyler put his hands on his cheeks and fake-shuddered. "Oooooh. I am sooo afraid," he said. But Sam noticed him look around to see if anyone was nearby.

"I'll tell you what," said Tyler, reaching a hand into the pocket of his sweatshirt and pulling out a black Sharpie. "I'll leave you alone, right after I write your name for you, so your sister and your girlfriend will recognize you."

He pushed Sam's bangs away from his forehead and spit.

"Gotta clear the board," he said, laughing as he wiped his sleeve across Sam's forehead.

Sam fought to hold in the tears pushing up from inside. He felt the pressure of the marker above his eyebrows, smelled its sharp, dizzying odor, and stopped struggling in hopes that when Tyler finished whatever horrid thing he was writing, he would be satisfied with the humiliation inflicted, and go away.

"There," said Tyler, capping the Sharpie and putting it back in his pocket. "All done. Now we're even for the bus thing."

He stood up, laughing. "Wanna see what it says?"

Sam rolled back over onto his stomach and pushed himself up, shaking his head. He brushed the mulch and dirt off as best he could and took a few steps away. Tyler walked around in front of him, holding out a hand to stop him.

"You don't want to see my artwork? That's rude. Are you crying?"

Sam pulled his bottom lip in and bit down on it. His hands

balled into fists, tight at his sides. Tyler grinned and waggled a finger.

"Do you wanna punch me? Because that would be a very bad idea, weirdo."

"What the hell?"

Both boys jerked their heads toward the voice coming from the direction of the picnic tables. Samantha was speed-walking toward them, a look of horror contorting her face. She looked the two over, assessing the situation.

"What did you do to him, Tyler?" she yelled, her voice biting with a ferocity that startled Sam.

But it wasn't just the ferocity that startled him. It was something else, something he was trying to pin down in his mind.

"Wait till I tell Aunt Evelyn. You can kiss football good-bye, Ty," she said, hands on her hips, leaning her glaring face toward Tyler's.

That was it! It was the familiarity in her tone. *Aunt Evelyn?* Samantha was related to this asshole?

"Wait, is *this* your girlfriend, weirdo? My derpy little cousin?" This seemed to momentarily disarm Samantha. Her cheeks flushed red. She turned her attention to Sam, a look of pity on her face that tore through him.

"I never said..." he started. "I mean..."

"Oh, just so you know. Your boyfriend has a new name. I wrote it down so he won't forget it." Tyler reached over and pushed up Sam's bangs. "LOSER!"

Samantha's brow furrowed and her eyes seemed to light on fire. She jumped forward, hands outstretched to push her cousin away, but he stepped to the side and she brushed past him instead.

"Aww. Look. Your girlfriend is trying to protect you," said Tyler, tilting his head at Sam and pushing out his bottom lip.

It was too much. The humiliation. The fact that the two were *family*. All of it. Sam took off running. He heard the cousins exchanging further insults in the background and Samantha calling out for him to wait. But it was too much.

Once out of sight of the park, Sam ducked behind a tree and leaned up against it, sobbing. He slid down to the ground and cupped his face in his hands, then wiped his eyes and looked around to get his bearings.

Plainfield Drive. Good. Christina would be walking Alvis this way on her way to the park. He could hide and wait.

His cousin! She's his cousin... and she's going to tell on him and make it even worse. If he can't play football, he'll kill me. It was all too much.

I understand.

Sam sniffed and wiped his sleeve across his nose. The little hairs on the back of his neck stood at attention against a cool breeze.

"Hello?" he said quietly, turning to see who was there.

The road and the sidewalk were both clear.

It's not fair.

It sounded close, like it was coming from the sidewalk next to where he was sitting.

"Hello? Are you the one who was in the culvert?"

Sam stood and stepped onto the sidewalk. Just on the other side, the road curved down under the concrete, disappearing into the gaping mouth of a storm drain like an asphalt waterfall.

"Are you down there?" He leaned over the side and squinted into the darkness.

I am, the voice echoed in his head.

"Can you come up here?"

Not yet. The light hurts my eyes. What is your name?

Sam hesitated. He wasn't exactly afraid, but the voice sounded so needy, and he couldn't shake the feeling that interacting with whatever was down there would have huge implications, though he wasn't sure what those could be, yet.

What is your name? it asked again, reaching into his mind and tugging, like a child vying for its mother's attention.

What could be the harm of just telling it his name? Sure, he wasn't supposed to talk to strangers, and he especially wasn't supposed to tell strangers his name. That had been programmed into him and pretty much every other kid on the planet by parents, teachers, and a variety of cartoon characters and puppets. What he wasn't certain of was whether or not this particular voice could be categorized as a *stranger*. What if he was on the cusp of discovering a new species of animal that could communicate with people? Would that animal be considered a *stranger*? Nobody got upset if you told a stray dog your name, or a snake, or a turtle, or...

"Sam. My name is Sam," he said, amply satisfied with his brain's skilled rationalization.

A pleasant vibration similar to the purr of a cat buzzed through him, pushing away thoughts of his recent humiliation. It was soothing, calming.

I don't have a name... Would you give one to me?

Something about the way this request was delivered sent a shiver down Sam's spine. He swallowed hard and welcomed his thumbnail between his teeth when it arrived there almost of its own accord.

"What do you mean?" he asked, more a means to buy time than a request for clarification.

Give me a name, Sam, so that we can be friends... connected. So that I can help you.

Loud barking erupted just down the street from where Sam was standing. He looked up. Alvis galloped toward him, leash trailing behind him, the plastic baggie container attached to its handle bouncing along the road and hopping up like a spastic grasshopper each time it encountered an obstacle. About a block behind the frantic dog, Christina was running and waving her arms, screaming for Alvis to come back. She stopped and bent over panting when it was obvious the dog was headed to Sam.

Sam braced himself for the usual jumping up and kissing that occurred when Alvis saw anyone in the family after any period of absence, no matter how short, but the dog was not even looking at him. Alvis's gaze, and his fury, were one hundred percent focused on the storm drain in front of the boy. He snarled and snapped, drool flying from his jowls when he approached the opening below the sidewalk, his hindquarters knocking Sam back and away.

"Alvis!" Sam called. "Alvis, it's okay. Come here, boy."

"What the hell is wrong with you?" asked Christina, finally reaching the pair and catching her breath. "Alvis, no!"

She clapped her hands together with a sound that made Sam think his sister's palms were going to be awfully sore in a few minutes, snapping Alvis out of his Oscar-winning Cujo performance. Then, she bent down to gather up the leash. The dog cocked his head to the side, leaning toward the drain, as if to verify that all danger had passed, then ran over to Sam, jumping up and covering his face with wet sloppy kisses.

"Hopefully Mom and Dad can get that trainer soon," said Christina. She leaned over and planted her hands on her knees, still winded. "Shit, my hands," she said, pulling them off her knees and looking at the palms.

She held them up toward Sam. They were the same color as the stop sign on the corner. He pulled a breath in through his teeth and squinted.

"Ouch."

"Yeah, ouch. Don't tell Mom and Dad, though. I don't want him to get into too much trouble. It's not like he actually ran away or anything. He took off when he saw you." She grinned. "Probably thought the raccoons were coming for you, with their switchblade teeth."

Sam nodded and forced a smile.

"What are you doing here, anyway? Weren't you supposed to hang out with your friend?"

His sister took a closer look at him, reached over, and brushed some mulch off his shoulder. Then, she leaned in, focusing on his forehead. Sam instinctively brought up his hand and pushed his bangs down. He turned to start walking, but she took ahold of his arm and stopped him.

"Sam, what the hell happened?"

Sobs bubbled up and tears began to flow. She gently brushed the hair off his forehead. He stared at the ground, making no attempt to stop her. When he looked up, he saw her expression turn from concern to big-sister, nobody-messes-with-my-brother-but-me rage.

"Who did this? Was it that little asshole up the street?" she asked, her tone leaving no room for denial.

Sam tried to answer, but his lips quivered and his throat

seized. He nodded. Christina let Alvis's leash slide down past her wrist. The dog was sitting obediently next to her, his dark soulful eyes trained on Sam. She pushed her brother's bangs back down over the writing and placed a hand on each of his shoulders.

"I'm the only one who's allowed to call you a loser," she said, looking him straight in the eyes and smirking.

This elicited the hint of a grin from Sam, who was chewing the side of his thumb full throttle. She gently pushed his hand down and pulled him in for a hug.

"Welp," she said. "Looks like I'm gonna have to squeeze an ass-whooping into my already busy schedule."

Sam's body stiffened and he pulled back.

"Please don't," he said. "It'll just get worse. Maybe he's done."

"In my expert opinion, gained during my two-plus years longer than you on this planet, he's not going to stop until someone makes him stop. And, if that someone is Mom or Dad..."

Sam's eyebrows bunched and his thumb went back up to his mouth. Christina once again moved it away.

"If it's Mom or Dad," she tilted her head down and lowered it more to his level, "which it won't be. You're right, it'll probably get worse. But, if that someone is *me*, aka older-high-school-sibling-with-friends threatening to kick his ass from here to Australia, well, that might just do the trick. In the meantime, maybe take Alvis when you go for walks. I'm sure that little prick won't come anywhere near you if he sees Alvis."

A smile snuck onto Sam's lips. He had, of course, heard his sister swear before. After all, she was in high school. But he'd never heard her swear this much in his presence and never in his defense, like this. It felt good.

"Now, let's get you home. We need to google how to get that off before dinner."

She tussled his hair. This time he didn't mind at all.

FOURTEEN

Sarah's phone vibrated in her pocket, announcing a text. She fished it out and looked at the screen, walking toward the front of the house. It was the one she'd been expecting. She paused for a moment to send a text of her own.

"Kids, finish up getting the table ready. Mr. Thomas is here."

She went into the office, Alvis at her heels.

"I'm going to shut Alvis in here," she told Greg, who was sitting at the desk working on his computer, "then let him out when Mr. Thomas is already in the kitchen. I read that it's better if the dog enters when the stranger is already there positively interacting with the family, as opposed to the stranger suddenly entering his territory. Even though," she glared down at Alvis, "Mr. Thomas is not really a stranger, is he? Since you were just fine with him the first five times you met."

Greg laughed and took ahold of Alvis's collar so he wouldn't follow Sarah out.

"Just let me know when, and I'll come out with him and

join you. Maybe holler something like 'release the hound!' or 'every man for himself!'"

Sarah rolled her eyes, the corner of her mouth turned up in a smirk, and shut the door. Then she headed to the door to the garage. She'd told Mr. Thomas to come that way so that Alvis wouldn't hear him come in. She'd also told him to pretend that Alvis wasn't even there and not to look him in the eye or reach down... everything she'd read in her internet search.

She took a deep breath and squared her shoulders, then opened the door and pushed the button to raise the automatic door to the outside. Mr. Thomas was there with a bottle in one hand and a plate wrapped in foil in the other.

"I told you not to bring anything," she said, shaking her head, though pleased at the gesture. "Unless your shining personality is wrapped up in that plate, you weren't listening."

Ben laughed and held out the items he was carrying.

"You know, my hearing has been going downhill lately. I guess you'll just have to accept these. Unless you are going to make an old man walk all the way back to his house."

"Of course not," she said, reaching out to receive his offerings. "Oh, I don't think we've tried this one." She examined the label of the wine bottle he handed her.

"I was told it pairs well with pizza," he said with a wink. "Oh, and I brought some of the most delicious cookies you'll ever taste, too. I don't get the credit for making them, though. Evelyn Whistler brought them over today. She always brings me way too many. And if they're in the house, I will eat every last one. Something my doctor has suggested I not do." He shrugged, patting his gut.

"Thank you," she said. "Come on in. Alvis is closed in the office. Hopefully, this little trick will help your reintroduction go smoothly. I really don't know what's got into him. He's never bitten anyone... in case you're worried."

Ben held up a hand and followed her into the kitchen. He didn't seem worried at all, which helped to set Sarah at ease. Dogs could sense fear.

"Hey there," said Ben when they turned the corner. Christina and Sam were putting napkins down at the place settings.

"Hi, Mr. Thomas," said Sam, walking over to them and eyeing the foil-covered plate.

"Sam told me you two have met." Sarah set the wine and cookies down, shooing Sam away with a hand. "This is my daughter, Christina."

"Nice to meet you, Christina." Ben extended a hand. "How do you like it here in our little town?" he asked, directing the question at all three.

"There are so many more creatures here than there were near our last place, in Indiana," Sam offered, his excitement obvious.

"I imagine that's because of the warmer climate down here in Texas," said Ben. "Whereabouts in Indiana? Mary and I lived there for a bit, among other places."

"We lived in Fort Wayne," said Sarah. "It's up near..."

"Oh, I know where it is," Ben jumped in. "Mary and I lived in Warsaw for a few years, has to have been at least fifteen years ago. Then we stayed in Wisconsin for a little stretch before moving here." He scratched the stubble poking through on his chin and his eyes drifted as if pulled by a memory.

"We moved a lot. I was in sales," he said finally, the look of reverie gone. "So, where's Alvis? Should I call out for your husband to 'release the hound'?"

Sarah snorted and grinned before regaining her composure.

"That's what Greg said I should say," she explained. "Greg, honey, you guys can come on out. We're ready." *As we'll ever be,* she added to herself.

The latch clicked and Alvis skittered down the hall and into the kitchen. He was heading toward Sarah with a look of *how-could-you-do-that-to-me* on his face when he noticed Ben.

"It's okay, Alvis," said Sarah, with an exaggerated smile. "Kids, relax and act like everything is normal."

"Everything *is* normal," said Christina, rolling her eyes. "You're the only one that looks nervous."

Sarah shot her daughter a glare and noticed Ben smirk from the corner of her eye.

"I'm Greg. Nice to finally meet you." Greg reached out and shook Ben's hand, watching the dog out of the corner of his eye. Alvis sniffed around their elderly neighbor, hackles at half-mast. The meeting seemed to be going well, so far.

"Ben Thomas. Nice to meet you, too. Hey, I got the nature pics you texted," Ben said, looking over at Sam. "You are quite the photographer."

"Did you print them?" Sam asked, a certain pride in his voice. "Mom, Mr. Thomas helped me scare out some crawfish and I got some amazing pics. He said he was going to print one and frame it."

He reached a hand around to his back pocket, then pulled it back.

"I left my phone in my jacket. Well, I can show you later."

"Here," said Ben, pulling out his phone. "Took me some

internet searches and a great deal of frustration, but I figured out how to make it my screen's background."

He held the phone out, turning to show the whole family a beautiful shot of one of the bright-colored creek-dwellers. While he was doing this, Alvis zeroed in on his pant pocket and began to sniff rather vigorously.

"Alvis, no," said Sarah, walking over to pull him away.

"It's okay," said Ben, holding up his hand. "I'm afraid he caught me, found my failsafe."

He laughed, reached into his pocket, and pulled out what appeared to be a large piece of some kind of jerky.

"I read that it's okay for dogs to have these... if it's okay with you, that is."

"It's fine," said Greg, looking over at Sarah, who nodded confirmation. "Besides, if you don't give it to him now that he's seen it, you'll end up back on his people-I-want-to-eat list."

"Ask him to sit, first," added Christina, "so you don't lose a finger giving it to him. I speak from experience."

Sam nodded vigorously, setting everyone laughing. Alvis sat when Ben asked him to and happily received his reward. And Sarah breathed a loud sigh of relief. A kitchen timer sounded.

"Let's eat before it gets cold," she said, waving her hand to the side to direct everyone to the table.

FIFTEEN

Dinner with Mr. Thomas was the perfect distraction. He had a million stories about creatures and cool things he did when he was younger. Sam wondered if there was anywhere his neighbor had not been. He was about to ask when the doorbell rang, sending Alvis into his usual stranger-at-the-door panic. Mom stood and grabbed his collar.

"Christina, could you see who's there, please?" she asked when she was finally able to calm Alvis enough to make herself heard.

Christina set down the piece of pizza she was working on. For a minute, it looked like she was going to complain about having to go, but she sighed and stood up instead. Sam was pretty sure it would have been a different story if Mr. Thomas hadn't been there. He grinned, keeping his head down so she wouldn't see. She trudged down the hall. Sam heard the door open and a short, muffled exchange.

"Sam, it's for you," she called.

He dropped his pizza and looked around, chewing the inside of his cheek. For him?

"Well?" Dad said. "Aren't you going to go see who it is?"

Mr. Thomas looked at Sam, brows raised. He made a slight nudging motion with his head and smiled.

"Oh, yeah," said Sam, pushing his chair back and standing. "Excuse me. I'll be right back."

He walked down the hall toward the door, wondering who it could be.

"Polite young man," said Mr. Thomas, loud enough for his voice to carry.

If his parents said anything in return, Sam didn't hear it. He was too busy staring at his sister, who had the door propped open and was just behind it smirking and blinking at him in an exaggerated way. She pursed her lips and pointed at the door, then swung it open for him to see Samantha standing on the front stoop. His stomach squeezed in an effort to squelch the swarm of butterflies coming to life in its pit.

"Oh... hey," he said, picking up his pace and sliding over to the door. "Thanks, you can go back to the table," he told Christina, nudging her with his elbow.

"Nice to meet you, Sam. Hope to see you again," said Christina, emphasizing *Sam* and grinning at her brother. She turned and went back to the kitchen.

Sam heard Mom ask who it was and his sister answer, "Sam's friend, Sam." He didn't quite hear what his mom said after that, but Christina followed with, "No, Mom. That would be weird. Let the kid have some space."

Note to self, you owe Christina big time, he thought, pulling the door closed behind him. He turned his attention to Samantha, who was holding something out in front of her. It was his phone.

"You dropped this at the park," she said. "It has a little crack, but it looks like it's only in the screen protector."

She reached out and handed it to him.

"Thanks," he said, not sure what else to say. He'd assumed the phone was in his jacket pocket.

The sting of embarrassment and the shock of finding out that she was related to his bully were still fresh. Christina had been able to get the Sharpie off his forehead with a combination of toothpaste and make-up remover, thanks to the internet. But seeing Samantha there in front of him with that expression of...

Sympathy, whispered the rational part of his brain.

Pity, corrected his pride.

His forehead burned.

"How did you know where I live?" He certainly didn't remember telling her, and there was no way she could have seen from the bus.

"Oh, I made him tell me when I found your phone," she said. Sam appreciated her not mentioning her cousin's name. "I told him I wouldn't tell on him if he showed me where you lived. Is that okay?"

Bonus points for Samantha. Maybe Tyler wouldn't kill him after all.

"Yeah," he said, his mouth turned in a half smile.

They stood in silence for a minute. It seemed more like an hour to Sam, and he spent most of it staring at the ground, concentrating on not chewing his thumbnail.

"Well, it sounds like you guys are having dinner. And my parents are waiting for me," said Samantha, breaking the trance. She stepped aside and pointed behind her to a car that was pulled alongside the curb with its engine running and headlights on. Then she locked her hands together and shrugged. "Sorry about Tyler. He's kind of a jerk. He's worse now that Uncle Frank moved out."

Sam's face scrunched. He had no idea what to say about that. It sounded almost like she was justifying her cousin's behavior. Like she thought there could be a good reason... any reason... for what he'd done. That feeling of *too much* was rising in his stomach, heading up his throat.

She must have noticed, because she immediately followed with, "He still shouldn't have done that to you. It was a jerk move. And if you want me to say something to Aunt Evelyn, I will even though I said I wouldn't."

Sam shook his head. "No. Don't," he said, his tone perhaps a little too panicked. He calmed his voice. "I mean, it's better if you don't. Thanks for bringing my phone."

She nodded and turned to go, looking back at him when she reached the sidewalk.

"See you on the bus, I guess. If your phone's okay, maybe you can show me those pics."

Then she hopped into the car and it drove away.

Sam stepped inside and closed the door, standing with his back pressed against it while he tried to process what had happened. He was glad to get his phone back, for sure. And she was right, it looked like only the screen protector was cracked. Still, he wasn't sure how he felt about his only potential friend in the world being so closely related to the kid who wanted to kick his ass just because he existed and was "ruining the view." He reached his hand up, lightly brushing his forehead with his fingers, and cringed. The skin was still tender. He wasn't surprised. Christina had to scrub pretty hard to get the Sharpie off, and when he'd looked in the mirror after, you could still see the word *loser*, only now it was red instead of black, and hot from the friction.

"It'll fade," said Christina, examining her work. "But you'll wanna keep your bangs down during dinner, for sure."

"Sweetie, are you coming back to the table?" Mom called. "If your friend is still there, you could invite him in for pizza."

"Coming. No, Sam just stopped by to drop off my phone. I guess it fell out of my pocket. Sam's parents were waiting in their car."

Two *Sams* equaled no lie. Besides, he was pretty sure that his mother would now be more focused on the phone part of his answer. And he was correct.

"That was lucky," she said, the tone of her voice changing from curious mom to teaching-a-lesson-mom. He could have mouthed the exact next words that came from the kitchen along with her. "You need to be more careful with your things."

Sam's shoulders slumped. He shoved the phone into his pocket. Alvis, who had been released once he confirmed that his friend was gone, met him in the hallway and followed him back to the kitchen.

"Too bad your friend couldn't stay for some pizza," said Mom when Sam came back into the kitchen. "You'll have to invite him another time so we can thank him for finding your phone. Nothing says thank you like homemade cookies."

She cocked her head and leaned toward Sam, putting a hand on his father's arm to get his attention. She was staring at his forehead.

Now, they were all staring at his forehead. Christina made a motion for him to brush his bangs down, but that ship had sailed. Mom stood up and walked over to Sam. He put his hand above his eyebrows to fix his hair, but she moved it aside and pushed his bangs completely to the side.

"What happened here?" she asked, her voice steady, its tone sharp. "Did that boy do this to you?"

She put a hand on each side of his shoulders and looked directly into his eyes, waiting for an answer. Sam squirmed and looked over at Mr. Thomas, trying to remind her that there was a guest in the house, pinching his mouth into a tight, lipless line.

"Greg," she said, ignoring Sam's cues and looking over at her husband. "We have got to do something about this boy up the street."

Dad lifted a brow and shifted his gaze between Mom and Sam.

"Has someone been messing with you, Sam?"

"It's the kid up the street," said Christina. "But Sam and I think that I can maybe talk to him, you know, without parents. Parents might make it worse."

She straightened in her seat and gave Sam a nod. He hoped that his eyes appropriately conveyed his gratitude.

"This isn't just teasing," Mom's voice shifted up an octave, shattering Sam's hopes that she would drop the issue. "This is *assault*."

She gently touched the red L, shaking her head when he flinched. Her eyes were on fire and her lips were pressed together so tightly that they were devoid of color. Alvis pressed against Sam's leg and whined until the boy reached down and set his hand on the dog's head.

"It's really not that bad, Mom. It was just a bad joke. Maybe he thought it would be easy to get off," said Sam, not believing a word he'd just uttered, but desperate to defuse his mother's anger before she did something crazy, like call Tyler's house. Or worse, march out the door and up the street.

"Calm down, Sarah."

Good. Dad was going to talk her down.

"You don't think we should talk to this kid's parents?" She lifted the bangs higher and pointed to the raised, irritated skin. "You think this was just a bad joke? He could get an infection, Greg."

"I just think that maybe we should let Christina try talking to the kid first. Sometimes the you'd-best-keep-your-hands-off-my-little-brother approach works better, especially when coming from a high schooler to a middle schooler." He held out his hands, palms up.

Sam could tell by his mother's expression that she was not convinced. He had just decided to feign sickness for the rest of the school year or to run away and join the grounds crew of a circus, when Mr. Thomas hesitantly raised a hand, reminding them all that he was still there.

"Was it Tyler?" he asked softly, catching Sam's eye. The boy nodded. "Well, maybe I could talk to him." His voice was calm and reasonable, matter-of-fact. "I know his parents and I've known him since he was little."

The room fell silent. Mom removed her hand from Sam's forehead and brought it to her chin, tapping it like she did when she was writing and stuck on a line or searching for a word—*word hunting* she liked to call it. Everyone else watched and waited. Her worry lines smoothed. She picked up a clean napkin from the table, walked to the refrigerator, and pushed a lever on the door to get some ice.

"Put that on your head," she told Sam, wrapping the ice and handing it to him. He did as instructed, his gaze never leaving her. "Do you want Mr. Thomas to talk to this Tyler kid?"

Sam looked over at Mr. Thomas, remembering how effectively his neighbor had scared Tyler off the day they met. He would have preferred Christina try first. That seemed like the least risky strategy to him. But it didn't look like that was going to be an option to which his mom would agree. Maybe this was the next best thing. Mr. Thomas had seen the earphone incident with his own eyes, so if he said something to Tyler about the bullying, it wouldn't necessarily mean that Sam ratted him out.

"I guess so," he said, nodding.

"Settled," Dad exclaimed, reaching over to give Sam a pat on the back. "Thank you, Mr. Thomas... Ben."

"Happy to help." Mr. Thomas winked at Sam. "Now that you have your phone back, you can show off the rest of the pictures you took at the creek." He turned his head toward Sam's parents. "Your son really is a talented nature photographer, even with just his phone. If he ever wants to learn how to use a professional camera, I still have Mary's laying around gathering dust somewhere. It has all the bells and whistles, and a big old manual to prove it."

"That would be awesome," said Sam, his eyes growing as wide as the tea saucers his mom was bringing over for dessert.

"I used to have an old film camera, but I haven't seen it since this last move," said Dad. "I'm sure it's not as nice as yours, though. Sounds like a good idea, right, Sarah? You're always saying the boy needs more hobbies. Maybe this would even be a good way for him to get more involved at school. He could take pictures for the yearbook or something."

If Mr. Thomas's intention had been to change the subject,

he was incredibly successful, and Sam was grateful. The rest of the evening was spent talking about cameras and creatures. Oh, and Mom even managed to loop in Christina's callback for auditions, to her great embarrassment, tying it into the *creature* discussions.

By the time their neighbor said goodnight, even Alvis was sad to see him leave.

SIXTEEN

Jacob Anderson opened his cold blue eyes, squinting against the beam of sunlight that had slipped through the space between the curtains and landed directly on his face. He groaned and rolled to his side. His hand drifted to the scar, the one that woke him most nights to remind him that he was *lucky to be alive*.

There'd been others since, but that was the first and the worst. His index finger traced the knotted line of skin from just below his sternum around and under his left rib cage. It was raging. He reached over to the wooden table next to the bed and fumbled about for the little orange plastic bottle that promised a modicum of relief, knocking it to its side. The crisp clicking of scattering pills against plastic, then wood, sounded. Good. The bottle was open. He wasn't sure he could have dealt with a child-proof cap right then.

He scooped up the pills closest to his fingers and shoved them into his mouth. What were they again? He wasn't sure, but whatever they were, they were better than nothing. After giving the pills time to soften the burn, Jacob reached back over to find the bottle. He held it up close enough for his eyes to focus on the label. His lips contorted, silently shaping out the words on the bottle as he read.

Julia Kline.

The name had no memory attached to it. But the substance was familiar. His mind wandered through the things he could recall about the day before, which were thinning like a forest full of lumberjacks.

The raging river of pain that ran along his scar slowed to a prickly trickle of discomfort. It was the best he could hope for. He closed his eyes and sighed.

"Thank you, Julia," he whispered, hoping she was still okay and able to receive the heartfelt gratitude he was sending telepathically. He couldn't always limit his damage, but there was a part of him that always made an effort.

An hour or two went by before he woke again, this time in a more tolerable condition. He swung his feet off the bed and sat up, looking around to find some reminder of where he was. Standard sappy wall art, stained gray polypropylene carpet, desk table topped with one beat-up coffee maker, and a packet of cheap, crappy coffee, hopefully not decaffeinated. It could be one of a million different motel chains in a million different towns.

He rubbed his eyes, bright masses of light exploding like fireworks when the heel of his hands pressed into the sockets. A stiff shove off the mattress launched him toward the window, where he pushed the heavy curtain aside just enough to peek out at the parking lot. No help there. Five cars with license plates from five different states, including his own beat-up Subaru Outback... Jimmy's Subaru Outback.

Hopeful that a few sips of coffee might jump-start his

memory, Jacob released the curtain and shuffled over to the coffee maker. He pushed aside a small pile of cash, knocking over a tower of quarters he vaguely remembered stacking the night before. The top two quarters landed on their sides, rolling along the table until they crashed into a heap of wallets and watches. He'd been busy the day before.

He knocked the heel of his hand against his temple a couple of times in a failed attempt to jar back his most recent activities. A glance down at his clothes reassured him. No blood. Well, at least he could be fairly certain he hadn't offed anyone... this time.

A scratchy laugh worked its way up his throat, exiting his lips in a dry, muffled chortle. He opened the machine, popped a coffee packet (caffeinated, thank god) up top and a disposable coffee cup below, then filled the tank using a half-empty water bottle laying on its side on the desk. Then he flipped on the power switch with one hand, giving his crotch a hardy scratch with the other.

Nothing.

Really?

His body ached for coffee.

"Piece of shit." He grabbed the machine and swung it back to throw it against the wall.

The card he'd used to pay for the room wasn't his anyway and whoever put this shitty joke of a coffee maker in here deserved the mess he was about to make. The cord swung around, smacking the plug against his lower back.

"Sonofabitch," he said, laughing. "Gotta plug the mother-fucker in first, I suppose."

He set the coffee maker back down and plugged in the cord.

"This is your lucky day," he told it, waggling his finger before jamming the digit against the power switch.

He closed his eyes and drew a deep breath when the sound of percolating filled his ears. Sure, it was most likely shit coffee, but shit coffee was better than no coffee, at least in most cases. Besides, he knew if he didn't get his morning caffeine fix, the headaches would ravage his brain later in the day. And he didn't see anything else caffeinated in the room.

When the little cup was full, he switched off the machine and brought the brew up to his nose. It looked like dirty dishwater and didn't smell much better. But it was caffeinated dishwater. He ripped open the tiny packet of sugar he found on the table and dumped it in. There were barely enough grains in it to flavor a thimble of coffee, never mind a cup. Grumbling his disdain, he downed the beverage in one gulp, holding his breath to neuter his tastebuds.

He looked at his watch... well, *his* now... and decided he should get on the road again before someone reported their credit card missing and figured out where he'd used it. People were slower to remember, and report, missing cards when he lifted them at bars. He just needed to keep an eye out for the loudest, most obnoxiously drunk patrons and wait for an opportunity to present itself. Then, as long as he got out of Dodge by the end of the next day, he was golden. The types of places he stayed didn't usually ask for an ID, and on those rare occasions that they did, well, he'd say he lost it and dip into his cash reserve.

"Why can't you be more like your brother was, bless his soul?" his mom used to ask, before Jacob finally got sick of it all and left.

I'm more like him than you'll ever know, he thought, snorting out a laugh.

Sure, Jimmy wasn't into drugs, a vice that had seized hold of Jacob thanks to the pain pills the doctor prescribed after *the incident*. And Jimmy never overdid it when it came to booze, something that Jacob readily admitted he himself occasionally did. But the church-going folks of their little Wisconsin town hadn't had a clue who the *real* Jimmy was. The only one who knew was Jacob, and he would take that shit to his grave, no matter how badly he wanted to rub it in his mother's face. His love for his brother far outweighed his hatred for her and everyone else in that holier-than-thou town of hypocrites.

He gathered up a duffle bag off the floor. One of its handles was hanging on by a thread, and it had the appearance of something that had been dragged behind the car, maybe even under it, though he religiously kept it in the seat next to him, at arm's length. He brushed at it. Most of the dirt and grime were not only on the bag, but an integral part of it. They'd been through a lot, he and this bag... and the car. They had history, but he might need to pick up a new one along the way if the opportunity presented itself.

"It's stupid to get sentimental about *things*," Jimmy always said. "*Things* are only worth something if you can sell 'em or use 'em. If not, best to get rid of 'em."

For now, it still served a purpose other than just reminding him of Jimmy, so he didn't feel like he was breaking the rules when he shoved his belongings, old and recently acquired, inside and zipped it shut.

On the way to the door, he picked up a paper he'd set on the nightstand. It was a newspaper article, printed out on a sheet of computer paper at the library at the beginning of this trip. It was actually the reason for this particular trip. The edges of the paper were crumpled, and creases, where it was being continuously refolded to fit snugly into his pocket, made portions of it illegible, as did the ugly brown circle stained onto the page, thanks to a leaky cup of coffee two or three motels ago. But the important bits were still legible. And, even if they somehow became illegible, they'd been burnt into his mind's eye as sure as if someone had seared them there with a branding iron.

At the top of the page, the word *Obituaries*, in thick, fancy, black cursive, reigned supreme above a scattering of photographs of the then-recently departed. About halfway down the page, Jacob had circled one of the black and white pictures and done some underlining below it. He gave it only a cursory glance before folding it and jamming it into the back pocket of his jeans.

When he stepped out the door into the parking lot, the sun hit his eyes like a hot poker. He squinted, reaching up with his free hand to rub his temples. Where the hell were his sunglasses? It was near impossible to think with the throbbing that was churning up in his head. He fumbled around in his pockets for the keys to the Outback, pushing through wads of cash and little balls of tin foil, remnants of those chocolate candy kisses he loved. At the very bottom of his left pocket, nestled in among the lint and frayed threads, his finger looped through the metal ring of the keychain he'd gifted his brother the year Jimmy bought the Outback, his first—and last—car. Tangled in the web of pocket threads, the keys put up a brief fight to stay put.

A quick yank and a twist of his hand freed them not only from the strings but from his hand. He watched the keys take flight, dragging the silver ring and the little Bart Simpson figure with them. After a sad little arch, they hit the asphalt and slid under the car parked next to his.

"Fuck," he said, leaning over to look under the red Dodge Charger, which was in considerably better shape than his Outback.

"Shit," he added when he saw where his keys had ended their journey. Bart and the ring were still visible, balanced on the edge of the bars of a sewer drain, which meant that the keys were now dangling down into said sewer.

"Do you mind?" asked an irritated voice nearby. "There are children."

He stood up and saw that the voice had come from a twenty-something-year-old brunette sitting in the driver's seat of the Charger with the windows down. She was wearing a tight mini-skirt and one of those cut-off sweaters that were less about staying warm and more about showing off the curves of a very well-tended body. She had a large band of her long, straight, silky hair tucked behind her ear and was peering at him, head tilted down, over a pair of oversized, expensive-looking sunglasses. She shifted her gaze to the backseat, once he was able to work his own up from her navel, past the sensuous suggestion of bare breasts visible just below the bottom of the sweater, and up to her eyes.

Jacob set his duffle bag on the ground and brushed his t-shirt down with both hands. He sauntered over to the car and leaned an elbow on the passenger side window, hoping that he didn't smell too bad. He had skipped his morning shower in favor of getting further down the road before the credit card he'd *borrowed* was missed. There was a truck stop about an hour away, a safer place for him to wash up.

Her sweet, tangy perfume met him at the window, filling his senses and tickling his imagination. He closed his eyes and pulled in a deep breath of her, his jeans suddenly tight at the crotch. The side of his mouth curled up into the impish grin that almost always ended up winning him some company. Though admittedly, he'd been so focused on this trip that it had been a while since he'd scored a piece of ass of her caliber.

He still had his room key and the shower in the motel room was more than big enough for two bodies, especially if those bodies were as close as he wanted his to be to hers. She pointed to the backseat, smiling, her bottom lip playfully tucked between her teeth. For a moment he thought she might want to meet him back there. He reached down to adjust himself, already imagining what he could do to her, even with the limited space the back of the Charger offered.

Something hit him on the side of the face. It was followed by a high-pitched victory cry and laughter. Jacob turned his attention to the backseat of the car, where a kid maybe seven or eight years old was holding a Nerf gun and giving him the stink eye.

"Potty mouth," the kid said before sticking out his tongue.

"Like I said, there are children. Watch the language." She started up the car and pushed the lever to roll up the window.

"Wait!" he yelled, remembering where his keys were currently located.

The bitch blew him a kiss and backed the car out of the space. He lunged for the keys as soon as the car was clear, snagging Bart just as he was heading over the edge of the bar and into the sewer. Then, he picked himself up off the asphalt and clutched the keys to his chest, panting. His knees were burning, and a quick glance down revealed two fresh tears in his jeans, the edges tinted red from the blood seeping from two ugly road rashes. The base of his throat tightened, a valve against the bile rising from his gut.

"Stupid bitch!" he yelled, running toward the Charger as it rolled backward.

He smashed a fist into the passenger door and rammed his shoulder against the window behind it. The woman jerked her body to the side, against the inside of her door, her face frozen in a gasp. She glared at him through the window, flipped him the bird, and shifted gears, propelling the car forward and throwing him off balance. As the car raced off, Jacob could see the face of the boy with the Nerf gun pressed against the back window, eyes wide and jaw slack.

"Bitch," Jacob said again, slapping his hand on the steering wheel, once he was back in his car.

He sat in the driver's seat of his Outback marinating in a stew of anger, embarrassment, and sexual frustration. The last of these was the easiest ingredient of the mix to deal with, and after a quick look around to make sure he was alone, he unzipped his jeans and got to work on a remedy while imagining all things he now wished to do to the bitch in the car, in front of her little shit kid, even. The way she had teased him... He wondered how hard he would have to bite down to burst one of those beautiful full breasts he'd seen peeking out from under her sweater.

He was almost there in his mind's eye, when he saw the boy at the edge of his field of vision, reflected in his window. The boy with the Nerf gun. The boy with terror etched onto his face. Something about the face was wrong, though. He turned his head to look at the image straight on and saw his own face reflected back.

SEVENTEEN

After dinner, Sarah put Christina and Greg to work clearing the table. Sam stepped over to help, but she waved a hand at him.

"You, come with me. I want to disinfect that and get some antibiotic on it," she said, motioning at his forehead.

He followed her to the back of the house, Alvis close behind him. When he stopped at the threshold of his parents' bathroom, Alvis brushed past.

"Come on in," Sarah said, rifling through the drawers below her husband's sink.

Sam stepped in and Sarah set to work dabbing his forehead with a ball of cotton freshly dampened with hydrogen peroxide.

"Sorry, sweetie," she said when he squinted and whimpered. "Was this Sharpie?"

He nodded.

"Did Christina scrub it off?"

Another nod.

"What did she use?"

She was careful to keep her tone soft, not to let the raging mother-bear seep into her voice. She didn't want him to think that she was angry at him. She was mad alright, but it was directed at pretty much everything but him. She was mad that she'd dragged the kids away from their last home, where Sam had a good friend, a best friend. Upset with Christina for not telling her what had happened. Mad at herself for whatever it was that she was doing that made the kids think they couldn't come to her. And furious with the kid up the street, Tyler, who for some reason had made it his mission to make sure Sam was miserable in his new town.

Sam explained the combination of techniques that they had used to get the Sharpie off his skin, making sure to emphasize that Christina had checked several trustworthy websites before doing anything. Sarah had to grin at this. Her kids fought a lot, bickered, and needled each other. But they were always quick to close ranks against outside threats or criticisms. Sometimes Sarah even felt a little jealous at how close they were and teased Christina about being Sam's *mom* 2.0.

"Mom, you're not going to go to his house and yell at him or anything, right?"

He must have seen the anger simmering at the edges of her pinched lips, peeking out behind the concern in her eyes. She looked him in the eye, taking a deep breath to steady her emotions, and smiled the most genuine and loving smile she could squeeze past her anger.

"Don't worry," she said. "Beating up little boys, whether or not they are assholes, is not in my repertoire."

"Mom!" said Sam, eyes wide, gasping, snorting, then breaking into a wave of giggles.

She smirked and raised her brows.

"Oops. Did I say that *out loud*?" She set the cotton ball on the counter and reached for a tube of antibiotics.

Sam's bangs crept back down and he reached a hand up to push them out of the way.

"Besides, didn't we decide to let Mr. Thomas talk to Tyler?"

He nodded, then held still while she painted over his angry skin with the gel. She had purposely grabbed the antibiotic with the label marked "with pain relief," hoping she could help soothe his physical pain, if not his embarrassment. The return of his smile, even if it had only been spurred by an unexpected swear from her lips, brought a warm feeling to her chest, as if that little bit of burning anger she'd let go from the pit of her stomach had warmed her heart on its way by.

"It's going to be okay, you know," she said, taping a large piece of gauze over his forehead to cover the shiny, greasy gel and keep it out of his hair.

She teased his bangs back down and turned him in front of her to face the mirror above the sink.

"See? Good as new."

He tilted his head and nodded, scrutinizing his reflection. A slight frown pulled down one side of his mouth.

"Don't worry," said Sarah, "You won't have to wear that to school. The red should be gone by then. And if it's not, we can call you in sick. I'll be home working on a story that's giving me some trouble. I keep jumping POVs like a grasshopper on a hot summer's road."

Sam raised a brow and cocked his head. Sarah laughed.

"Never mind that last part. If your skin is still even a little red, you can stay home, is the point."

He smiled at her in the mirror, gratitude shining in his eyes.

"We'll get this sorted. And I know you are going to make lots of friends here. Sometimes it just takes a little while. And sometimes we make friends when and where we least expect it."

When she uttered these last words, an odd vibration rumbled through her. She left one hand on Sam's shoulder and placed the other palm down on the bathroom counter to steady herself. The sensation rippled through her inner ear, creating a sound, a high-pitched ring. Sarah blinked hard, giving her head a little shake. She noticed Alvis staring up at her, ears perked, head tilted. The source of the vibration seemed to be her son. She lifted her hand off his shoulder and lowered it again, noting that, though it did not completely disappear, it was definitely much softer when she was not in contact.

Time to go back to the ENT, she thought, taking a deep breath.

"You okay, Mom?" Sam's expression slipped into one of concern. He turned around to face her.

"It's that weird inner ear thing. Don't worry about it. Anyway, I was saying... you will make friends. I mean, it looks like you've made one already. Sam, right?"

The vibration stopped. Sam was still smiling, but it was hard to read his expression.

"I guess," he said, a hint of uncertainty in his voice.

She wished she could figure out a way to boost his self-confidence. First things first, though. They needed to deal with this Tyler kid. Sarah would keep her promise and not get involved, let Mr. Thomas talk to him first. But, if that didn't work, all bets were off.

. . .

THE NEXT MORNING, Sarah and Alvis ran into Ben while on their morning walk.

"Good morning," he said, waving.

Alvis slowed and lowered his head, seemingly unsure as to whether he would be facing friend or foe. Mr. Thomas reached a hand into his pocket and pulled out a piece of jerky. The dog's head popped back up and his ears perked. He gave a sharp but friendly bark followed by a whine and a tail wag.

"You have his attention now," said Sarah, telling Alvis to sit.

Alvis sat, body trembling and tail wagging, hind quarters rising and falling each time Ben's shoes hit the pavement, scooting forward until his leash was taut.

"Good boy," said Ben, tossing the jerky when he was a few steps away. Alvis snapped it out of the air, then stood and walked over to lean into Ben's legs, happily absorbing the attention the elderly man showered on him.

"Looks like you are officially his new favorite person."

"Thanks to my beef jerky bribes." Ben winked.

"And how is my new favorite family doing today?" he asked.

"Ah, the dinner bribe worked, too, then." Sarah laughed. "We're okay. Sorry about the excitement last night... and thank you for offering to talk to the boy bullying Sam. Sam was sure relieved that I wasn't going to go busting down their door, She-Hulk style."

"Not that I ever would," she added, reminding herself that Ben didn't know her that well.

"Of course not," he said, his grin reassuring her that he got her sarcasm. "Tyler is supposed to come help me do some yard work. I'll have a little talk with him then. How's Sam doing?"

"I let him stay home today," said Sarah. "The writing on his forehead is pretty much gone, but I thought he could use a day off. He's watching nature documentaries. His teachers are going to email his homework later."

"I'll bet he's relieved he'll be getting his homework," said Ben, adding a hearty laugh and showing that he, too, was fluent in sarcasm.

Sarah grinned and nodded. "It'll be the highlight of his day. In the meantime, I just have to make sure I don't inadvertently add anything about... say... the mating habits of hissing cockroaches into the article I'm working on."

"If you need a nature documentary break while you work, you can send Sam over my way. I don't have anything going on after I go grab my mail." The corners of his eyes crinkled.

"I wouldn't want to impose," she said instinctively, though she could see by his expression that it would be no imposition.

It must be lonely, she thought, trying to imagine her life without Greg and the kids and all the pleasant pandemonium they brought to each day, happy her memories of before them had all but faded, and that more recent memories of almost losing it all had lost most of their sting.

"I dug around and found Mary's camera when I got home last night. I could use some help trying to figure it out. The print in those darn manuals is always so tiny."

"I'll let him know you offered," she said. "If he can tear himself away from Sir Attenborough, I'm sure he'll be over. What time is Tyler coming over to help you? It's probably best we keep some distance between them for now."

"Not until early evening," said Ben. "His mom has a

meeting tonight and I told her Tyler could stay for dinner at my place."

He rolled his lips in and passed a hand over his beard stubble like he was trying to decide whether or not to add something. He sighed hard through his nose and nodded slightly, seeming to give himself permission.

"His dad kind of flaked out on them this past summer."

Ben shook his head. His brows cinched together and the corners of his mouth turned down, in an expression that seemed alien on his kind face.

"I'm being too kind. I thought I knew the man. Thought he was a solid responsible husband and father. And I tend to give him too much of the benefit of the doubt, which isn't fair to Evelyn."

Sarah watched him, a lump rising in her throat. He wore his inner struggle in a pained expression. She didn't know Tyler or his family. And with the image of the raw raised skin on Sam's face so fresh in her mind, it was difficult for her to summon feelings of sympathy. Still, she listened out of respect for Ben.

He took a deep breath through his nose and let it escape in a puff, hardening his expression and looking from the ground to Sarah. She lifted her head slightly to meet his gaze, wearing a pinched, understanding smile.

"I don't like to gossip," he started. "It's a nasty business, any way you cut it. And, when people confide in me, I take their trust and the responsibilities that come with it very seriously."

Sarah nodded. She one hundred percent believed that he did.

"But I think you should know some things, things that are public knowledge, but of which you are probably unaware, due to the fact that you are new to our town."

Another nod.

"Frank Whistler just up and left his wife and son this past summer. No warning. No... what do you call 'em... *red flags*. He up and left and took up with someone else. Someone with kids. Someone in town. Says he's trying to *find himself*. Well, it'd be better if he were looking somewhere else completely, in my opinion."

Ben's eyebrows scrunched and his mouth twisted, as if he'd just tasted something rancid. A cold hollow ache took hold in Sarah's chest.

"It'd be better if he just left town, left the state, the country even. That boy, Tyler, was a sweet kid... a kind kid. And it just eats my insides to see him acting out like this, treating your boy this way. To see Evelyn struggling the way she is, but always smiling, keeping that upper lip stiffer than steel. Worrying about the likes of me, when she has enough to worry about already."

He took another deep breath and let the worry lines on his face smooth.

"It in no way excuses the way he's been acting toward Sam, mind you. And believe you me, we'll be chatting plenty about that over dinner tonight. I just wanted you to know. And that's all I'll say about it."

He gave one more final nod as if to punctuate, and the gentle, light-hearted smile Sarah had come to know him for reclaimed its rightful place. She nodded, empathy winding through her. She felt guilty for thoughts over which she'd had no control, for judging on impulse and without all the information. Her face relaxed, neutral and controlled.

"I appreciate your honesty and the information. I promise you I will keep it all in mind."

She looked at her watch, then at Alvis. The dog whined and walked away from Ben, hopping a bit on his front paws and looking toward the park up the street.

"Well, I'd better get moving so that Alvis can finish his business and work off some energy. When I get home from our walk, I'll send Sam over. That'll give you plenty of time to get your mail and to get some caffeine in you so you're ready for the full summary of the documentaries he's been absorbing since he woke up this morning." She laughed.

"It's been a pleasure as usual," said Ben, giving a little bow. "I look forward to learning about... what was it you mentioned?" He squinted and looked up to the left, then back at Sarah. "Hissing cockroaches, wasn't it?"

She nodded and chuckled. "Looks like you were paying attention. And thanks for having him."

When they went their separate ways, Sarah's mind kept hopping from planning out the rest of the story she was working on to the information Ben had relayed about the Whistlers. Her heart was already softening regarding the boy, Tyler, and she sincerely hoped that Ben could get through to him. Her own childhood had not been an easy one, and she herself could bring to mind at least one instance when she'd lashed out at someone undeserving as a result. And how would Sam have reacted if she and Greg hadn't patched things up, if she hadn't given him another chance? She had no way of knowing. She did know how easy it was for the sins of the father... or mother... or grandfather to wreak havoc on the mind, on one's self-worth. She understood the importance of trying to give children a feeling of safety and stability.

She wondered why Ben and Mary had not had any children of their own, or adopted if they were unable. From what she'd heard, Mary had been a delightful and caring woman. And Ben most certainly would have been an excellent father and one of those grandfathers she'd dreamed of having when she was little. One like the one Christina and Sam lost when Greg's father passed away last year. One very unlike the one she'd had, the one who had raised her.

Of course, she would never ask Ben such a question. In her experience, it was best not to pry. If people wanted to share their business, they would do so in their own time. Besides, as friendly as he was, Sarah had a feeling he liked to keep his business to himself. She had a sixth sense about people and their tolerance for scrutiny. It was one of the things that made her a good journalist. And though most of the things she wrote in the new job were fluff pieces, she liked to keep her sense for people tuned.

Besides, she fully understood the preference to keep some things private... things that deserved to be buried deep down in the bottom-most layers of one's mind. Things that were better off closed behind impenetrable doors with locks and no key.

The leash went taut, jerking both Sarah's arm and her attention back. She looked around, following the length of the leash with her gaze, right up to the ring where it was attached to Alvis. He was seated on the edge of the sidewalk farthest from the street, collar cinched up to the base of his head, and he was growling. She turned her head to look at the path they were walking, already sure of what she would see. The deep rumbling vibration, and conversation-like whispers of rushing water, alerted her to the presence of a storm drain somewhere nearby. She walked back to the dog, changing their direction away from the drain. And, in her dreamy, pensive state, she imagined two words floating up from below to meet her ears.

I understand.

EIGHTEEN

"Seriously?" said Sam, his attention turning from the impressive Goliath frog on the television screen to his mom. He picked up the remote and paused his show. "He said he wants me to help with his camera? Cool. Maybe I can learn to take nature pics with a *real* camera! Then we could make one of those rooms where you develop the film yourself in our basement and hang them from string tied across the ceiling with those wooden pinchy things." He made a claw with his hand and pinched his fingers together to illustrate.

"Clothes pins?"

"Yeah, those. And the creepy red light."

Sarah scratched her forehead and ran her hand through her hair, her mouth pinched over to one side.

"Where have you ever seen a darkroom?" she asked.

"I saw a little bit of *Stranger Things* on TV with Dad when you and Christina were out doing a girl's night. But we stopped when it got too scary."

Sarah raised her brows and closed her eyes, shaking her head.

"Don't tell him I told you." He clasped his hands together and shot her some puppy-dog eyes.

She raised both hands, shoulder height. "Far be it from me to interfere in father-son bonding time. Anyhow, you are getting a little ahead of the game, buddy. Why don't you head over to Mr. Thomas's house and help him with the camera? If you eventually do show an interest in photography, and if you show that you not only want to do it but that you'll take the time to learn to do it right, we can talk about cameras and dark-rooms and pinchy things."

She pinched her fingers together, her hands up like crab claws.

"What I don't want is another *skateboard* incident. You know, like when you really really wanted to learn to skate-board and you were going to skateboard everywhere, even to school. Then, we got you a nice expensive longboard for your birthday. You tried riding it a few times, and now it sits gathering dust in the garage."

"That was different, Mom. Skateboards are *dangerous*. And I totally sucked at it. You heard Mr. Thomas, I'm really *good* at photography." He grinned matter-of-factly.

"He did say that. Well, your birthday is coming up. Start researching options—reasonably priced options—and your dad and I will think about it. Now, scoot on over there, if you want to go. I asked the school to let me know when the teachers email your homework. I will text you when you need to come home and do it."

Sam turned off the television and ran over to put his shoes and jacket on. Alvis bounced around him, barking.

"Sorry, buddy. You gotta stay here with Mom," said Sam, scratching behind the dog's ear.

Sarah stepped over, gave him a hug, and took ahold of Alvis's collar so Sam could get out the door without being followed.

"Have fun," she said.

The door shut behind him, muffling Alvis's protests at being left behind.

Sam rushed across the street and onto the sidewalk in front of Mr. Thomas's house. He stopped and looked around. The little hairs on his neck were raised, as if pulled by static electricity. He licked his hand and passed it between his collar and his skin. This relaxed the hairs but did nothing to alleviate a feeling that he was being watched. He looked back at his house. Next to a glint of sunlight reflecting off the office window, he could see Alvis's face. His nose was pressed against the glass, and it looked like his hackles were up. It was hard to make out details with the sunlight so brightly reflected, but Sam could see Alvis's eyes, and they looked... intense.

That must be it, he thought, rubbing the back of his neck again.

He started up the walk to Mr. Thomas's door, glancing back at the sidewalk, at the cement lip above the opening to the storm drain, when he heard...

Name me, Sam.

NINETEEN

Jacob wandered around the truck-stop convenience store waiting for his number to be called. Each time he walked up an aisle toward the front of the store, he caught the cashier's eye and flashed her a grin and a wink. And each time, she cast her eyes down, blushing and giggling, the tips of her fingers brushing along her bottom lip. It was driving him insane.

When he had handed her the twelve bucks to purchase his shower time, he was distracted, calculating how many more miles he could drive before having to stop for gas, how much cash he still had on hand, and where to get more, mulling over the bitch in the Charger. He would also need to swap out the credit cards he used the day before. Best not to use the same ones more than once. Also, one of the cards he'd lifted had turned out to be one of those prepaid Visa gift cards with a grand total of $5 on it, which was not only a disappointment but had thrown things off.

"Here's your ticket with the code."

The soft, melodious voice had cut through his thoughts like a laser through Crisco, and he had looked up to see a young blonde woman standing on the other side of the counter, manning the register. She was holding out a receipt, a pleasant, somewhat awkward smile gracing her lips.

"We'll, ummm, call your number when a stall opens. Make sure you, ummm, punch the code in within ten minutes... after that."

Her wavy honey-colored locks swayed when she spoke, a hypnotizing web loosely gathered into a ponytail that sat to the left of center behind her head. Every few words, she bit her lip as if she wasn't quite sure of what she was saying and her eyes flicked to the right or left, maybe in search of her manager... or a senior employee.

"New here?" he asked, letting his eyes lead his imagination on a field trip around her curves.

She was young, but not off-limits young, based on her abundantly developed body. Her expression screamed inno-cence, but there was something just under the surface that told him not to believe it. He'd been scammed plenty by *innocent* girls... innocent-*looking* girls... especially when he was younger and had just struck out on his own. Blindly letting your cock take the lead was a great way to end up with an empty wallet... and possibly even naked and beat up at the side of a rest area parking lot, lucky to still have a vehicle because you had enough sense to at least stash your keys before getting down to business. Live and learn.

"Yeah," the girl said, chewing the inside of her lip. "It's my first shift alone. I've never done a shower alone before." She blushed a deep crimson red and brought her hand to her face, shaking her head. "I mean, I've never rung up a shower purchase by myself." Her eyes slowly wandered back up to meet his gaze, embarrassment still illuminating her cheeks.

Jacob had swung his duffle bag to the back of his shoulder and put both palms on the counter in front of her, leaning in to read the name printed on her uniform, just above her left breast. An impish grin crept across his lips.

"Well, Kit," he said in a growly whisper, "I'm glad to hear that you do occasionally shower alone. Though," he leaned a little closer, turning up the intensity of his gaze and running his tongue over his drying lips, "you are welcome to join me in mine if you so desire. I certainly wouldn't complain."

He backed up to let his words sink in, donning an overly innocent smile on his rakishly handsome face while he watched her like an archer who, having just released his bowstring, was waiting to see if he would hit his mark. She giggled again; this time her whole face flushed and her hand floated down to rest on the top curves of her breasts, which rose and fell with her quick, shallow breaths.

"Oh... ummm... sir," she said, looking around.

"Jacob," he offered. "And I don't think your manager is here right now. Don't worry."

He had smiled and reached for his receipt, noting two things. One, that she did not release it right away when he pinched his fingers down on his end. And two, that she was crawling over him with her eyes, the very corner of her lips curved into a painfully seductive grin.

"Think you can step away from the counter for a bit," he pressed, shifting to adjust himself and conscious of the fact that she'd noticed.

"Mmmm," she said, finally letting go of her half of the ticket. "I'm not gonna lie. I'm tempted." She brought her hand up to the base of her neck, wrapping her fingers around a lock of hair that had escaped her ponytail. "But I really need this job and I'm pretty sure showering with customers is a fireable offense."

She had caressed the loose hairs between her thumb and fingers and lifted a shoulder, letting her bottom lip slip forward into a pout. He had battled an urge to jump over the counter, to push her up against the register and release everything that was pent up inside, pulsing, into her. To suck her shiny protruding bottom lip in between his teeth, push his hand between the buttons of her uniform onto her breasts and hear her sigh. He squeezed the strap of his duffle bag and stepped back, ticket in hand, not attempting in any way to hide the bulge now pushing out his jeans. She looked down, her eyes lingering.

"I get off at two. That's just a few hours from now."

His lips parted and curled upward.

"I could get you off sooner..."

She giggled again and leaned back against the cigarette display on the counter behind her.

"I bet you could," she'd said, then straightened and brushed her uniform down, her mouth morphing into a neutral how-can-I-help-you smile.

"Okay, sir. You are all set. Just wait to hear your number. And remember, once you hear it, you have ten minutes to put in your code. There is no set limit on shower time, but we ask that you keep it to about half an hour. Thank you and have a lovely day."

Jacob tilted his head and gave a nod.

"Thank you, Miss. You have been extremely helpful."

He swung his bag off his shoulder and positioned it in front of his jeans, then turned. As expected, the manager was standing a few feet behind him, scrutinizing his underling. Jacob flashed his widest smile and waved his ticket.

"What a delightful young lady," he'd said to the manager, who didn't look like he was much older than the girl behind the desk. "You should give her a raise."

He winked at the guy, whose pale skinny arms were positioned in a V in front of him, ending in hands that clasped a clipboard, then Jacob walked down the closest aisle, turning when he got to the end. The manager was talking to the girl, holding up the clipboard to show her something. But her attention was not on whatever it held. Her gaze kept wandering over the top of it, past her boss, and onto Jacob. The almost certain knowledge that she'd been studying his ass as he walked away nudged his arousal up another notch. Hopefully, that shower stall would be ready soon.

As if he had willed it with his mind, a voice came over the intercom calling out his number. Jacob wasn't surprised; the store was almost empty. He made his way to the back, studying the paper in his hand. When he got to the keypad, he punched in his code and slipped inside.

The first year after leaving home, he'd relied on whatever motel he could afford, when he could afford one, and the occasional campground shower to keep himself cleaned up. Once in a while, he found a woman interested in taking him in like a stray dog, fawning over him and spoiling him for a time. Though it never lasted long, he took full advantage while he had the run of a house with a clean bathroom and a stocked fridge. But, when his welcome inevitably ran out, or he sensed that things might be getting a little too serious, it was back to the road.

Truck stop showers were a more recent discovery for him,

and they beat both motel and campground facilities by leaps and bounds. Weaponizing the good looks nature had seen fit to bestow upon him would mean nothing if he was dirty and smelled bad, after all. If he wanted to have a shot at replenishing his supplies later that night at the bars he'd mapped out on the way, he needed to look the part he'd decided on: a clean-cut college student on his way back to campus.

He turned on the water in the shower in case it needed a moment to heat up, then set his duffle bag on the shiny white tile counter in the bathroom section of the stall, pulled out some clean, folded clothes and some bottles of pills, and set them neatly next to the bag. He then peeled off his dirty clothes, crinkling his nose at the pungent odor of last night's bar. The reflection of his bare, muscular body in the mirror above the sink caught the corner of his eye.

Not too bad, he thought, scanning the image. Despite the abuse he put his body through on a regular basis, he looked toned, healthy.

"Good genes," his mother used to say when she lined the boys up on Sunday mornings before church... when they used to go to church... before the incident, "aren't always a blessing." She always focused in on Jacob at this point. "You have your father's good looks, but he never did a thing in his life to deserve 'em. Bastard sure fooled me."

A knock at the door pulled Jacob out of his thoughts.

Shit. What now? he thought, wrapping the fluffy white towel that was hanging from the bar next to the shower part of the stall around his waist.

It wasn't a bad card. He'd used cash to pay for the shower. And though he was still feeling a little fuzzy, thanks to the pills he'd *borrowed* from Julia What's-her-face, he was certain he had not made any missteps. He hadn't *really* bit through that bitch's breasts, had he? It was a daydream... a wish, right? He took a deep breath and closed his eyes. No, he hadn't done anything to her or to the shitty little brat in the back. His clothes were dirty, but there wasn't any blood on them other than the small stains around the holes in his jeans, and that was *his* blood. The things he wanted, still wanted very much, to do to her would result in a lot more blood than the stains on his knees. He let out his breath in a slow soothing stream and opened his eyes, checking his friendly smile and innocent expression in the mirror before walking over to the door.

"This one's occupied," he said, hoping that would resolve things quickly.

The knock came again, this time to the tune of *Shave and a Haircut*, piquing his curiosity. He cracked the door just a little to look out.

"I think you have the wrong..."

The blonde from the register slipped in and pushed the door shut with her behind. For a moment, Jacob's brows seemed to defy gravity. His jaw dropped and he blinked hard, not sure he was seeing things straight. His right hand tightened around the ends of the towel about his waist. The other still rested on the door handle, effectively cornering his company against the sink bowl. His body was quick to react, pressing closer. His mind scrambled to catch up.

"Well, hello there, Kit." The name came to him as his focus sharpened. "What an enormously pleasant surprise. And just in time," he added, adjusting his towel, then letting it drop altogether.

Kit gasped and stepped closer, undoing the buttons of her blouse while he reached around and up underneath it to unfasten her bra. She hung her blouse on the door hook and pushed her hand into her pocket, pulling out a condom and grinning. He nodded and ripped the packet open, raising both hands when she grabbed its contents from him and reached down to slide it onto him.

"I thought showering with customers was a fireable offense," he said, groaning when her cold hands made contact.

She unbuttoned her uniform khakis, brushing against his upper thigh. "Well, we don't actually have to *shower* together," she whispered, pressing her fingertips to his lips. He opened his mouth to welcome them in, running his tongue along the edges of her nails. "Shari told the manager I got my period and had to clean up. She's at the register filling in. She owes me since I saw her pocket a pack of Newports the other day. We got about fifteen minutes."

She let her pants drop and Jacob quickly slid his hands into her panties to explore while she wiggled out of them. He pulled in a deep breath of her, then he reached around to her buttocks and pulled her up and onto him, exhaling.

"I can work with that," he said, sealing his mouth over hers and moving with her through the steam and into the shower stall.

When they emerged from the shower, she picked up his towel off the floor and handed it to him, grabbing another one off the bar for herself. She dried herself off and turned to watch him do the same, tracing the details of his body with her eyes. Then, she slipped into her panties and khakis and turned to watch him wrap the towel around his waist and reach into his duffle bag to pull out a small travel case.

"I need to shave while I've got the stall," he explained.

Kit nodded and finished getting dressed. She stepped

closer, her attention focused on his torso, and extended a hand toward his scar. He took ahold of it before she could touch the long knotty rope of reddish-pink flesh, shaking his head when he released her hand away from him. She looked from the scar to his eyes and back again, tilting her head and tightening her mouth.

"Where'd you get it?" she asked. "Motorcycle accident or something?"

He laughed and shook his head. "Mountain lion."

It was a mountain lion, kid. A goddamn mountain lion and nothing more. Probably had some cubs nearby.

Her eyes widened and she pulled her head back, then forward again, scrutinizing the scar.

"No shit?"

"No shit," he said.

A mountain lion. You are one lucky little bastard to be alive.

"Damn," she said, whistling her amazement.

"Well, you should probably slip back out there before the manager gets suspicious." As much as he'd needed this unexpected and immensely enjoyable release, he needed to get cleaned up and on the road. And talking about his scar had been the perfect reminder.

"Oh, don't worry about Kevin. The word *period* will keep him from nosing around anywhere near the bathrooms." Kit sighed and looked around at the stall, a dreamy expression on her face. Jacob hoped she was reliving her time in there with him, but a thought occurred to him.

"You don't want anything else, right?" He hesitated, biting his lip. "Because I don't have any money or anything."

She scrunched up her face and shook her head, a hint of

offense shining in her blue-green eyes. Then she relaxed and giggled, stepping closer until she was leaning the front of her breasts against his bare chest. "Why, Mr. Jacob. I'm not that kind of girl."

She kissed him softly on the lips and turned to leave. Jacob watched her until the door closed and latched behind her, perfectly content with the kind of girl she was.

TWENTY

Ben had gone through his mail and was leafing through the instruction manual to Mary's camera, sipping on his second cup of coffee, when the doorbell rang announcing Sam's arrival. The camera and all its various lenses and attachments lay spread across the kitchen table.

"Be right there," he called out, heading to the door.

When he pulled the front door open, Ben thought he heard the boy talking to someone. But, when he leaned out and looked around, he saw that Sam was alone at the bottom of the steps, facing away, toward the street.

"Hey there," said Ben, startling the boy. "Come on in and help me figure this thing out, won't you?" He held up the manual, turning the cover toward Sam.

The boy looked a little dazed, like he'd been deep in a daydream and still hadn't quite worked his way back.

"Everything okay, Sam?"

"Oh... yeah, Mr. Thomas. I'm good." Sam turned and blinked a few times, rubbing a hand across his eyes. "I guess my eyes hurt a little. I've been inside all day and it's so sunny out here."

"Well, come on in. I'll open up the kitchen windows so you can get some fresh air while we look at the camera. If we get it up and running, maybe we can take a walk and get some nature pictures. We could start by snapping a few in the front yard. I think I saw a rabbit out there earlier." Ben waved the boy up and turned to hold the door for him.

Sam followed him, smiling and giving him a nod on his way into the house. When he stepped into the foyer, the boy froze and looked at the walls on either side.

"Whoa," he said. "Did you guys take all these yourselves? Or did you buy some?"

His eyes scanned the photographs lining the walls. Frames stretched all the way down the corridor. One side was adorned with pictures of all sorts of creatures, from spiders to elephants. The other side held photos of buildings and people.

"Mary took most of the nature photos. The city and people ones are a mix. Let's put it this way, the ones that look professional are hers and the rest are mine." Ben chuckled. "All taken with the camera I'm about to show you."

Sam walked down the hall, stopping every couple of steps so he could examine each picture. He glanced over at the people side. The structures captured were rundown and mostly devoid of color and the people were definitely not of the happy persuasion. In one, an enraged man seemed to be charging the camera. He pointed to that one.

"He doesn't look all that happy to get his picture taken," he said.

Understatement of the century, thought Ben, shaking his

head and trying not to remember the events following the shot. "No, Sam, he was not."

The boy walked closer to the nature side, obviously more drawn to the assortment of creatures. At every stop, he smiled and whispered the names of the subjects Mary had captured on film.

"Dude! That's a loggerhead sea turtle! Did you know that scientists have discovered that loggerhead females lay multiple clutches of eggs in the same season? Sometimes they're even miles away from each other so the species has a better chance at survival." He turned with wide eyes and looked at Ben, who was laughing. He didn't recall ever having been called *dude* before. "You guys swam with loggerheads? They can be pretty shy, you know."

"Mary had a way with the creatures," said Ben. He sighed.

"Wait a minute," said Sam, pointing to a picture near the end of the row. "That's a Mojave rattlesnake. Mrs. Thomas took that?"

Ben nodded, his mind wandering back to the exact day she took the photo.

"Seriously? Look at its tail." Sam moved his index finger over the image of the snake's tail, moving it in a tight circle. "It looks like it's about to strike. Mojave rattlesnakes have one of the most powerful venoms in the world, you know. How close were you guys?"

Sam aimed an incredulous stare at him; intensity and curiosity radiated from the boy like waves of heat off blacktop in summer.

"Too close," said Ben, chuckling. "That's what *I* thought, at least. And I told her so at the time. But Mary had a way with even the most dangerous creatures. It was almost as if she could communicate with them, and they with her. She told me that this guy," he tapped the picture, keeping his finger to the side of the snake, as if he were afraid it would strike him through the glass frame, "was just giving us a warning. That he didn't want to harm us, as long as we respected his space. And, you know what?" He tapped the back of that same finger on the tip of his nose and pointed it at Sam, who was frozen in place, waiting for the rest of the story. "She was right. She took that picture and we backed away. Call me crazy, but I'm pretty sure I saw it give her a wink."

The side of Sam's mouth curled up, pulling his nose to the side, and he laughed. Ben grinned.

"Are you calling me crazy?"

This brought even more giggles from the boy, which were only interrupted after he saw the very last picture on the wall.

"Is that..."—he craned his neck closer to the frame—"my picture?"

Ben nodded, touched by the expression of pride spreading across the boy's face, as he stood staring at the picture of the most beautiful crawfish they saw that day. His head listed slightly, giving him a statuesque appearance of reverie.

"One of the prettiest here," said Ben, smiling. "And you took that with your *phone*. Just imagine what you could do with a camera like Mary's."

The boy blushed and bit his bottom lip, limiting his grin to half his face.

"I'm being totally serious." Sam looked like he was suspicious about the sincerity of the compliment. "Look closely at the picture you took, the angle. It looks like the little fellow's trying to tell you his story."

They both leaned closer and stared for another moment.

"I guess... maybe," the boy said, scratching his head.

"A lot of photography is about timing. Especially when you're using a film camera. It's not like the cameras they have now, where you can sometimes move backward and forward from the still shot to find the best image. And you seem to have a knack for timing."

Sam squared his shoulders, seemingly more confident now.

"Yeah, I don't use the *live* setting on my camera. The pics take up too much space on my phone."

"Come on in here and I'll show you Mary's camera." Ben walked into the kitchen waving an arm at Sam. "I'll put on some water for hot chocolate. I'm pretty sure your mom doesn't want me giving you coffee. And I'll grab some cookies from the pantry. You go ahead and take a look. Feel free to fiddle with anything and everything."

Sam approached the table, his gaze wandering over the parts that were spread out and arranged in groups. Lenses on one side of the table, next to a backpack camera bag. Lens cloths, a mini screwdriver set, and a weird-looking plastic balloon thing with a tube on the other. His eyes focused in on the center of the table. He took a few more steps and reached out a hand, looking over at Ben.

"Can I?" he asked, his fingers hovering just over the camera with the word Nikon printed above the aperture ring.

Ben walked out of the pantry, cookies in hand, and nodded. "Of course you can. Go ahead and pick it up. Get a feel for it."

"It's heavier than I thought it would be," said Sam, cradling the camera in his hands. He tilted it this way and that, examining all the levers and buttons. "This is how you focus it, right?" He turned the focusing ring delicately, using the very tips of his fingers.

"Yes, sir."

Sam put the strap over his head and held the camera up to his face, centering the viewfinder over his right eye, and turned slowly, adjusting the focusing ring as he pivoted.

"How does it feel in your hands?" asked Ben, setting the cookies down on the table.

"Good," said Sam, continuing his journey. "It feels balanced." He brought the camera down to his chest, still holding it with both hands. "Like it wants me to take a picture."

Ben shook his head, his mouth a tight line. "That is exactly what Mary used to say. Incredible. Boy, do I wish you two could have met."

Sam pulled the strap back over his head and set the camera down. He sat down, propped an elbow on the table, and chewed the edge of his thumbnail.

"Mr. Thomas?"

"Yes, Sam?" He handed the boy a cookie and turned to tend to the kettle on the stovetop.

"How come you and Mrs. Thomas didn't have any kids?"

Ben's hand clasped the handle of the kettle. He curled his lips in and looked up at the ceiling, taking a deep breath. He certainly wasn't expecting that. Not from a child. That was usually the prying question he got from neighbors or new acquaintances... adult acquaintances. But there was something in the way Sam had asked the question that made it more palatable, less nosy. His tone was one of pure matter-of-fact curiosity. It almost seemed more of a statement of fact, as if the words had been "I just don't get it, you would have been wonderful parents," or something to that effect.

Ben turned to bring the kettle over to the counter, where he had arranged a mug preloaded with chocolate powder and a little bowl filled with the tiny marshmallows Mary had always kept on hand in case any neighborhood kids stopped by, though they rarely had. The marshmallows had been in the pantry for a very long time, but Ben was pretty sure that those things had a shelf-life that would far outlive his time on this earth. He poured hot water into the mug, set the kettle back on the stove, and brought the mug and the marshmallows over to Sam.

Sam pushed the cookie into his mouth and took the mug with both hands. Instead of setting it on the table to add marshmallows, he held it with one hand and grabbed a handful of the tiny white sugar bombs with the other, carefully lowering his hand as close as he could before releasing them. He seemed extremely conscious of the spread on the table when he did this, as if he were afraid the hot liquid would jump from the mug and douse the whole shebang.

"It's okay if you don't wanna answer," he said and took a careful sip of his hot chocolate after blowing on it. "Sometimes I ask too many questions. Christina says I'm nosy."

"Not at all," said Ben. "Mrs. Thomas couldn't have kids and I guess we were so happy together, that was okay."

"And Mrs. Thomas was friends with all the creatures, too. Right?" Sam contemplated the steam floating over his mug, passing his hand through it to make it swirl.

Ben poured himself a cup of coffee and sat down across from the boy.

"You could say that," he said, nodding.

"I get it," said Sam. "Sometimes—most of the time—I like animals more than people. It's easier to guess what they're thinking. I mean, people can talk, sure, but sometimes that just makes it harder to understand what they're really thinking." He cupped the mug with both hands and took another sip.

Ben nodded. The kid was pretty perceptive. He observed the boy over his coffee cup. Sam seemed to be contemplating the photos on the hallway wall, or at least staring in their general direction.

"Well, my boy, don't give up on humanity completely."

He said this in a playful tone, but a part of him couldn't help but worry. Mary had been so isolated and distant when he first met her. It had taken time to earn her trust, and then to help her trust in people again in general. And there had certainly been bumps along the way... horrible, gruesome bumps. It was a lonely world if you didn't have friends you could trust. Thankfully, this boy had a loving family to help him through this awkward, sometimes painful, stage of life.

"Do you think..." Sam paused, turning his head to face Ben. He squinted and bit his lip, as if trying to decide whether or not to continue. Ben kept quiet, giving the boy time to work out his thoughts. "Do you think that Mrs. Thomas could actually communicate with creatures?"

Ben leaned an elbow on the table and brought his hand up to massage his beard stubble.

"You mean actually talk to them, like I'm talking to you?"

The boy gave the side of his thumbnail a nibble and let his eyes wander. Then he shook his head.

"Not exactly." He reached out and took a few marshmallows from the bowl, this time popping them into his mouth instead of his mug. "Different animals have different ways of talking, like with movements or chemicals or lights. I don't know. Maybe some of them are talking to each other telepathically and we just don't know it."

"I don't think so, but sometimes it sure seemed like it. Sounds like you've been doing some research. I'm betting you'll be hanging out with the likes of Sir Attenborough when you grow up."

This kid was going to be a famous naturalist for sure. Ben would have no qualms about betting good money on that.

"That would be amazing. He's one of my heroes," said Sam, a dreamy look clouding his eyes.

Ben guessed he was most likely imagining himself hanging out with his hero. Then, his lips tightened and he looked at Ben.

"What if someone discovers an animal that *can* talk to people, maybe telepathically? Wouldn't that be cool?"

Ben set his coffee on the table. Sam was staring into his mug, as if waiting to receive a message from the marshmallows floating in his hot chocolate. He looked like he was drifting off into another daydream.

"I guess that would depend on what the animal had to say," said Ben, a sharpness in his voice that he had not meant to add.

Sam looked up, startled.

"I mean," he softened his tone, "wouldn't you then have the same problem you have with people? Not knowing if what they *say* is what they *mean*?"

Like making a vow and not following through, he thought. The hairs on his arm stood straight and he could feel sweat building on his brow.

"Do *you* think there might be animals out there that can

talk to people?" asked Ben, his gaze pinning the boy like an insect on a board. Sam squirmed a little in his chair, his shoulders sliding up in a half-shrug.

"Nah. Of course not," he said, a little too quickly. "I just think it might be cool." He shifted his attention back to the table, reaching over to pick something up. "What's this plastic balloon thingy?" he asked, turning it in his hand.

Ben hesitated, then decided that he, too, would welcome a change in topic.

"I don't know what it's called," he said. "But it is used to clean the camera. Squeeze the balloon end and a puff of air will shoot out the little straw thing."

Sam gave the bulb a squeeze with the straw aiming up, and they both laughed when a puff of air lifted his bangs.

"I'll tell you what," said Ben, picking up the manual and running his thumb over the pages so they fanned out like a peacock's tail feathers. "Why don't we start looking through this to figure out what the parts are called? When your mom says you have to head home, you can take the manual with you, so you can figure out how it all works. Then, the next time you come over, we can give it a whirl... maybe go take some pictures at the stream."

Sam nodded. "That would be awesome. Even if the stream is pretty boring compared to the places you guys went." He perked up, head tilted, eyes squinted. "Hey, did you guys ever go to the Andaman Islands or the Galapagos?"

"Nah," said Ben, shaking his head. "I traveled a bit before I met Mary, Mrs. Thomas. But she was afraid to fly. We tried a ship once, but she said she felt trapped. So, we drove everywhere in our trusty pop top. All the way down through South America."

"What's a *pop top*?"

"It's a van that turns into a camper of sorts. I retired ole Ginnie—that's what we called our pop top—when Mrs. Thomas took ill. Bought that little number parked in the drive-way. Ginnie's short for Virginia West because she's a VW."

The boy was staring at him intently with one of those looks kids make when they aren't quite following, but don't want to admit it.

"Anyway," he said. "She's parked in the garage if you want to take a peek."

"Cool," said Sam, nodding.

Ben walked the boy out the front door, grabbing a small fob on the way. They continued around to the garage. He stepped past the double door closest to the house and stopped in front of the isolated, third, single door. He held up the fob, took a deep breath, and pushed the button. The door complained with a series of creaks and pops, making Ben worry that the chain or springs might be broken. After a final couple of clicks, it lifted, revealing an old, orange VW pop top camper.

One of the tires was flat and it was in definite need of a scrub, the perfect target for those kids that write *wash me* with their fingers on the backs of dirt-crusted cars and trucks in parking lots. But the memories of so many road trips with Mary painted rose-colored glasses across Ben's eyes.

"She's a beaut, isn't she?" he said, his voice sounding like that of a salesman, throwing out his best pitch.

"Can I see inside?" Sam stood, lips parted and eyes wide, taking in the sight of this rare beast.

Ben took a step toward the vehicle, intending to say yes, but held back when he noticed that the long sliding door was open a crack. He didn't remember leaving it like that. Of course, he didn't remember much at all about the day he and Mary had decided it was time for Ginnie to be retired and put to pasture in the section of the garage that they'd had walled off. The access door inside the main garage was always locked and this was the first time he'd used the fob since they'd parked it there.

He thought about the hole he'd just repaired in the main garage wall and wondered if he'd find one in here, too. Maybe Princess had somehow slipped in to visit her old travel bed one last time. Once he thought of her, the darker memories began to rise from the place he kept them closed in his mind. The picture in the corridor flashed behind his eyes. Why had she wanted to keep that picture, knowing what had happened?

It's a reminder, Ben. A reminder of the darkness among us. Of the necessity of all God's creatures.

He glanced over at the boy, who was still waiting for permission to enter the garage.

"Umm, let's do that another time. I want to clean it a little, first."

He stepped back, extending his hand to guide Sam back with him, and pressed the button on the fob once more.

TWENTY-ONE

"Take your coat, it's chilly out there. Oh, and take your brother with you. I can't deal with him right now."

Ten-year-old Jacob smiled up at his older brother at his mother's voice, floating in from the family room, where she was watching her shows. Though it was less of a float and more of a drop, since the words were delivered with the delicacy of a pro-wrestler. Jacob had already asked if he could go with his older brother, anyway. He didn't even care where they were going. He just wanted to go. To Jacob, everything Jimmy did was exciting and cool... and much better than having to stay home trying to avoid the wrath of their mother.

Jimmy ruffled his brother's hair and grabbed two jackets off the rusty nails pounded into the wall by the back door.

"Think fast," he said tossing one hard at the boy.

Jacob wasn't quite fast enough to grab it out of the air but managed to get ahold of his jacket before it slid to the ground off his face.

"Thanks, asshole," he said, sliding his arms into the upside-down sleeves and flipping it over his head.

"Stop putting your jacket on like a dork," said Jimmy. "You want kids to pick on you? Cause they're gonna if they see you putting your jacket on like a preschooler."

Jacob frowned and looked at his shoes. He didn't bother telling his brother that kids already picked on him for any number of things: where he lived, his dirty clothes, dorky hair. He was pretty sure it didn't matter how he put his jacket on.

"Never mind. Come on," said Jimmy, giving him a swat on the side of the shoulder. "Let's get the fuck outta here."

Jacob looked up at his brother and grinned.

"Did I hear the F word out there? Jacob, did you say the F word again? The Lord don't like it when you cuss."

Jimmy lifted a finger and wagged it at his little brother, adding a little "tsk, tsk, tsk," for effect.

Jacob rolled his eyes. Of course, Mom thought it was him, even when it *obviously* wasn't. His voice was like two octaves higher than Jimmy's... something else he got teased about. But his older brother could do no wrong in her eyes. Jimmy was handsome. Jimmy was fit. Jimmy was a star football player. Jimmy had a million girlfriends. And Jimmy's father had been a saint-like figure, tragically lost in a car accident, while Jacob's dad was a no-good piece of crap, or so she said. He hadn't seen his dad in years, didn't even remember what he looked like. Anyway, Jacob was sure that the Lord wouldn't like a whole lot of the things his mom did, either, so he wasn't particularly worried.

Jimmy grabbed the collar of Jacob's coat and pulled him out the door. They climbed into the blue Outback parked along the two strips of dirt that were supposed to be a drive-way. Jacob crinkled his nose when he settled in. The car still smelled like whatever chemicals they used to clean them up to sell.

"When is that smell gonna go away?" he said, waving a hand in front of his face, then rolling down his window.

Jimmy took a deep breath, eyes closed, and released it all at once with an *aaaahhh*.

"I hope never. That, my friend, is the smell of a new car."

Jacob made a face like he was going to vomit. His brother jammed the keys into the ignition, then tapped the little figure hanging from the keychain with his pointer finger to set it swinging and kissed the green stone on the bulky silver class ring all the football players had. His ritual completed, he started the car. He reached his right arm back, making sure to smack Jacob's head on the way by, and grabbed onto the passenger seat, leaning and turning his head for a clear view while he backed out. When he got to the end of the path, he slowed and maneuvered onto the grass to avoid the mailbox, which was hanging halfway off its base, its door sticking out like a hound dog's tongue. The Outback was Jimmy's baby and he was going to keep it in mint condition as long as he could.

"Wow, honey. They must be paying you a lot at the Arby's," their mom had said the day he brought it home. "Well, they know a hard worker when they see one, I s'pose. Gotta pay ya well to keep ya. Think you can get 'em to hire on your brother? We could use the cash."

"Ma, you gotta be fifteen to work there."

"Great, so he'll be leachin' off us another five years."

It would only end up being another three. Turned out, as long as you *looked* old enough to drive, and followed traffic laws, chances were you'd be left alone. And, if your mother had multiple warrants out, she wouldn't dare file a report when you took your dead brother's car, which is what he would have wanted anyway.

"Got a box of nails in the back. Let's go reload the trap," said Jimmy, a mischievous grin pasted on his lips.

Sometime after taking off cruising down the road, Jacob had dozed off. When he opened his eyes, they were turning into an old, abandoned rest area with nothing but trees and pastures around. There were signs up on the main road warning motorists that the area was "under construction." They always elicited a snort and a chuckle from Jimmy, because there was never any construction going on and everyone who lived nearby knew there never would be. They'd already built a fancy new rest stop, complete with a restaurant and gas station, down the road, the next town over. Now, this one had become the perfect place to drink and smoke pot. And a place where Jimmy liked to hang out and *help* any unfortunate motorists who were unfamiliar with the area and had the bad luck of ending up there with car trouble.

"Bingo," said Jimmy, stopping the car and pointing to a couple at the far end of the area, standing next to a camper van pulling one of those self-move trailers.

The vehicle was at a funny angle and the man was waving his hands in the air, kicking one of its tires.

"Looks like a flat. What say I go give them a hand?"

The overcast sky and forest around them made it difficult to make out details, but they looked like an older couple to Jacob. He yawned and rubbed his eyes.

"I'm hungry," he said, scooting up in his seat. "Can we go get something to eat?"

"Why don't you just scooch back down and I'll just be a

minute. Then we can go wherever you want, and if my gut is correct, you can eat as much as you want."

He slid down low in his seat. He knew the drill. Jimmy would go over and offer to change the tire, for a price. It was a much better gig than Arby's, he'd said. And, since you never knew who you'd meet in a rest area, it would be safer for Jacob to stay out of sight. Jimmy nodded at him and reached across to open the glove box, where he kept his switchblade and a gun. Jacob sat on his hands; he knew better than to touch either. His brother's hand hovered over the two and after taking another look at the couple, he grabbed the gun.

"They don't look like they could be too much trouble, but you never know. Bonnie and Clyde probably looked like a sweet couple, too." He smiled, closed the glove box, and got out of the car, slipping the gun into the back of the waistband of his pants before pulling his hood up over his head and walking over to talk to the couple.

Jacob drummed his hands on the seat while he waited, tucked down just far enough so that he was out of sight, but could still watch. Jimmy had taught him how to change a tire just the other day so that maybe he could start helping at the rest area. He liked watching his brother spin the tire iron to loosen, then tighten the bolts with the skill and ease of a professional.

The man waved a finger at Jimmy, shook his head, and walked back over to his van. He must not have liked the price. A lot of them didn't like the price, but what did they think... that his brother would change it for free? They were lucky he was there to help. Jimmy walked closer to the couple. Then the woman also wagged a finger and held up a hand. It looked like they were going to change their own tire. There went lunch.

He heard a loud discussion, then yelling broke out over by the couple's vehicle. Jacob pushed himself up higher to see what was going on. He saw his brother pull the gun out of his pants and approach the woman. The man raised his hands and handed Jimmy what looked like a wallet.

Jacob reached into the glove box and took out the knife. He was sure his brother wouldn't mind in this case. It looked like he might need help. He cracked the door open and slipped out, keeping low to the ground and out of sight. He could get pretty close without being seen if he ducked into the woods. He popped the blade out and crept along the tree line, keeping his brother in sight. Jimmy was next to the woman now. He had the gun pointed at her head and was telling the man to take off his watch. Jacob cocked his head to the side. He must have heard wrong. This wasn't what was supposed to happen.

A sudden ear-piercing shriek knocked him back off his feet. It was followed by the sound of a gun being fired. He rolled to the side, gasping when he felt the blade of the knife puncture the skin just under his sternum. He pulled the knife back, flinging it to the side, and looked down. He brought his hand to the wound, lifted his shirt to take a look. It was bleeding, but not too badly. Jimmy was definitely gonna lecture him on not touching his stuff, maybe cuff him upside the head.

Pushing himself up on all fours, he looked over to see where the sounds had come from. The old man was kneeling over the woman, his hands on her shoulders. He was shaking her gently, saying, "Mary Mary Mary," over and over again. He leaned down to hug her, lifting the top of her body up to him. The man's back was to Jacob, and when the woman's face peeked up over his shoulder, Jacob screamed. At least he tried to scream. His mouth was open, but it felt as if his stomach had twisted up and around his lungs, cutting off access to air... and sound.

The woman's eyes were open, staring right at him, through him. And, something was terribly wrong with them, the color and the shape of them. He only fully understood what when she blinked and nictitating membranes slid from one side of each of her green-yellow eyes to the other, like a reptile.

"Jimmy," he whispered as loudly as his strangled lungs would allow, crouched frozen among the shadows. "Jimmy, where are you? Jimmy, help me."

Jacob inched forward out of the woods, but away from the couple... away from those terrifying unnatural eyes. He pushed himself up to his feet and spun frantically on his heels trying to locate his brother. A hiss, similar to the sound a truck makes when it brakes, pulled his attention to something protruding from behind the trailer, something that was sliding away from him. He squinted and caught sight of a pair of sneakers, toes pointing up, just as they disappeared behind the trailer.

Jimmy's sneakers. Those were Jimmy's sneakers! Jacob scrambled after them, a raspy squeak escaping his lips when he came upon one of his brother's shoes now discarded on the pavement. He took another step and found the other sneaker. It was still on Jimmy's foot, laying laces-down on its side.

"Jimmy," he whispered, his eyes turning to follow the length of his brother's motionless legs... until he was no longer looking at Jimmy, but at something that was in front of his brother, blocking his view.

It was on top of Jimmy's torso, a dark shadowy something, shimmering, oozing, as if it had been dipped in raw egg whites. And the sound it was making... the nauseating sound of slurping and sucking and chewing. Jacob felt acid rise from his stomach, tasted it in his mouth. Just under the sound of the something, he could hear Jimmy... what was left of Jimmy... gurgling. Jacob turned, doubled over, and vomited on the pavement. He wiped his mouth with his sleeve and stumbled back a step.

No, he told his body. *No! You're going the wrong way. You need to help Jimmy. You need to get that thing off him!*

He looked around on the ground for something to throw... anything.

Jimmy's knife. I need to find the knife.

He turned and hurried toward the trees to look for the switchblade, tripping over his own feet and falling when he heard scraping and sliding behind him. For a moment he stayed on his stomach, afraid to get up, to look back. Warm, rancid air caressed the back of his neck in spurts. Something hot and wet touched his skin. He slid his hands under his chest and skittered forward, pushing off with the toes of his sneakers and his knees.

Something grabbed his leg, clamped down around his calf, and flipped him to his back. He squeezed his eyes shut. His breaths sputtered out in uncontrollable hiccups, and tears and snot ran down his face like ice cream melting down a cone on a summer's afternoon. Something warm and wet caressed his face, licked it, purring when it tasted him. He moaned, began to tremble. Then, he felt it lick him again, this time just below his ribs where he had stabbed himself. The purring grew louder, vibrating through him, a mix of excitement and pleasure.

Jacob sobbed. He reached out his hands to push it away, but they slid off its body, the slimy, egg-white film sticking to his fingers. A numbness oozed across his torso, relaxing his muscles, calming him. He opened his eyes and looked down at his body. The something was on top of him, but he could not feel its weight, could not feel its shimmering brown scales pressed against him. It had pushed up his shirt and was examining his wound, licking the area around it, its long, thin, smooth tongue flicking here and there, but he couldn't feel that either. He whimpered, tried to move his arms. No matter how hard he willed them, they refused to obey, refused to exist.

"Stop," he whispered, feeling the words rush from his lips like the air from a deflating balloon. "*Please, stop.*"

The creature didn't look up, and he was grateful. He had no wish to see its face, its eyes. Though he was almost certain he already knew what those looked like. It lifted a claw, clicking and purring, and inserted it into him, into his wound. Then, as he watched, helpless to stop it, the something pulled the claw along the skin under his ribs. He couldn't feel it, but it made the sound a bedsheet makes when you tear it apart. He watched his blood trickle from the new, longer wound. Dizziness clouded his head, and through blurred eyes he watched the creature cover the entire wound with its face. A gentle pressure filled him, followed by a kind of euphoric release.

It's inside me now, he thought. *It's emptying me. I'm going to die.*

"Mary!" a voice screamed. "Mary Thomas, make her stop! He's just a child, Mary! Make her stop or I will!"

"I can't." The woman's voice was spent and barely audible. "She's too strong, Ben."

"You stop her right now, or I will shoot her," the other voice, the man, insisted.

Jacob blacked out.

When he opened his eyes again, he was strapped to some

kind of platform, floating... no, bouncing. Bright lights flashed in his eyes and voices filled his head.

"I think he's coming out of it," said one.

"Shit. This kid is lucky to be alive. Lucky someone heard shots and called it in. Did you see his brother?" asked another.

"Not much left to see."

"It's been a while since we've had an attack like this. Must've been some cubs nearby."

"You think this was a mountain lion?"

"What else would leave a claw mark like that?"

Jacob felt a cold hand brush across his ribs.

"What about that slimy stuff?"

"I don't know, maybe it was rabid or something. Anyway, Fish and Wildlife are out searching for it. Hoping the kids at least nicked it when they shot at it. Looking for some kind of blood trail. Anyhow, that's their problem."

A MOUNTAIN LION. *It was a mountain lion, kid. You tell 'em anything else and they'll put you in a little padded room. Mom'll be happy to be rid of you. It was a mountain lion, understand?*

TWENTY-TWO

"Sir? Sir, are you okay?"

Knocking, then pounding, vibrated against a door.

"I think I hear the sink running. Go set a new code for the door. Sir? We're going to come in, sir."

"Shit. Do you think he's dead in there? Should I call 911?"

"Bring it down a notch, Kevin. He probably just fell asleep or something. The guy looked like he's been having a rough time."

Jimmy? Where are you, Jimmy?

Jacob wondered if the voices were part of a dream. He didn't feel the straps anymore. His hand went to the wound under his ribs. No slime. No blood. Instead, a tight, raised rope of skin.

Another few bangs on the door jarred him the rest of the way awake. He looked around and saw that he was splayed out on some kind of tile floor. A bathroom floor. The truck-stop shower. Kit. His brain began to sift through dream versus reality. He pressed his hand against his forehead and wiped it down the length of his face and around the back of his neck.

"Okay, punch in the code. Sir? We're coming in."

"Whoa whoa whoa," he called out, sitting up and scooting himself against the door. "Don't come in. I'm fine. I'm okay. Don't come in."

"Sir, you've been in there for almost an hour. Are you sure you're okay?"

Jacob took a deep breath, wet his lips, and looked around. He was wearing a towel around his waist. His shaving kit was up on a counter near the sink next to a pile of clean folded clothes. He moved his hand, to help push himself up to his feet. A cap-less, plastic pill bottle went skittering across the tile floor. Empty, by the sound of it. He reached over, grabbed it (yeah, empty), and tossed it up into the sink.

"I'm fine. I think I slipped and maybe knocked my head, but I'm fine."

"Would you like us to call an ambulance, sir?"

He tried sorting out the voices. The my-voice-hasn't-quite-changed-yet, late pubescent boy, panicky voice must be the manager. The other voice, an older female, he thought, didn't sound like Kit. It must be another employee.

"No, thank you. Those things are crazy expensive. Give me a minute and I'll get dressed and come out."

"Alright, sir. So sorry this happened, sir. Would you like some coffee or orange juice or something?"

"Coffee would be great, thanks. I'll be right out."

"We'll have it waiting for you, sir."

Jacob knew that all the "sir"-ing and pleasantry was most likely a CYA technique. They were probably worried about a lawsuit or something. Sure, it would be an interesting scam to run, but lawsuits took forever. He knew that from the one his mother had filed against the town for negligence, claiming they'd failed to maintain the rest area... leading to his injury and his brother's death. If they had maintained the area, her lawyer/boyfriend-of-the-month had claimed, it wouldn't have been infested by mountain lions and there would have been a working phone to call for help when they had been trapped away from their car, as was the hypothesis. He hadn't seen a dime of that money, of course, but it was probably another reason why his mother didn't care that he'd eventually taken the Outback.

Anyway, it didn't matter. He had neither the time nor the patience for a slip-and-fall scam. He needed to hit the road, to settle some things.

"Thank you kindly."

He looked around the stall, trying to remember if he'd showered or not and if the thing with Kit had been real or his imagination. He lifted an arm and sniffed, deciding that even if he had already taken his shower, he should freshen up again. The sink would do just fine.

When he opened the door, the manager greeted him with a cup of coffee and a handful of creamer and sugar packets.

"I wasn't sure how you wanted it, sir," he said, handing over the coffee and extending the hand with the extras.

"Black is fine, thank you." Jacob brought it to his lips and lowered it again, deciding it was still a little hot.

"We got some real creamer in the break room fridge if you want. That'd cool it down."

This kid was starting to get a little annoying, like a clingy little puppy dog.

Keep your cool, he thought. *Just play along and you'll be on your way.*

"No need. It just needs a minute to cool. Hey, you might want to put some kind of non-slip mat in there, maybe a warning sign." He chuckled to show that he wasn't quite a threat.

"We are going to do both of those things, right away, sir."

"And don't worry... I'm only a law *student*, not a lawyer, yet." He winked and watched Kevin squirm and swallow hard while congratulating himself on his little improvisation.

"Oh," said Kevin, smiling a stiff mannequin smile. "Well, we would like to offer you our sincere apologies, and this gas card and a gift card for our store. You can also use it at our restaurant. It's good for any of our truck stops."

He reached into his back pocket and pulled out two plastic cards, each in the amount of $200.

"Are you sure you don't want us to call an ambulance for you? Head injuries can be tricky, sir."

"I'm fine..."—he leaned a little closer and eyed the name badge on his shirt—"Kevin. Thank you for the concern, and I do appreciate the gift cards. Law school, as I'm sure you are aware, can get pricey."

He took the cards and slid them into the side pocket of his duffle bag, giving a nod, then headed for the door. It was time to get out of there while he was ahead, and he was definitely ahead, now that he wouldn't have to figure out how to build up his gas or food money for a while. On the way out, he looked over at the cash register, searching for Kit. A short stocky brunette stood manning the counter. There was no sign of the blonde he had paid when he got there, the one who had snuck into the stall with him... maybe.

The woman at the register waved as he walked by to the

door. He gave a quick wave back and grabbed the door handle, ready to get the heck out of there, questioning the events of the past few hours.

TWENTY-THREE

A few hours after Sam got his text to return home to start on homework, Ben's doorbell sounded again.

"We're getting more company these days than we've had since the reception after you left," he said to the picture of Mary after he placed it back on its shelf. "Sure, lots of people dropped off food and everyone said hello then, but it's nice to have *company* company... the kind you serve coffee, tea, or hot chocolate and cookies to."

He wiped some dust from the shelf and turned.

"I suppose it's also a lot safer to have company these days..."

The doorbell rang again, spurring him to walk a little faster.

"I'm coming. I'm coming. Hold your horses. I'm not as young as I used to be."

He opened the door to a scowling preteen dressed in old jeans and a jersey with what he guessed must be the name of some band the kids liked these days scrawled across it above a depiction of a skull and flames. The boy was carrying a small canvas shopping bag, which he extended toward the door the moment it opened.

"My mom wants me to give this to you. I think it's cookies or something."

"Wonderful," said Ben. "We can have some after we get some yard work done. Come on in, Tyler."

Tyler scrunched up the left corner of his mouth and rolled his eyes, then stepped into the foyer. He pinned the back of one shoe with the front of the other and started to slide it off.

"Oh... you don't have to take your shoes off. We're going to head right out back, and I need to clean the floors later anyway."

The boy pushed his heel back down and shrugged, his angsty glare fixed on the floor.

"Don't worry. There really isn't that much to do. Mostly some raking, and maybe a bit of digging to get the dead plants and weeds cleared from the vegetable garden. I want to try to get that going again next spring."

"Sure. Whatever."

They walked down the hall into the kitchen and to the door that led out to the backyard.

"So, anything new and exciting happening with you?"

Tyler shrugged.

"Think you're ready for high school?"

Another shrug.

"Your mom told me you're going to be playing football again this year. I'd love to come see some games. I need to start getting out more. Mrs. Thomas and I used to travel a lot, you know. I've pretty much been in the house since she passed."

Ben opened the door for him, watching for any kind of sign that he could get through the wall the boy was throwing up to repel each question. He wondered whether this particular adolescent wall was one of solid steel or maybe of a more fallible material, one he could soften up with some good old-fashioned yard work and, of course, hot chocolate and cookies.

Tyler glanced at him as he walked through the door.

"Yeah... sorry about Mrs. Thomas. She was nice."

"Thank you, Tyler. Yes, she was."

Well, it was a start. He handed the boy some work gloves, and one of two rakes that were leaning against the side of the house, taking the other for himself and slipping on his own gloves. For the first ten or fifteen minutes they worked in silence, pulling together piles of maple and oak leaves and building them into hills around the yard. Ben figured he'd let the boy get some work under his belt before trying to poke at that wall again.

"How long have we known each other, Tyler?" he asked when the boy set his rake down to tie his shoe.

Tyler finished his knot, picked up his rake, and looked at Ben. Effort had melted the scowl into a more neutral expression, though there was still no trace of a smile. He shrugged but kept eye contact... a slight improvement in Ben's opinion.

"I don't know. I guess since I was little."

"You are correct," he said. "I think you were around two or three when we moved here. You used to run up and down the sidewalk dragging that blue rabbit of yours everywhere. I forget what you called it. Mega something... right?"

Ben thought he saw the hint of a grin, a crack in the wall.

"Mighty Max," the boy said, shaking his head. "Stupid name."

"Mighty Max, that's right. I remembered it was a pretty powerful name for a rabbit," said Ben. "Intimidating, even."

The boy's grin took on a shade of contempt and his eyes flicked upward in a partial eye roll.

"No, really. Most kids name their stuffed animals things like Bun Bun or Fluffy... cutesy names like that. You picked a solid, confident name for your rabbit. I was impressed."

Tyler shrugged and started raking again.

"Do you remember when that little yappy dog down the street got ahold of it? Tore its arm right off?"

The rake stopped moving and Tyler looked over at him again. He was squinting and chewing his bottom lip.

"Yeah. Gator. He was a rat terrier. He was always trying to grab it from me."

Ben nodded and smiled.

"Gator... that was it."

"Mrs. Thomas sewed Max's arm back on and gave me some candy." A grin spread across his face.

"She liked to fix things, no matter how broken or torn they were."

"I remember she asked me if I wanted the clear thread or something brighter so Max could show off his scar."

Ben heard a quick puff of air escape Tyler's nose. Almost a laugh. Another crack in the wall.

"Of course, you chose the brightest color thread after she said that."

The boy nodded, then went back to work.

"We should probably start bagging these up," said Ben. "We've made so many hills, it looks like a giant mole's been through here. Wait here and I'll get the lawn bags."

When he came back with the bags, Tyler had leaned the rake back against the house and was fiddling with the grill on the patio.

"How come it's tied shut?" he asked. "The knot's pretty tight. I could open it and clean it for you, if you want."

Ben dropped the bags and rushed over. He waved the boy back, picked up a dirty blanket that was in a pile on the ground nearby, and threw it over the grill. Then he took a deep breath to stop his heart from slamming into his ribcage, or at least to slow it. Tyler was staring at him, his mouth slightly open.

"Sorry," said Tyler, though it was clear he wasn't quite sure what he was apologizing for.

"No, Tyler. I'm sorry. I didn't mean to be so gruff. It's just... the inside of that grill is pretty nasty. I'm thinking I might just throw it out and get a new one. I burned some stuff in there that I probably shouldn't have. I don't want any fumes to get you sick."

The excuse sounded ridiculous to his own ears the moment it escaped his lips. But it was the only thing he could come up with on the fly. Besides, he was talking to a middle schooler. They were naturally skeptical of *anything* adults said, if he remembered correctly. He probably could have just told the boy the god-honest truth, and the kid would have thought Ben was joshing him.

Oh, don't open that. I incinerated some monster eggs in there when I was in a rage. The fumes could be toxic. Better safe than sorry.

Ben walked over and pulled one of the large paper lawn bags from the bundle. Tyler approached and helped him open it.

"Thanks, Tyler." He hoped that the grill incident hadn't fortified the wall.

"Sure, Mr. Thomas. I actually might be able to clean that grill for you. I mean, if you air it out for a while first."

"It is very kind of you to offer. I will keep that in mind."

"Dad and I put our grill together a few years back, so I know the different parts. I'm pretty good at making burgers on it, too."

"I'm impressed," said Ben, noting that the wall seemed to have crumbled altogether. "Mrs. Thomas used to make the best burgers... oh... and steaks. She had this secret mix of spices and sauces she used. All I had to do was flip them when they were ready to be flipped. And, if I recall correctly, your dad was the one who put that one together." He pointed at the blanket-covered grill. "I tried to give him a hand, but I'm pretty sure I was just in the way. I'm not great at that kind of thing."

Tyler's mouth turned. He leaned over, gathered a handful of leaves, and threw them in the bag, then wiped the back of his sleeve across his face. Ben didn't think it was for sweat.

"Want to take a break and get some hot chocolate? Maybe dip into those cookies your mom sent over?"

Tyler sniffed, scrunching up his nose, and nodded.

They went into the kitchen and Ben directed the boy to sit while he lit a burner, set the water to boil, then reached into the bag Tyler's mom had sent over with him.

"I'm sure she won't mind if we start with dessert," said Ben. "I have some pizzas for dinner later on. Your mom said she has a meeting tonight?"

"Yeah. It's conference night at the school. She said she'd pick me up on the way home." His shoulders slumped when he said the word *conference*.

Ben set the hot chocolate powder and the cookies, snicker-doodles this time, on the table.

"Now we just wait for the water to boil," he said. "But we

can go ahead and start on these cookies. Your mom makes the best cookies."

Tyler nodded and took a cookie. He turned it over in his hands a few times, took a nibble, and set it on the table.

"You know, if you want to get something off your chest, you can tell me," said Ben, taking a cookie for himself. "Everything okay at school?"

Tyler shrugged and took another bite of his cookie. The kettle called Ben back with a long strident whistle. He removed it from the stovetop, poured hot water into two mugs, and brought them to the table. He then tossed a tea bag into his, opened the container of chocolate powder for Tyler, and grabbed a spoon for each of them.

"Do you have any marshmallows?" asked Tyler, scooping some chocolate into the water.

"Of course. I can't believe I forgot the marshmallows." Ben stepped into the pantry and came out with a bag of mini marshmallows.

Tyler grabbed a handful and put them into his mug, watching them melt into the liquid. They sat quietly, enjoying their drinks and occasionally taking a bite of their cookies.

"How's your mom doing?" Ben chanced.

"She's okay, I guess," said the boy.

"How about you?"

Tyler shrugged. He squirmed in his chair a little, then stood up.

"Where's the bathroom?" he asked.

Ben pointed down the hall. "Last door on the left, before you reach the entryway."

Tyler disappeared down the hall, leaving Ben at the table with his thoughts.

"He's a tough one to crack, Mary," he said just above a whisper and took another cookie for himself.

On his way back to the kitchen, the boy stopped to examine the pictures on the wall.

"Cool," he said. "Did you take these?"

"Mrs. Thomas took most of them. All of the good ones. Oh, and Sam Parker took the one on the end, the one of the crawfish."

He watched Tyler closely when he mentioned Sam and noticed the corner of the boy's mouth twitch.

"You know Sam, right?"

Tyler's lips pinched together, his mouth a thin, level line. Once again, his answer came in the form of a shrug. He was staring at the picture. Ben was pretty sure he was thinking of the earphone-in-the-tree incident. No use denying the obvious.

"Great pic, don't you think?"

This time he didn't even get a shrug.

"You know, Tyler, Sam's a nice kid. You two would probably get along if you got to know him."

Ben brought a hand up to scratch at his beard stubble. Tyler was still looking up at the photo, but his brows were furrowed and it was more of a glare now.

"Tyler?"

The boy turned to look at him. Not only was the wall back up, but it looked like it had been fortified.

"You don't have to be friends. Though, I think you guys probably have a lot more in common than you think."

At this, the boy's head shook slightly back and forth and the corner of his mouth pulled back in a sneer. Ben decided to go for broke.

"You don't have to be friends, but do you think you could leave him alone?"

"What did he tell you?" Tyler's voice was cold, accusatory. He was staring at the floor now.

"He didn't tell me anything. I saw you guys outside when you threw his earphones in the tree. And your mom mentioned that you are having some trouble at school and that if you get into any more trouble, you won't be able to play football. You worked so hard this summer, Tyler. I saw you out practicing with your dad almost every day."

"My dad's an asshole," the boy snapped. "And that Sam kid is weird."

Ben sighed and leaned back in his chair. Silently pleading to Mary for strength, he cleared his throat and made sure to keep his voice calm but clear, his best Gentle Ben voice.

"You have every right to be angry with your dad, and if you ever want to talk about it, that's fine, and if you never want to talk about it, still fine."

Tyler shook his head and glared at the ground, his eyes fixed as if he were willing the wooden planks to burst into flames.

"As far as Sam is concerned, I know you will do the right thing and stay away from him. Now, what say we get back out there and clear the garden? It's getting close to dinner time and you look like you could benefit from some weed-ripping therapy."

Ben smiled and stood, sweeping his hands to the side to direct Tyler to the back door. The boy trudged past the table, eyes cast down, and back out to the yard. They spent the next couple hours clearing the garden in complete silence. But Ben thought maybe he'd gotten through, at least a little. Tyler's face had slowly smoothed from an angry scowl while he was ripping out weeds, and Ben was confident the boy did not want to risk his chance to play on the football team, no matter how much he hated his father or Sam at the moment.

Dinner was also very quiet, with Tyler giving one- or two-word answers at the most in response to any questions Ben could think of to ask the boy. It wasn't tense. Ben understood that Tyler needed space to think things over.

"Thanks for the pizza, Mr. Thomas," said Tyler after his mom texted to let them know she was on her way. He stood and brought his dishes to the sink.

"You are very welcome. You worked hard out there. And if I get a new grill, I will definitely be calling you to give me a hand at assembling it. I'll also be asking your mom for the football schedule. I'd love to catch some games this year."

Tyler nodded. He walked back to gather up a few more items to help clean. When everything was cleared away, they walked to the front door together. Tyler took his phone out of his pocket and checked it.

"My mom's here."

Ben nodded and opened the door, just as Evelyn's jeep pulled into the driveway. Tyler stepped out and trudged down the steps, looking like he was in no hurry to find out how parent-teacher conferences went. Evelyn waved up at Ben and mouthed the words "thank you." Then, she held up a hand with her thumb and pinky finger extended and put them to the side of her head like a phone, twirling her index finger straight after.

She'll call me later, thought Ben, interpreting the hand signals. He nodded and gave a thumbs-up.

Tyler was almost to the car when the Parkers' door burst

open across the street. Sam appeared, carrying a large trash bag and headed to the bin they'd set out for pick-up the next morning. Mr. Parker stepped out a second or two after, calling his son's name. Ben couldn't quite make out what he was saying but saw Sam turn and hold the trash bag open with both hands. His dad made a motion like the star basketball player going for the winning shot and tossed a wad of what looked like duct tape into the air. Sam set his feet, moved the opening of the bag, and caught the object in flight. They both cheered. Ben chuckled. Sam jogged the rest of the way to the end of his driveway and tossed the bag into the bin. Ben waved, but the boy seemed to be in his own little world.

Sam was already back on his front stoop high-fiving his dad when Ben noticed Tyler. He was standing with his hand on the handle to the passenger door of his mom's car, white-knuckled and rigid against the dusky sky. His face was set in an angry scowl. If facial expressions were sounds, Ben was sure Tyler's would reach his ears as a deep throaty growl.

A familiar feeling of static and excitement charged the air, raising the hairs on Ben's neck. His breath caught in his throat. Sam, who was about to enter his home, paused and cocked his head to the side.

TWENTY-FOUR

Jacob drove until exhaustion forced him to call it a day. Whatever it was that had happened to him at the truck stop (his mind was still a little fuzzy on the details thanks to the pills... maybe?) had drained him. He had pushed through for as long as possible. Falling asleep at the wheel, or swerving and catching the attention of the police, would end his adventure before the conclusion he needed it to reach.

He pulled into a rest area and took out his phone to search for a place to stay that would not take him too far off the Interstate. In the pocket with the phone, he found the folded obituary he'd been carrying around with him, since printing it off the internet. He smoothed the paper and stared at the picture of the woman, framed in a crooked circle drawn in black marker. She looked older—the obit was published around nine years after he'd seen her in person—and her eyes were different, human. But it was her. He had no doubt.

Mary Thomas, make her stop or I will.

He traced the words under her photo with his pointer finger, feeling suddenly cold. His lips trembled.

"Mary Thomas is survived by her adoring husband, Benjamin Thomas."

I can't, Ben. She's too strong.

So many times over the years, he'd typed those two names into search engines together. Thomas was a common name. It was less common to find the two names together, but happened often enough that when her obituary had popped up, he'd almost missed it. He was packing up his things to leave the library, to let it go for another bit, when he saw the woman in the photo staring up at him. And now he had the name of a town.

It was solid evidence that he wasn't crazy, that he had not hallucinated the couple in the rest area. There was no mountain lion in his dreams. The face from his nightmares was there in front of him. Sure, her eyes were normal in the picture, but he recognized her face all the same. Besides, *that*—those lizard-like eyes—was something he could have imagined. He'd been just a kid when it happened, a terrified, traumatized kid. And it couldn't be a coincidence that the name was the one he remembered.

Mary Thomas, make her stop.

Jacob shuddered, closed his eyes. He reached a hand up under his shirt and traced his scar. It pulsated under his fingers, a small section in the center now raised like a target, swollen and hot to the touch. The sudden need for relief flooded through him, as it had so many times before, and he found himself rifling through his bag looking for the pills he knew he'd finished.

This time was different, though. This time he just wanted to take the edge off the pain, to ease the burn that pushed up through his scar. He didn't want to dull his senses, to lose himself in an ocean of nothingness. He didn't want to forget.

He tilted his head down, eyes closed, and saw the creature in his mind. It was straddling him. Its inky tongue flicked across his skin, through his scar, into him. He could feel it snaking through to his spine. It was probing for something, something it wanted, something it needed. His body went limp, his mind lost down a dark tunnel. Somewhere from the darkness, a thought traveled to meet him, to welcome him.

Come back. I need you.

JACOB OPENED his eyes and stretched. He was still parked in the rest area, phone in his lap. The sun had set, and a quick look at the cell phone showed that a couple hours had gone by since he pulled in to research a place to stay. He slid his finger on the screen, flipping to his travel app. The GPS indicated that he was around twelve hours away from his destination now.

Though his plan had been to find a place for the night, his accidental power nap had left him feeling not only recharged, but reinvigorated. He looked at the blue line tracing the road he still needed to travel and typed in the name of the truck stop where he would be able to use his gift cards. Two popped up along the way. Perfect. With all this information, he decided to drive as long as he could through the night. He would load up on energy drinks, maybe try to score some pills, at the next truck stop. There were plenty of places to stop if exhaustion reared its head again.

TWENTY-FIVE

Try as he might, Sam was unable to convince his mother that he should stay home another day. The red on his forehead had faded completely, and the fever he desperately tried to will into existence never materialized.

"You'll be fine," she said. "I'll walk with you to the bus stop..."

Sam moaned and kicked at the floor. He opened his mouth to protest, but his mother raised a hand.

"I'm not going to walk *with* you," she clarified. "I'll be walking Alvis on the other side of the street. When you get to the bus stop, I'll pretend to train Alvis. None of the other kids will even know I'm your mom. But I will be there in case something happens. Once you're on the bus, just sit far away from him. If he tries anything, let the bus driver know. Okay?"

Sam scrunched his lips to one side and nodded.

It turned out not to be an issue. Tyler wasn't at the stop when he arrived. He ran up the street last minute when Sam was already aboard and seated by himself near the front of the bus. Sam turned his head to look out the window when Tyler passed him on his way down the aisle, giving a slight nod to his mother to let her know all was well.

"Loser."

The word was uttered at a whisper, barely loud enough for Sam to hear. So he pretended not to, tapping his fingers on his legs as if to some snappy tune lodged in his brain. And though he was facing the window at an angle that would make it impossible for Tyler to see his face, he pasted a hapless smile across his lips to complete the illusion, just in case.

The bus slowed and came to a stop again. Sam flinched when a hand reached over from behind and moved his bag.

"Sorry. I didn't mean to startle you," said Samantha, sliding into the seat next to him before any of the kids now boarding could.

"What about your brother?" asked Sam, edging closer to the window to give her more space. "Aren't you supposed to sit with him?"

"He'll be fine. My mom worries too much. It's not like someone's gonna kidnap him through the bus window or anything."

Sam's bottom lip quivered, and a smile forced its way across his face.

"Ha! Made ya laugh. Seriously, though, how are you? Does your phone work okay?"

His shoulders relaxed, making him aware of just how tense he had been.

"Yeah."

"Great. Can you show me the pics you took?"

Sam nodded and pulled out his phone, relieved she wasn't bringing up the incident in the park. They spent the rest of the ride to school looking through the nature pics he had taken with Mr. Thomas.

"Those are pretty cool, and your neighbor's camera sounds amazing. I can't wait to see the pics you take with a camera like that," she said when the bus pulled up to the school. "As soon as Ms. Liz opens the door, book it out. I'll stand and stall a little in the aisle to give you more time."

Sam chewed his lip and looked up at the rearview mirror above the driver. Samantha had said that last bit a little loud for his taste. His eyes met Ms. Liz's in the reflection, confirming his fears that she'd heard. He swallowed hard. The driver winked and nodded. A sigh eased past the lump in his throat.

"Okay," he whispered. "Thanks."

The rest of the day slipped by without anything noteworthy happening. Sam was on heightened alert and thankful for the fact that Tyler was wearing his red and white team shirt. Easy to spot meant easy to avoid. And the shirt also served as a pleasant reminder that Tyler would be at practice after school and not on the bus ride home.

Sadly, Samantha was also not on the afternoon bus. She'd told him on the way to school that she had a dental appointment so her mom would be picking her up early. He settled into a seat in the middle of the bus. The hum of the engine as the bus bounced rhythmically along its route lulled him into daydreams inhabited by creatures, cameras, and Samantha.

A familiar face passed by his seat, penetrating the enjoyable haze of his daydreams. His mind focused in like a freshly jumpstarted car and he realized that the bus was at his stop. He shook his head, casting off his residual fog, and grabbed his backpack. He was the last one up to the front of the bus, but had fallen in before the kid in front of him reached the stairs.

"See you tomorrow," said Ms. Liz when he passed by.

"See you tomorrow," he said, his hand raising in a half-wave.

He hopped off the last step and rushed home to do his homework. He didn't have much but wanted to finish quickly so he'd have time to go to the stream before dinner. The echo of claws tip-tapping down the hall sounded the moment he pushed his key into the lock. When the door swung open, Alvis was there to greet him. He leaned down to ruffle the dog's fur, taking care to scratch behind his ears. Alvis leaned past him, looking out the door and emitting a low grumble, which tickled the hairs on Sam's arms. When Sam shut the door, the dog transformed back to his happy, bouncy self again.

"Mom?" Sam called out. The house was quiet except for the sounds of Alvis's claws on the hardwood floor.

Sam headed for the garage to see if his mom's car was there. A door closed somewhere in the back of the house.

"Is that you, sweetie?"

His mother's voice drifted in from the back bedroom. She stepped into the family room a few moments later, smiling when she saw him.

"Got any homework?"

"Yeah, a little. Can I go to the stream when I'm done?" Sam pressed his hands together and raised his brows.

"Are you sure that's a good idea?" Mom was giving him a knowing look now, her lips pursed.

Sam took a deep breath and parried with a confident look of his own.

"Tyler has football practice today if that's what you're

worried about. Besides, I'll bring my phone. I can call if anything happens."

"I hate to bring this up, but you had your phone the other day at the park, too."

Sam's bottom lip slipped in between his teeth, and he looked down at his feet. He was thankful she didn't know about the previous incident at the stream.

"Well, I didn't want you to know what happened. But now you know so I'll call if I need to."

He looked up at her, grinning to defuse the spark he saw in her eyes.

"I'll call and you can bring Alvis. When I see you, I'll yell 'release the hound!'"

The spark turned to a sparkle. A grin followed.

"Okay. You'd better get going on your homework so you'll have enough time to go before dinner. Any plans to get together with Mr. Thomas to figure out his camera?"

"I have the manual here. I'm almost finished looking through it. Can we invite him for dinner again?"

"He is pretty nice, for an enemy spy," she said, winking.

Sam winced, heat rushing to his cheeks.

"Sure. I think we should invite him again. He seems lonely and it was fun having him as a dinner guest. He sure has traveled a lot."

"Yeah, he's pretty cool. He kind of reminds me a little of Grandpa," said Sam.

The thought had come out of nowhere and stirred a twinge of guilt, like he might be trying to replace his grandfather. He felt the salty beginnings of a tear working its way out of the corner of his eye and quickly wiped it away.

"You're right," said Mom, nodding. "I see it. Grandpa

could always cheer you up and he loved hearing about all the creatures you found, didn't he? I know you miss him. I actually think that Grandpa and Mr. Thomas would have been good friends if they'd met."

Sam nodded. It made him feel better to think of the two of them hanging out, maybe even playing cards or fishing together, or whatever old people did to bond. It felt less like replacing Grandpa and more like having a mutual friend. He wiped away some more pre-tear humidity.

Mom stepped closer and pulled him in for a hug, wrapping her arms all the way around to his backpack and tugging on the top handle.

"Good lord, how do you even lift this thing?" she asked, stepping back and sliding her hands to his shoulders. "You can do your work on the kitchen table. I'll make you some popcorn to snack on. Okay?"

Sam smiled and nodded.

After a quick wrestle with linear functions, and a bit of a word skirmish involving an essay on a poem they read in class that day (poems were definitely not his thing. He was more of a literal, matter-of-fact kid and did not understand why he couldn't just be tested on scientific tomes for English class. It *was* still English, after all.), Sam packed up his books and took his empty popcorn bowl to the sink. He put his backpack in its place by the door to the garage and got a resealable baggie from the pantry to protect his phone. He looked up at the clock above the pantry door and bit his bottom lip. Christina would still be at her school for a while. There was some kind of meeting planned after they found out their parts.

He didn't want to admit it to his mom, but he was a little nervous about going to the stream alone and would have preferred the company of his big sister. But Tyler wasn't on the bus, so Sam was sure he was at practice, and the weather was perfect for herping. He might even get a glimpse of that big snapper that had been so elusive during his recent trips. He wanted to show Mr. Thomas the turtle when they went, but there was no sign of it. If he saw it today, he would get a picture.

"Mom! I'm done with my homework," he called toward the office. His mom was probably writing and he didn't want to burst in and disturb her.

He ambled toward the door to the garage, giving her time to respond. If she didn't answer by the time he got his shoes on, he would leave her a note on the little chalkboard by the door. She knew that's where he was going, so he wasn't worried he'd get in trouble.

"Okay, honey. Be careful at the stream. And please be home by five."

TWENTY-SIX

The sky was an analogous color palette of blues and grays, striped with clouds that masked the fading brilliance of a sun well along the latter half of its daily journey. Occasional beams shone down through openings in the thinner cloud cover, like cones of light cast by giant flashlights hidden in the heavens. The shadows they cast swayed along with their three-dimensional counterparts in the cool breeze rustling Sam's hair. He wasn't worried about finding the creatures he sought at the stream. There was still more than enough sunlight for them to be searching out its warmth. Nor was he concerned about the setting sun. He would have to be home for dinner before it got dark anyway. He set his phone alarm for 4:45. That would give him a little under an hour… better than nothing. He grabbed his waders and some supplies from the garage and started down the street.

When he was about a block away from the stream, Sam began scanning the ground under the trees. He picked up and tossed aside several sticks before settling on a long smooth branch he found under one of the larger birches. Somewhere between four to five feet long, it was a thick, sturdy specimen with a secondary branch sprouting off near the end, giving it the rough appearance of a two-pronged fork. This would be perfect until he saved up enough allowance money to buy the snake hook he wanted. It was definitely a keeper.

Rush hour traffic whooshed along somewhere beyond the end of the neighborhood and out of sight, the rush of its steady flow masking, then mingling with, the gurgling water of the stream as he approached. Sam crept closer to the bank, the sounds of his footsteps covered by the symphony of white noise. He sat tucked low on the grassy incline, his gaze sweeping the landscape, searching for the shyer creatures that would disappear the moment they sensed his presence.

Water striders scooted along the surfaces of stagnant mini-ponds created where the flowing waters had pooled, cut off from the stream by pebbles, sticks, and leaves. Tiny indents glimmered under their feet, as if they were perched upon gelatin. Sam focused in on the spastic creatures, a gasp of pure giddiness flooding his lungs when a frog popped up from under the water and grabbed one. Movement near a large rock in the center of the stream bed pulled his attention. He slowed his breathing, staying as still as his excitement would allow. A string of bubbles meandered up from under the rock.

Sam carefully scooted forward, doing his best not to rustle the drier grasses around him. He leaned forward and observed a smaller triangular rock protruding from the silt. A grin crept up along his lips, lifting his cheeks and crinkling the corners of his eyes. Moments later, another string of bubbles. When he squinted, focusing in on the area, he could make out two tiny marble-like circles on either side of the smaller rock. Definitely a turtle. And, by the rough shape of its head and its tiny almost pig-like nose, a snapper.

He pulled out his phone and zoomed in. The picture wasn't going to come out that great. He'd have to point out where the turtle was, and even then, would probably have to explain exactly what was in the shot. But he took it all the same, in case he wasn't able to get a better one. He only took one, though, because his hope was to lure the turtle out into the open for a better picture. And if he could lure it out far enough to get a good look at its tail, he'd be able to tell whether it was a male or a female from afar.

Please be a female, he thought, closing his eyes and crossing his fingers, then shoved his phone back into the baggie and his pants pocket.

The sandy bank on the other side of the stream would be perfect for a female snapping turtle looking for a place to lay her annual clutch of eggs. If this was a female, he would be on the lookout for patches of freshly turned sand nearby when laying season rolled around. Of course, he would be on the lookout anyway, but this would give him more hope of actually finding a clutch to monitor until the hatchlings emerged.

He reached into his jacket and pulled out a plastic spoon and a small tube containing dead flies he'd collected for just such an occasion. The breeze had all but disappeared, so success would be totally dependent on his aim, and he'd been practicing. He opened the tube, tipped it, and tapped on its side with a finger until a fly slid out onto the spoon. After closing the tube and taking a deep breath in, releasing it slowly to steady himself, he gripped the handle of the spoon with his left hand and pressed his index finger down on the edge of the bowl. The spoon bowed slightly under the pressure. He lined up his sights—knuckle, spoon, and turtle—and released the bowl. The dead fly took off in a graceful un-fly-like arc, gliding over the grassy bank and hitting the water not far from where the bubbles had erupted into the air.

Sam tucked his lips between his teeth. With each shallow breath through his nose, he willed the turtle to go for the insect, which was now floating just above. The tiny ripples caused by the fly's landing rapidly dissipated, along with Sam's hopes that the turtle would go for this first fly. Without movement, it would no longer look like a tempting snack. He was unscrewing the cap of the tube again when a dark, crusty-looking head shot up from below the water and snatched the dead fly in its jaws.

"Yes," Sam whispered, then covered his mouth. He didn't want to scare his find.

The turtle pushed itself the rest of the way out of the silt with its two front legs, using them to navigate to the edge of the stream. Sam grabbed the tube and slid another fly onto the spoon, this time aiming for the area just in front of the turtle. Once again, his aim was true, and once again the turtle gobbled up its snack, not seeming to mind that it was stale.

Sam reached his arm back and felt for his phone, keeping his gaze locked onto the turtle. Snappers were geniuses at camouflage and he was afraid that if he looked away, the turtle would dart back under the water, kicking up silt to disguise its path to a new hiding place. He held the phone in front of him, turning it on and swiping back to his camera without losing sight of the snapping turtle. He took several pictures, giddiness rippling through him when the turtle continued up the bank and out of the water. It was a female.

Leaning forward onto his elbows, Sam inched closer, letting his knees unfold until he was laying on his stomach, phone held firmly in both hands. The turtle's head jerked to the side, in his direction. Had he made too much noise? He snapped a few more pictures right before his subject jettisoned itself back into the water, then lowered the phone and watched silt explode up from the stream bed like a rolling thunder-cloud, obscuring his view of everything below the water's sparkling surface.

He shrugged, still satisfied with the pictures he was able to get before the turtle skittered away.

Mr. Thomas is going to love these, he thought, pulling one of his knees up underneath him and pushing up with his elbows.

On his way up, his back met with resistance, and before his mind could register what was happening, something shoved him, pinning him down. When his face made contact with the ground, his mouth filled with an earthy mix of grass and dirt. He spat, the coppery taste of blood washing over his tongue, mixing with the other undesired flavors. He made another attempt to get to his feet, but a weight on top of his back held him in place. A slight turn of his head revealed Tyler in his peripheral.

"Well, look who we have here," Tyler snarled. "It's the weirdo snitch. You tryin' to get me thrown off the football team, snitch?"

Sam shook his head vigorously, an airy moan slipping past his lips when Tyler sat down hard on top of him.

"Ever heard the saying *snitches get stitches*, weirdo?"

"I didn't say anything to anyone," Sam mumbled, suspecting it wouldn't do him any good.

He scanned the ground around him, looking for something that might help him escape, wishing that one of the snakes his attacker was so afraid of would appear. Tyler grabbed a handful of hair at the back of Sam's head and pushed his face into the ground. Sam squirmed and spat out his second mouthful of dirt, but Tyler held firm.

"I swear I didn't say anything," said Sam, his fingertips pressing into the ground.

His arms were sprawled out in front of him, making him look like a superhero in flight. He tried to army-crawl forward, but the pressure Tyler was applying between his shoulders kept him from effectively using his upper body. And one of Tyler's legs was tucked up behind the bully across the backs of Sam's knees. Sam let his body relax, hoping that a total surrender would satisfy the bigger boy. It did not.

"I guess the question now is... where do you want your stitches to be?" Tyler rolled his hand into a fist and launched it toward the side of Sam's face. Sam turned his head to the other side a moment before impact, taking the hit on the back of his head.

With his head turned to the other side, he noticed the stick he'd brought with him to use as a snake hook was within reach. He stretched his arm and wrapped his fingers around the end closest to him, then yanked his hand up and back, swinging the two-pronged branch into Tyler's side. It wasn't a hard blow by any means, but it threw the bigger boy off his balance when he raised his arm to block the hit. Sam rolled away from the stick, bringing it along and giving Tyler another whack on his way.

"What the fuck?" yelled Tyler, once again throwing an arm up to block.

The stick cracked hard against his wrist. As he rolled, Sam saw his bully's face flush a red the color of freshly spilt blood, his eyes shrinking to a squint at impact, then widening and turning to meet Sam's. His glare was a furious beam of hatred. Sam scrambled to get his legs underneath him, pushing away in a half-crawl, before regaining his balance. He sprinted across the grass away from Tyler and toward the culvert at the far end of the stream.

Sam's heart skipped like fireworks in his chest, each beat an explosion reaching up into his head. He ran, eyes fixed on the dark opening before him, ears unable to hear anything other than the sounds of his own frantic breaths and the pounding of his heart. When he arrived at the culvert, he turned his head just far enough to see that Tyler was not far behind, face contorted and creased with rage, a terrifying canvas streaked with reds, grays, and yellows.

With one hand against the concrete opening, Sam steadied himself turning to face his assailant. Tyler slowed, approaching like a wolf closing in on its prey. A grin crept up one corner of his mouth.

"Where ya gonna go now, weirdo?"

With his spine pressed against the entrance to the culvert, Sam reached a hand back to his pocket. His lip quivered slightly when he realized his phone was not there.

"Looking for this?" asked Tyler, holding up Sam's phone with his thumb and index finger, before tossing it over his back.

Sam stepped into the stream with his back to the mouth of the culvert, not daring to take his gaze off Tyler. He tilted his head to the side, listening for sounds of movement inside the tunnel.

"You think I can't get you in there?" Tyler laughed.

"There are snakes in there," said Sam, his voice shaking with shallow breaths. "The venomous kind."

"I'll take my chances," said Tyler dismissively, moving closer. He leaned down to pick up a rock and folded his hand around it in a fist.

Sam stepped back into the shadows, a miasma of stagnant water, blooming with algae and bacteria, assailing his nostrils. He crinkled his nose, tried to slow his breathing to limit the burn in his sinuses. Each step back echoed across the walls of cement, mingling with the stirring and dripping of water. He thought he heard several splashes further back in the dark, most likely frogs startled by his entrance. If he moved slowly and noisily, he was certain any water moccasins in the area would swim away. And even if one did approach, his neoprene waders would protect him. With any luck, it would swim toward Tyler, scare him away, but Sam was not feeling particularly lucky at the moment.

"There's nowhere to go, weirdo. Come on out and it'll be over faster." Tyler's cold, cruel voice echoed through the tunnel and into the marrow of Sam's spine.

Splosh!

Sam turned toward the sound behind him, with no expectation of seeing its source. Even if his eyes had time to adjust to the darkness that now lay before him, the sound had come from back just beyond the world of shadowy forms, where a curtain of profound nothingness was drawn. Yet there it was, a vague shape somehow even darker than the void, an impossible shadow cast upon the curtain of nothingness. It moved toward him. Tiny waves lapped against his waders, tapping against him to announce its arrival. Winding closer in a hypnotic zigzag.

I understand.

"Whisper, is that you?" he asked. The name he had chosen, thus far uttered only in his mind, hissed from his lips.

"What did you say, weirdo?" Tyler's voice rumbled through the culvert. He stood a few feet from its mouth, illuminated by the rays of a sinking sun, striped by the shadows of trees.

Sam straightened and took a step toward him, an inexplicable rush of moxie pushing him forward. His sudden courage seemed to confuse Tyler, whose face had smoothed from anger to contemplation.

"What the fuck is up with your eyes, weir... What the hell is that?!" Tyler stumbled backward to the shadowy stream bank, landing hard on his backside.

Sam smiled, the world around him bathed in colors, shapes, and depths he had never before perceived. He moved toward Tyler, now a trembling mass on the ground. Fear emanated from his bully's body like bright green waves of radiation lifted by the rage that had preceded and washed over Sam, warming him, exciting him. He tilted his head, aware that they had switched places. Predator was now prey. He stepped closer, even as his body remained at the entrance of the culvert, rapt.

For he was no longer Sam. He was Whisper. And Whisper was hungry. Famished from days of settling for scraps when that for which he truly hungered eluded him, taunting from an insurmountable distance. The connection he had established with the boy, however faint in its beginnings, electrified him. The possibilities it opened coursed through his body in shivers as he approached his first truly nourishing meal.

He eyed the boy laying helpless in the grass, shadows adorning his young form. Took in the beauty of him, like a cool drink on a hot summer's day, before allowing his dark, slick, viscous body to slide alongside his prey. The boy was positioned on his side, eyes closed, curled tight in a feeble attempt to deny him. With a leg on each side, he lifted his body and flipped the boy onto his stomach, a shiver running the length of him when his scales made contact with a small strip of the boy's smooth, exposed, pink skin.

With one webbed hand, he pinned the trembling boy's shoulder. Using the weight of his hindquarters to keep the boy's legs still, he slid the other hand up under his shirt, pushing it up to expose the subtle mounds of his spine. This was the easiest route, the simplest path to success for a first-timer. A knowledge instilled in him during incubation. He leaned his face closer, taking in the sweet smell of sweat and adrenaline, watching his hot breath tickle the downy hairs on the back of his prey's neck, hairs that stood at attention like the hackles of a dog.

The boy whimpered and sobbed, tried to pull himself forward, snapping Whisper back from his revelry to the task at hand, his first true meal. He set his chin gently on the boy's back at the base of his spine, allowing his long sharp tongue to explore the length of it, his body quivering along with that of the boy at each flickering brush along his warm salty skin. He decided on his point of entry, a smooth, supple patch of skin at the base of the boy's neck, close to his prize. He slid a claw over to the spot and made a small satisfying slit, then slipped his tongue inside. The moment he connected, his tongue spindling into the bundled nerves, he tasted the boy's anger, a deep well, fresh and filling.

Whisper lay pressed against his prey, feeding on a pool of his warmth and aggression, drawing it out with his straw-like tongue. Each gentle pull filled him with newfound strength, heightening his excitement. Until the pool began to dwindle. She had warned him of this, the one who created him. Warned him before he ever knew of her. In some, the rage that nourished was a shallow puddle, in others a bottomless quarry. The youngest of them usually fell into the first category.

He quelled his frustration with reminders of promises made before air ever filled his lungs, tickled his scales. This was just his first, and once marked, could be easily accessed for future feedings until nothing remained to feed upon, until there was nothing left to replenish, the package consumed. In the meantime, he needed to strengthen the connection he'd begun to forge, his sight into their world... his access door. And there was only one way to do that. He withdrew his tongue, static tickling through him as it unwound and detached from Tyler, who lay pale and unconscious.

Through his eyes, Sam had seen what the creature could do, how he could help the boy. Now, an act of mutual sacrifice was needed to seal their bond. Whisper turned toward Sam, looked into his eyes, their eyes, and saw no resistance. The boy welcomed him forward, his face frozen in a dreamy smile, lips slightly parted, arms outstretched.

The creature flicked his tongue against his own extended arm, creating an opening, a portal for his part of the sacrifice. Then he approached Sam. His scaled body tensed with anticipation. His eyes squeezed and widened, a thin translucent film gliding over them and back again, replenishing the shimmering layer of protective slime. He drew himself up to the height of the boy before him, a slight arch to his back, and spread out his arms as if to receive Sam into a loving embrace.

And it would be, even more than that. If the stories upon which he fed through the membrane that nourished him, body and mind, were true, he was about to experience a surge of power and life that would eclipse everything and anything he could ever get from a mere feeding, no matter how rich or seemingly endless the source. It would be a power he could replenish upon request for the life of his host, a life that he would protect with his very being, tooth and claw until it no longer provided.

Whisper was close enough to see the heat generated by the boy's warm-blooded body, to feel it, when a beige-colored flurry of hair appeared in his peripheral, speeding toward him. Before he could comprehend, it expanded to include pink gums and rows of sharp ivory-colored teeth, the longest of which caught the last of the fading sunlight as they rocketed toward him. He turned to confront his attacker, but was ill-prepared for the onslaught of claws and teeth launched onto him by the dog's powerful hind legs.

He hissed and scuttled to the side after taking the full brunt of the initial attack.

"Alvis! No!" screamed Sam.

The words came out with a fury, from a snarl that had never before graced the boy's lips, confusing the dog. Alvis paused, head tilted, and observed his boy with deep, expressive eyes, a quiet whimper squeaking from his throat.

The creature dropped lower to the ground, taking advantage of the dog's confusion to attempt another approach, desperate to finish what he started, unaware that his inexperience and eagerness were working against him. Catching this movement, Alvis placed himself between Sam and Whisper, snarling and snapping to drive the dark hissing bundle of scales and slime back again.

Whisper eyed the dog's throat, his tongue flickering from side to side. He mentally calculated the distance he would need to leap in order to latch on and gain access. The limited connection he had with the boy didn't allow him to draw direct energy, and he realized that his first meal had been so immensely satisfying, first and foremost because it had been just that, his first. In reality, it had not provided much more than a quick surge, a taste of possibility.

What their connection did allow was shared sight. The moment the creature focused in on Alvis's neck, Sam knew its intentions. He reached a hand down and nestled it into the soft warm fur on Alvis's back. The dog wagged his tail, backing his hindquarters against Sam's leg, like he always did when he wanted more attention. Then he let out a tirade of barks in the direction of the creature, driving it back further still, until it was a step inside the culvert.

"Alvis!" A voice called from the direction of the neighborhood homes. "Alvis, where the hell are you? Sam? Are you down there? Alvis slipped his collar."

The creature darted into the dark sanctuary of the culvert, now painfully aware that his moment had passed. He would have to wait. To complete their connection another time. In the meantime, he had a source of the nourishing food he so desired, needed, in Tyler, once the boy recovered and replenished his reservoir.

Sam blinked hard a few times, shaking his head. He sank

to the ground and threw his arms around Alvis, who wiggled and covered his face with kisses. Then the dog squirmed free and ran to Tyler, nudging the boy's cheek with his cold wet nose.

"Sam?" This time the voice was much closer. "Sam, is that you? Is Alvis with you? He ran this way. Sam?"

"We're both here," he called back. "Alvis is fine, though he looks a little naked without his collar."

Laughing peppered the nearby panting sounds.

"Hey, guess what? I got the part of Charlotte," said Christina, appearing at the top of the hill. She paused a moment to catch her breath, hands on her hips.

"Are you okay?" she asked Sam when she noticed Tyler, who was now sitting up and trying to fend off Alvis's assault of affection.

Sam nodded. He bit his lip and shifted his gaze from his sister over to Tyler, worried about what the other boy might say.

"Okay, okay, stop," said Tyler, standing and scratching the dog behind his ears.

Tyler appeared both exhausted and confused. He looked around, letting his sleepy gaze pause first on Christina, then on Sam.

"What happened?" He reached a hand behind his neck and rubbed. There was no sign of the anger Sam fully expected to erupt from the boy.

"You slipped on the bank," chanced Sam. "Remember? We were watching the snapping turtle I found, and you slipped."

Sam walked over and picked his phone up off the ground where Tyler had tossed it. He opened the screen and scrolled to his pictures, now fully committed to selling his version of events.

"Remember?" He walked over to Tyler holding out the pictures he'd taken of the turtle on the bank of the stream.

Tyler leaned forward, squinting to get a better look at the screen. Christina eyed them both through squinted eyes, brows and lips pinched.

"Are you okay? You went down pretty hard." Sam brushed some dried grass from his bully's shoulder and gave him a pat on the back.

"Yeah, I think so. I just feel a little bit tired. Cool turtle." He reached down to pet Alvis some more.

Christina walked down the hill, holding out the collar which, unlike the dog, was still attached to the leash. She slipped it over Alvis's head, all the while regarding the two boys incredulously, as if waiting for someone to deliver the punchline of this obvious joke.

"Umm. Okay. Well, it's time for you to head back home, Sam," she said, still staring, eyebrows bunched, creating a mountain range of creases across the top of her nose.

"Wanna walk with us?" Sam asked Tyler. He wanted to keep an eye on him, to see if he remembered anything, if he was really okay.

"Sure, I guess," said Tyler, his voice neutral, matter-of-fact.

The three walked side by side in silence up to the road, Alvis leading the way. When they arrived at their house, Sam held a finger up to Christina.

"You go ahead. I'll be right there," he said.

His sister shrugged, said a quick, baffled goodbye to Tyler, and coaxed a resistant Alvis toward the front door. The boys walked a few steps further up the road before Sam reached out and touched Tyler's arm. Tyler flinched, then settled.

"Are you really sure you're okay?"

"Yeah, I guess. But..." he reached his hand up and passed it down his forehead, pinching the skin on either side of his eyes on the way. "I don't remember what happened. Like, I can't remember looking at that turtle or falling or anything."

"What do you remember?" asked Sam, trying to keep his tone nonchalant, with a touch of concern. The concern part was not at all hard to relay.

Tyler looked at his shoes, his top lip tucked between his teeth. He took a deep breath and held it for a moment before letting it out. Then he shrugged, his eyebrows darting up when he shook his head.

"I remember walking to the stream. I think I was angry at you... like really angry. But I don't remember why."

"Are you angry at me now?"

Tyler shook his head.

"No. I don't think so. I'm just tired... and hungry."

"Yeah. It is time for dinner," said Sam, nodding.

Tyler nodded, too. He looked like he was okay physically, but something was off. Sam saw no trace of the angry bully who'd come after him time and time again. Something was definitely wrong. Though to be honest, Sam much preferred this version of him.

"You okay to walk home, or do you want me to go with you?"

"I'm fine, I guess. See you tomorrow."

Tyler waved and walked away toward his house.

"Hang on," said Sam. "There's something stuck on the back of your shirt."

He trotted over and pulled some dead leaves off the back of Tyler's shirt collar, lowering it to get ahold of a leaf that was working its way inside the boy's shirt. A quiet gasp pulled air through his lips when he noticed a dime-sized bruise on the back of Tyler's neck, with what looked like a small, raised, red line crusted with a fleck of blood in its center. It looked almost like a target.

TWENTY-SEVEN

When Sam turned to head home, he noticed Mr. Thomas staring at them from his front window. He raised a hand and waved, hoping that his forced smile looked more natural than it felt. Mr. Thomas waved back, but Sam couldn't help but notice his confusion.

Understandable. The kid who had been trying to kick Sam's ass since he moved in was suddenly exchanging pleasantries with him out in public. Sam was pretty confused himself. Well, that and the whole "monster in the culvert" thing. But Mr. Thomas didn't know anything about that.

Whisper, he thought, his own memory of the events at the stream growing as fuzzy as the skin of a sweet Georgia peach. *My new friend, Whisper.*

Something tugged at him as he walked toward his house, a thin thread in the back of his mind. He had that bothersome feeling of having forgotten to do something, of needing to complete something. Had he finished all his homework? He thought so, but would check when he got home. He looked at his phone, then stopped walking and scratched the back of his head. Maybe he had time to swing by the stream for a few minutes more before heading home. Maybe he'd left something there. Sure, it was starting to get dark, but it would only be for a couple minutes.

"Sam, everything okay?" Mr. Thomas called from his new position, outside his front door. He nodded toward Tyler, who had almost disappeared down his driveway up at the top of the street, then cocked his head and raised his brows.

"Oh, yeah. It's all good. Thanks, Mr. Thomas," said Sam, flashing a lipless line of a smile accompanied by a thumbs-up.

"Good," his neighbor said, voice a little hesitant. "Well, I think I figured some things out with the camera if you want to come over tomorrow after school."

Sam gave another thumbs-up and turned toward his house. His mom was now standing at their front door, motioning for him to pick up the pace. Sam growled ever so slightly in the back of his throat, gave up his plans to head back to the stream, and ran home.

TWENTY-EIGHT

"Was that that Tyler kid you were talking to outside?" Sarah asked Sam when the family was seated at the table for dinner.

She held out a bun for his hotdog, pulling it back slightly when he reached for it, as if leveraging for an answer. Greg looked up from his meal. He glanced from Sarah to Sam, to Christina, seemingly searching for a way into a circle of information of which he obviously was not a part. Christina shrugged.

"Tyler? The bully kid?" he asked.

"Yeah," said Sam, taking the hotdog bun and looking at his parents, one by one.

His eyes were wide and innocent, but Sarah could see that he was chewing the inside of his cheek, one of his usual tells when he was trying to hide something. When he took a nibble at the side of his thumb, her concern grew.

"Was he threatening you, or something?"

"No, Mom. Nothing like that. We were talking about turtles and stuff. I guess whatever Mr. Thomas told him worked."

Sam took an oversized bite of his hotdog, smiling with the innocence of a baby harp seal as he chewed. Sarah wondered if filling his mouth was an attempt to avoid further conversation on the matter.

"Buddy," said Greg, laughing, apparently oblivious to his son's strategy. "Slow down. There are plenty more hotdogs. You don't have to swallow them whole."

Sarah waited for him to finish chewing and threw in a comment before he could fill his mouth again.

"So, after all that, he's not only going to leave you alone, but you guys are suddenly friends?"

She turned her mom-scan on him full power. He squirmed, then straightened in his chair.

"Really, Mom. It's fine. I don't know what Mr. Thomas told him. Maybe Tyler's worried he'll get thrown off the football team."

"That sounds reasonable," said Greg, nodding.

Sarah shot her husband a glare. He raised his hands, palms up, and mouthed the word "what?" then set both hands on the table, shrugged a you're-on-your-own at Sam, and picked up his hotdog.

"Really, Mom. Ask Christina. We were talking about turtles. She walked back with us. Hey, did she tell you she got the part of Charlotte in the play? Isn't that awesome?"

"Yes, she did, sweetie. And yes, it is awesome. You walked the boys home, Christina?"

He had successfully shifted all attention to Christina, who stopped mid-chew when Sarah turned her gaze, then nodded, pinching the corner of her mouth and hunching the corresponding shoulder. She swallowed the contents of her mouth and took a quick drink of water.

"Yeah... and they were talking about turtles. I mean, that's what they were talking about when I got there, anyway. I thought it was weird, too."

"I got some cool pics. Then Tyler slipped and bumped his head, so I helped him up. Want to see the pics?" Sam's voice squeaked. He cleared his throat.

"You start showing me selfies of the two of you and I'm going to start wondering just how hard that bump on the head was." Sarah's brows were still furrowed, but her mouth had smoothed into a slight smile.

Sam laughed. It was a little overzealous. Maybe he was trying to sell a story. But Sarah decided to let it drop. She took a deep breath, her brows shifting back into neutral. At least Sam looked a lot happier than he had the other night. She would have to remember to stop over at Ben's house to thank him for whatever magical spell he had cast on Tyler Whistler.

"No cell phone at the table. You know that," she said, relaxing into her chair. "You can show me the pictures after dinner."

She held the plate of hotdogs toward him, happy to see him snatch one and reach out for another bun.

"It was a *female* snapping turtle, Mom. Do you know what that means?"

She shook her head, preparing for the inevitable onslaught of snapping turtle trivia. Christina rolled her eyes, obviously prepared for the same.

"It means she'll probably lay a clutch of eggs—that's what a bunch of turtle eggs are called, a clutch—on the stream bank in late spring. I'm gonna start looking for them in May. When you're looking for snapping turtle eggs, you need to look for places where the sand has been dug up a little in a pile."

Sam paused to catch his breath and to make sure that his audience was still with him.

"Sounds interesting," said Greg, grinning. "But, no bringing any little snappers home as pets, please. Alvis would get jealous."

At the mention of his name, Alvis perked up from his place next to the table.

"Of course not, Dad," replied Sam behind his widest how-could-you-even-think-that eyes. "Though, let's say one of them was hurt and needed rebilitation."

"Rehabilitation, doofus?" asked Christina.

"Yeah, that," said Sam, ignoring the insult part. "I couldn't just leave an injured turtle to be eaten by the raccoons, could I?"

"There are things called *animal rescues*, you know." Christina flicked a breadcrumb at her brother.

"Well, someone would have to bring the turtle to the animal rescue," he countered, dodging the yeasty missile. "And I think Alvis would be fine with a baby turtle."

The second mention of his name sent Alvis into a series of whimpers and anxious whines. He was staring at the plate of hotdogs, still sitting but scooting forward ever so slightly with each desperate sound.

"Can I give him one, Mom?" asked Sam. "He was a good boy today."

"Yeah, except he slipped his collar when I was walking him," said Christina, glaring at the dog. "Almost pulled me right off my feet."

"Because he was coming to help m-m... Tyler. He ran over to Tyler after he fell and made sure he was okay."

Sarah held up her hands, palms out.

"Okay, okay. Enough with the bickering." She pointed at Sam. "Yes, you can give Alvis a hotdog, but not from the table. Put it into his bowl." Then she turned to Christina. "Please help clear the table." And, when she saw that her daughter was about to protest, she followed up with, "I don't care whose turn it is tonight, just please help without complaining. I have some work I need to finish."

"I'll do it, Mom," said Sam, popping up from his seat and tossing a hotdog toward Alvis's dish.

It bounced once and was promptly snatched up and swallowed by the dog, who had leapt forward when he saw the boy's arm swing back. Sam spun back toward the table and began to gather plates. He grinned over at Christina. It was clear they'd struck some kind of clandestine deal between them, which was fine with Sarah, as long as the table got cleared.

"Go ahead, honey," said Greg, standing to bring his plate to the sink. "I'll make some coffee and bring it to you in the office. Unless you'd prefer some limoncello or Sambuca." He flashed her a mischievous smile.

"There's what I'd prefer, then there's what I need." She pulled in a deep breath and expelled it in a long sigh. "This is definitely a coffee night."

He gave her a thumbs-up and turned. "Coffee, it is."

Once she was situated in the office, coffee on the desk and Alvis curled up in his usual spot in the corner, she opened her laptop and pulled up the article she was in the process of writing. A fluff piece, of course. She'd been told that in this new job, the road to serious articles was paved with fluff. Lately, she was wondering just how long this road would be.

She sighed, silently chastising herself for once again letting doubt slip into her thoughts. Sure, she'd had more serious assignments in her last job, but this move would be good for them in the end. Of this she was certain. The passing of Greg's dad had been the last little tug to unravel any and all knots tying them to the area. And, though time had a way of softening the sharp corners of bad memories in a kind of mental erosion, there were things from which she simply needed more distance. Greg had agreed. Of course, he had. Some of those memories involved him directly.

"It'll be an adventure. A fresh start," he'd said.

And he had been true to his word so far, a full partner in finding a place to move on. A place where they had both secured new jobs. Jobs that gave them more time with the kids and each other.

"'How to Enjoy an Empty Nest,'" she read, chuckling. "Does anyone really read this shit? Would they still read it if they knew that it was written by someone whose nest is nowhere near empty?"

She wrapped her hands around the back of her neck and pulled as she tilted back her head until her spine crackled like Pop Rocks in soda. Then, stretching her arms out in front of her, she shook her hands a few times. Time to get to work.

A few hours later, the kids were in bed and she could hear the music from one of Greg's crime shows coming in from the family room, *CSI Something-Or-Other*. There were too many for her to keep up with. She reread what she'd written one more time, rubbing her burning eyes between paragraphs, and decided that it was quitting time.

Pushing the laptop closed, she yawned and reached out to turn off the office light, her finger lingering on the switch. Her head felt heavy but clear, as if she'd successfully emptied out the words that usually resided up there, a tornado of phrases and expressions, onto the computer leaving only images that came in and out of focus as they whirled by. It wasn't an unpleasant feeling, floating in snapshots of her life, illustrations of her thoughts and feelings.

Cold air kissed her cheek, bringing her focus back to the present. In her reverie, she had made her way to the office window. Alvis sat at her feet staring up at her, a patient but anticipatory expression on his face. She set a hand on his head.

"We'll head to bed in a minute," she said, giving him a pat.

The plantation shutters were parted just enough to allow the cold aura around the window glass to snake through. She peeked out into the night. The moon wasn't quite full. She gazed at it, the question of whether it was waxing or waning tickling her thoughts.

Last year I would have known, she mused. *Last year when Sam was studying the phases of the moon in school.*

Her mind shifted gears, heading down a trail to thoughts of how quickly time was passing. One minute your son was studying the moon and the next he'd moved on to the elements. One minute your daughter was too shy to talk to her kindergarten teacher and the next she's mooning after boys and has the lead in her high school play. One minute your son is getting the crap kicked out of him by the neighborhood bully, and the next the two are best buddies. In her current state of exhaustion, it all fit into a perfectly logical and natural progression of events.

She stood with her forehead pressed against the shutters, watching shadows cast by strips of clouds crossing the moon, scurry across the yard. The light was on in Ben's front room.

"I'm glad you've decided Mr. Thomas is okay after all," she

said, giving Alvis a scratch behind the ears. "Even if it is because he bribed you with food."

The dog sat a bit taller, growling at the window.

"Seriously? You changing your mind? Holding out for more jerky, maybe?"

Alvis stood at attention, emitting a short, muffled "woof."

Sarah looked outside in time to catch the passing of a shadow that didn't quite fit with the others. It was somehow darker, its sleek movements not the two-dimensional slide of those shadows cast by the clouds obscuring the light of the moon. It slithered a twisty curving path just under the window where she stood and disappeared into the bushes that hid the dull gray foundation as per the HOA's request.

A shiver slid down Sarah's spine. She crossed her arms in front of her in a tight hug, leaning forward to see if she could spot the shadow. Something glided up the side of the house, along the brick. Alvis leaned against her leg, his nose pointing in that very direction. He looked up at Sarah, then back at the side of the house, then back at her, as if to say, "Did you see that?"

Sarah focused on the brick; moonlit shadows from a crepe myrtle set nearby danced on the house, stirred by a sudden breeze.

"Silly boy," she leaned over to tell the dog. "It's just the wind moving the leaves."

She rubbed her hands up and down the tops of her arms before releasing her self-hug, and blew out a puff of air.

"Okay. It is obviously time for both of us to get some sleep. We're getting paranoid. You know what they say about a good night's sleep."

She squinted her eyes and scratched the top of her head.

"Never mind. I'm too tired to remember."

Sarah closed the shutters and left the office, Alvis trotting along behind her. On the way past the front door, she checked to make sure the lock was secure. And, before stopping by the family room to let Greg know she was heading to bed, she went upstairs to the kids' rooms to check their windows, peeking under the shade in Sam's room when she heard scratching, which turned out to be a branch bowing against the house in the wind.

"What?" she asked Alvis in a whisper, prompting the dog to tilt his head. "Paranoia aside, one can never be too careful."

Once reassured that the house was a proper level of secure, she kissed at the dog to follow, a completely unnecessary task, considering that ninety-nine percent of the time Alvis was at her heels, even under her feet, when she was home. On the way down the stairs, she couldn't help but be reminded of her days living alone in the city and the nightly lock-checks.

TWENTY-NINE

When he pulled onto Main Street, Jacob couldn't help but sneer. Bile crept up his throat to the back of his tongue. This is where they had lived, comfy-cozy after murdering his brother and maiming him. He wondered what their house looked like. Or maybe they lived in an apartment. No, a house would be more likely, considering the unconventional pet they were keeping, concealing.

He drove the main strip of the town, glaring at the shops and restaurants. This is where they had walked along arm in arm, stopping to peek inside the row of quaint mom-and-pop stores, maybe grabbing a coffee at the little café, while he scraped by on whatever food his grief-struck mother remembered to bring home, when she remembered to come home.

He turned Jimmy's Subaru into the first available parking lot and pulled into one of the spots furthest from the shops. Tears competed to access the ducts he attempted to cut off with a concentrated squint and a swipe of his sleeve.

Was he sad? Shit, no. They were tears of anger, the tears of someone who'd had one too many things stolen from him. It didn't matter what the town looked like. To him, its mere existence represented the continuation of life without any regret for the past, for what they'd done. To actually be here, watching families stroll along the sidewalks, mothers carrying their babies, parents swinging their children along between them, was infuriating. And the tears that did find their way past his defenses fell like lighter fluid on a flame.

He glanced around to make sure nobody was watching before sliding a plastic baggie out of his pocket. The inside of the baggie was clouded with dust, its pastel colors obscuring the contents. He opened the top to reveal a variety of pills gathered at the bottom, each tainted by stray particles of the others. Reaching in with his index finger, he hooked one and closed a thumb over it, then popped it onto his tongue. He was grasping for another when a memory washed over him with the first wave of comfort delivered by the pill dissolving in his mouth. The numbness.

He remembered the numbness that had overcome him when the creature slid on top of him, tasted him. He knew there were frogs and salamanders that had toxins on their skin. His brother's buddies used to joke about going toad-licking. He'd looked into it when he was a kid. It didn't sound very appealing to him at the time. Whatever it was that had killed his brother and marked him, whatever *that* was, was a helluva lot bigger than any salamander he'd ever seen. And, that tongue...

His finger twirled around the pills in the baggie, taking on a dusty hue. He yanked it out and shoved the bag back into his pocket, then jammed his chalky finger between his lips, sucking off the remnants of the drugs.

One to take the edge off. Just one to take the edge off.

When he felt up to it, Jacob pulled out of the lot and continued his tour of the town. He'd been in plenty of towns just like it over the years. Little shit towns that tried to hide their blemishes under layers of fresh paint and pretty plastic playgrounds. As if washing the streets at night with those glorified spinning-toothbrush-pushing truck-lets could rid the place of the stench of human nature.

He was sure as shit he could find the underbelly of this town with little to no effort. Every town had one, at least every town he'd been to. The burning under his scar had subsided, but the little raised welt still had a certain itch to it... the kind that once you think about it, you can't stop. He was reaching under his shirt to give it a scratch when he saw a sign for the local library. The perfect place for a little research.

The map on his cellphone showed that this little Podunk town was experiencing the same suburban sprawl that was infecting the rest of the country. He needed to narrow down the area of his search. In the library, he could ask about local papers, dig around a bit. And if worse came to worst, he could try the "I'm looking for my long-lost Grannie and Grandpapa" act his brain had been perfecting. First, though, he wanted to find a motel where he could stash his things and get cleaned up... look respectable.

THIRTY

When Sarah stopped by the next morning, the first thing Ben saw upon opening the door was the dog sitting, not exactly patiently, on his front stoop. His leash was lax, but Alvis's muscles were tensed, and he looked like a furry beige spring, ready to release. He lifted his two front paws, shifting his weight between them as if the cement under them were made of lava.

Ben looked down at the dog, whose ears perked up and tail swayed the moment they made eye contact.

"Good morning," said Ben, risking releasing the spring by reaching down to pat Alvis's head.

Sarah, anticipating the move, drew up the slack in the leash, limiting Alvis to a slight scoot forward, which he punctuated with an impatient whine.

"Good morning, Ben. I brought your new best friend over to say hello on our way back from his walk." She smiled. "Also, I wanted to thank you for talking to Tyler. Whatever you said seems to have worked."

Ben nodded and scratched at his beard stubble. He was

curious to hear what Sam had told his mother about his most recent encounter with Tyler.

"Why don't the two of you come on in," he said, motioning to the door. "I have some coffee on and plenty of cookies and jerky in the pantry."

"Are you sure?" asked Sarah, casting a glance at Alvis, who despite being at the end of his walk, looked like a greyhound positioned for the starting box to open.

"Absolutely," said Ben, opening the door for them. "Head straight down the hall to the kitchen. He'll be fine. And, if he gets antsy, he can run in the backyard. The privacy fence is nice and sturdy, and Tyler helped me clear out the weeds the other day. I would say it's dog-ready."

"Well, you'd better warn any squirrels or rabbits if we do let him out. He loses his mind when he sees them."

Ben nodded and laughed, adding, "I haven't seen any signs of rabbits or squirrels back there in a very long time." Then, he thought to himself, *They figured out pretty quickly that it wasn't a good idea to come to our yard.*

Sarah and Alvis entered the house, followed by Ben.

"Sam is right, these pictures are amazing." Sarah tossed a glance accompanied by a smile back over her shoulder at Ben. She stopped in front of a picture at the end of the hall and pointed. "That's the one Sam took, right? He is so happy that you printed and framed it."

Ben nodded. "It's a beautiful shot. The boy's a natural, if you ask me. He has a way with angles and lighting. In fact, I wanted to ask you and Greg if it would be okay to give him Mary's camera."

Sarah's brows climbed and her lips parted.

"Are you sure about that? I saw the manual. That's a very

expensive camera for a kid Sam's age. I mean, that's very generous, but I'm not sure we can accept."

Ben's signature gentle smile curled up onto his face, pushing his wrinkles into pleasant arcs that framed his mouth like parentheses. He swept a hand toward the kitchen table.

"Sit, and I will bring some coffee and cookies." He smiled at Alvis. "And jerky."

When they were settled at the table, each armed with a cup of hot coffee, and Alvis was nose-first into his own little dish of jerky, Ben brought up the camera again.

"It's just sitting in a box gathering dust," he said, pointing to the counter where he had set the camera after going through the parts with Sam.

"Maybe we could buy it from you," said Sarah, between sips of her coffee.

"Absolutely not," said Ben, his firm, faux-outrage quickly contradicted by a playful smile. He set his coffee down and placed his hands, palms down, on the table. "Mary would want Sam to have it. She would have adored your whole family, especially Sam with his incredible knowledge of nature and love for the creatures she also loved. They would have been out hunting for all sorts of creepy crawlies together if she were still here. I always went with her on her explorations, but I was never passionate about it like she was. I just went along to be with her..." The pain of her absence wound itself around his words, tightening his throat and causing his voice to trail off.

Alvis, sensing sadness, lifted his head from his bowl and nuzzled it against Ben's side.

"Aww, thanks," said Ben, reaching down to pat the dog.

"Wow, you really are his new best friend," said Sarah. "I

have honestly never seen him do that to anyone outside the family." She smirked. "What did you put in that jerky?"

They both laughed and Alvis tilted his head, confused by the sudden mood shift.

"If it really means that much to you, Ben, Sam's birthday is coming up in a month. You can give it to him then. In the meantime, you can teach him to properly maintain such an expensive piece of equipment. We are talking about a kid who didn't even notice that he'd left his cell phone at the park the other day."

Ben extended a hand across the table, which Sarah accepted and shook.

"It's a deal. I'll teach him how to care for it, while we both figure out how to use all its bells and whistles. Then, when his birthday rolls around, I'll surprise him with it."

His face softened. He took a deep breath through his nose, swallowing hard to keep nostalgia from creeping up into his heart after all the talk of Mary. But he found that the sadness had dissipated on its own, leaving only a trace of bitterness. He took a sip of his coffee and chased it with a sugar cookie, letting the sweetness melt in his mouth to overpower the bitterness.

More and more lately, thoughts of Mary stirred anger in his soul. More and more, guilt and contempt wrangled for position when he asked himself if he had fought hard enough for her. Maybe his gentle nature, one of the things Mary loved him for, had made him weak. He had shared her, been a weight on the other extreme, balancing the scales for her, when he should have been her knight, fighting fiercely to free her.

"Ben?" He felt Sarah's hand on top of his and flinched.

"Sorry, I drifted. One of the hazards of getting old, I guess."

"Oh please, I drift all the time. Unless... are you calling me old?" Sarah laughed in an obvious attempt to lighten the mood once more.

"I would never," said Ben. He chuckled and found that a smile had once again worked its way onto his face.

A sound pulled their attention to the door from the kitchen to the garage. Alvis had wandered over and was scratching at the base of the door and whining.

"Alvis, no," said Sarah, standing and rushing over to grab his collar. She turned to Ben. "I am so sorry. I hope he didn't leave any marks."

Ben waved a hand at her and smiled. "No worries. That door has so many scratches, it looks like Jack Torrance tried to break in... or out."

A wide grin spread across Sarah's lips. "So, you *have* read some Stephen King."

Ben laughed. "A book here and there. But horror isn't really my genre. Too many horrible things in the real world for me to fill my head with them in my leisure time. Maybe Alvis needs to go out?" He stood and went to the back door.

"He shouldn't. We just got back from a three-mile walk." She looked down at the dog. "Do you have to go out?" At the word *out*, Alvis cocked his head and answered with a short bark.

"I should probably just walk him home. I would hate for him to dirty your lawn."

"Nonsense," said Ben. "You haven't even made a dent in your coffee. We can let him out so he can explore while we finish. Maybe I can convince you to have a few more cookies, too, so I don't eat them all. Unless you have somewhere you need to be, of course."

"I do eventually have to get home. But, if you're sure you don't mind, I can stay a little while longer. I'm not going to promise anything on the cookies, but I will definitely finish my coffee. Maybe I'll even pester you for a second cup. I need all the energy I can get to start the article I've been assigned to write." She sighed.

Ben opened the back door and they both watched Alvis dart through it like a racehorse fresh out of the gates. He sniffed around, marking trees and bushes as he went, then plopped himself down in the grass and tilted his head to the sky, a sunbather catching the rays.

"Little stinker," said Sarah, shaking her head.

"It's fine," said Ben. "I guess he just wanted to enjoy the sunshine. We could move outside, too, to the little patio table, if you'd like."

Sarah wrapped her arms around herself and shivered.

"Too cold for me. Not sure how I ever survived in the North. I am definitely a warm-weather gal."

She slipped back over to the table and sat down, wrapping both hands around her coffee cup. Ben shut the door and went over to retrieve the carafe of coffee warming in its home on the coffee maker. Sarah held up her cup and he added to it, topping her off. Fingers of steam snaked up from the hot beverage, veering for her face when she breathed them in.

"Thank you," she said, adding a spoonful of sugar from the porcelain bowl in front of her and stirring.

Ben closed both eyes and tipped his head in a slight bow. "Of course. Is that why you moved here? For the warmer weather?"

Sarah took a careful sip, then set the coffee on the table,

both hands still swaddling the cup. She stared at it, biting at the side of her bottom lip.

"If you don't mind me asking," Ben added, concerned that he may have crossed the line from friendly to nosy. When Mary was alive, they had occasionally been guests at someone else's house, mainly the Whistlers, and only when they knew Princess was full and in her resting phase. But, they rarely had people over to their house, and though he was loving his new role as host, he still wasn't quite confident in it.

"No, it's fine," said Sarah, pulling in another deep breath and releasing it in a sigh. "The weather is part of it, for sure. But we mainly came here for a fresh start."

"That is always a good reason for a move," said Ben, smiling. "Of course, the trick is to make sure your demons don't move with you."

Sarah flinched ever so slightly, then grinned and nodded to cover.

"True. I just hope it turns out to be the right move for Sam. Christina hasn't had any trouble making friends and loves her new school. Sam loves all the creepy crawlies that come with the warmer weather, but friend-wise... Well, you've seen how that has been."

"Second guessing, always my sport of choice," said Ben with a gentle laugh. "I suppose it's even more of a sport when you are a parent."

Sarah nodded. "Definitely."

"Well, Sam is a smart, likable kid. Maybe now that the bullying seems to have stopped, he can come out of his shell a little more so the other kids can see what they're missing. He did tell me that he's been striking up a friendship with a certain Sam. Hopefully, that will blossom. I know her family. Good people."

Sarah's brow raised and a sly grin pushed a dimple into her cheek. The moment he saw that grin, Ben realized his mistake. He whistled.

"Uh oh, I am in trouble."

"So, Sam is a *Samantha*," said Sarah, propping an elbow on the table and leaning her chin on her thumb, her index finger hooked in front of her lips. "Do tell."

Ben sealed his lips in a tight thin line and shook his head, then raised his brows in surrender. "I promised the kid I wouldn't tell. Some friend I am."

"Don't worry, I won't say anything. Though it's really tempting." She grinned and reached over to give Ben a pat on the side of his shoulder. "I certainly won't tell him that you let it slip. Though, now my mission will be to *accidentally* find out."

"Well, thanks for not telling on me." He pressed his palms together in front of his chest.

"Oh, hey," said Sarah, her brows rising with her tone. "With all the talk about the camera and moving, I totally forgot to ask what you said to Tyler to help convince him to leave Sam alone."

Ben reached a hand up to rub his beard stubble. It made a scraping sound as the dry skin on his palms moved across the stiff gray hairs poking through on his chin.

"Honestly, I wasn't sure I'd convinced him at all. That is, until I saw the boys talking yesterday." His hand slid from his chin to his neck, working its way around to the back before dropping into his lap. "He's been a pretty angry kid since the thing with his dad. I do think that under different circumstances, those two would have struck up a friendship from the start. Interesting fact, Samantha is actually Tyler's cousin. I wonder if she may have had something to do with Tyler's change of heart, as well."

He put both elbows on the table, clasping his hands and leaning forward, his gaze set squarely on Sarah. "What did Sam say about yesterday?"

"Something about looking for turtles with Tyler at the stream, and I guess Tyler fell and bumped his head or something. He was kind of vague. Honestly, I was a little suspicious at first. I thought maybe Tyler had threatened him not to say anything." She furrowed her brows and looked away, then her face smoothed and she shrugged and shifted her gaze back to his. "But Christina confirmed that the boys were talking about turtles when she got to the stream with Alvis. Speaking of Alvis, I should probably gather him from your yard and head home. What is it they say about not looking a gift horse in the mouth? Don't question miracles and all that?"

She stood and grabbed the leash from where she'd hung it on the back of her chair. Ben nodded and stood to accompany her to the back door. Alvis was no longer sunbathing. He had walked over to a corner of the yard and was standing alert, a low growl, barely audible, rising from his throat.

"Alvis!" Sarah called, kissing and clicking at him. "Alvis, come on."

She clapped her hands a few times to get his attention, but he wouldn't budge, so she walked toward him. Ben followed, the hairs on the back of his neck up like needles in a pincushion.

The dog was aimed at the corner of the yard near the garage, where he'd pushed the grill. He'd cleaned it out right after Tyler left his house the other night. Just beyond the grill was a small mound of dirt, the only indication of the deep hole —as deep as he could quickly manage—where he had buried the putrid ashes he pulled from inside the old Weber.

"Silly dog, you are literally growling at a grill. I guess I can add that to the list of inanimate objects that scare you." Sarah raised a palm to her forehead. "What the heck, Alvis?"

"Oh, it's not his fault." Ben stepped between the grill and the dog and pulled a piece of jerky from his pocket.

"Do you always carry jerky in your pockets?" asked Sarah, laughing.

He smiled. "Best friends have to be prepared. Anyway, something crawled into the grill and died a while back." He waved a hand in front of his nose. "I just finally cleaned it the other day. He probably smells it. I'm going to throw it away when trash day rolls around. Definitely not tossing any more burgers on that old thing. It was pretty gross."

Sarah scrunched her nose and her lips rolled back in disgust. She reached out and grabbed Alvis's collar, clicking the leash around its metal ring and giving the dog a tug.

"That does sound pretty gross. Come on, Alvis. Whatever it was though, it's dead now and still qualifies as inanimate."

Alvis slowly backed away, still mumbling a muffled growl. When they reached the door to the house, he turned and scooted inside ahead of them, relaxing once the door closed, then perked up again and pointed at the door to the garage, the one he had previously scratched. Sarah pulled him back.

"Boy, you are just all kinds of trouble today, aren't you?" she said, directing the dog to the hallway. "Someone needs some lessons on good guest manners."

"No worries, really," said Ben, passing them in the hall and opening the front door for them.

He said his goodbyes, then rushed back down the hallway, through the kitchen, and out the back door. He walked over to the grill, his attention riveted on the thin line of ash leading away from the dirt mound to the outer wall of the garage. Just above the grass line, opposite from where he had tried to patch the wall from the inside, was a hole. Something had clawed through the quick-dry cement. Not only that, but when he pushed down on the grass to get a better look at the hole, he realized that it was wider and deeper than it had first appeared. He grabbed a stick from the ground, not wanting to use his hand, and poked it down into the hole. Not only did it go to the garage wall, but by turning the stick back and forth, he could feel no resistance, leading him to believe that it tunneled both directions along the wall.

The claw marks along the cement told him he was dealing with something bigger than a squirrel or a rat.

THIRTY-ONE

Ben was leaning a dirt-caked shovel against the side of the house when the doorbell rang. He looked at his watch. Could it already be three p.m.? He stood with his palm pressed against the top of the shovel for a moment, trying to account for the time. His mind was fuzzy, each thought navigating through what felt like a brain filled with wet cement. His last clear memory was running back to the yard after Sarah had left with Alvis, though he vaguely remembered another trip to the hardware store on the way to an appointment with the notary at his bank.

He released the shovel and wiped his forehead with his sleeve and the back of his hand then assessed the yard. A dirt trench stretched alongside the foundation of his home. The grass had been pulled away from the house, presumably by him—some memory of the labor involved ached in his muscles — and formed a fuzzy green hill along the edge of his work. He approached and looked down into the fresh earthen moat. The hole that he'd patched in the wall to the main garage was not the only one. His efforts had revealed two more holes, one into the house itself where the laundry room was located, and another leading into the smaller garage used to store the old camper van. He had a feeling that if he removed the junk lining the wall between the garages, he might just find another hole.

The doorbell rang again. Three o'clock. Already knowing who would be there when he answered, he hurried into the house and ducked into the powder room on his way down the hall to the front door. He grimaced at his dirt-splotched face in the mirror, wet the hand towel next to the sink, and swiped from forehead to chin. When the bell rang a third time, he abandoned the towel on the edge of the sink and walked over to answer the door.

"Sorry about that, Tyler," he said to the boy leaning against the railing, staring off into space. "I was out back getting a head start on the yard work."

Tyler yawned, a smile pasted on his face that Ben could only describe as *neutral*. Gone was the moody, grumpy kid from the last visit.

"Everything okay?" asked Ben, holding the door open to let the boy in.

"Yeah, Mr. Thomas. I'm just tired." Tyler sighed and stepped into the house. "But don't worry. I can still help with your yard."

"How about some hot chocolate and cookies first, to wake you up?"

Tyler nodded and lumbered down the hall, only turning when he reached the kitchen. It looked like someone had flipped a switch on the boy, cutting off his power.

"Anything exciting happen at school today?" asked Ben, in an exaggerated jovial tone in an attempt to energize the boy.

"Did you have practice this morning?" An early morning practice followed by school would explain his current state for sure.

Tyler shook his head and sat in the closest chair. He rested his elbows on the kitchen table, curving his back like a bow in full draw.

"No practice today, sir." Another yawn.

Ben walked over to the stove and lit the burner under his tea kettle. Then he headed to the pantry to pull out the hot chocolate mix and a variety of cookies. By the time he had set everything on the table and fetched spoons and mugs, the kettle of recently heated water was whistling. He filled both mugs, setting a tea bag in his own and popping open the canister of sweet powdery chocolate in front of Tyler.

On his way to set the kettle back on the stove, he gave the boy an instinctive pat on the shoulder. When his pinky finger brushed against the base of Tyler's neck, an icy shiver traveled the length of his spine. He stood frozen for a moment that stretched out into decades in his mind, his hand resting on the boy's shoulder.

"Did you hurt your neck when you fell the other day?" he asked, trying not to let his voice reflect the terror churning through his gut. His hand floated up to rub the back of his own neck while he spoke.

Tyler waited until he finished chewing the cookie he'd just popped into his mouth. "No, sir," he said, his hand turning the spoon in his mug, creating a chocolate whirlpool. "I think something bit me."

"Do you mind if I take a look? I have some after-bite creams in the medicine cabinet."

"Sure. It doesn't itch or hurt or anything anymore, though."

Ben took a deep breath and squeezed his eyes closed,

mouthing a brief but intense supplication. He pulled back the boy's collar just enough to look at the raised skin he'd felt through the t-shirt. There it was, a raised red patch of skin about the size and shape of a lifesaver candy. In the center of the raised circle of skin, a tiny blood blister the shape of a thin line.

He released the shirt and took a step back, once more bringing his hand to his own version of this oddly symmetrical rash. Only once had Princess fed on him. Only once had he allowed his anger to get the best of him during his years with Mary. Princess had saved them from a violent man who had intended to rob them in a rest area. She had saved them but had not stopped after dispensing the thief. There was a little boy, a little boy with terrified, icy-blue eyes. Only Ben's intense anger had drawn her away.

He had called from the very next payphone while Mary sat in the van with the engine running, not wanting help to arrive while they were still there. The newspaper article they found later on said the kid had survived. Said it was a mountain lion attack. Ben never forgot the look on that boy's face. Or the feeling of doubt that had overwhelmed him, despite everything that Mary had told him. He had found himself hating everything that Princess was, wondering how much of Mary was still there, and how much of what she said was the creature justifying its own existence. Wondering until the numbness, until his anger and doubt were drawn out of him.

Mary had apologized for Princess, reminded him that creatures like her had been with man from the beginning of time, that they served a purpose like all of God's creatures. Reminded him of his promises to her, of how she only allowed Princess to intervene, to feed on those who caused harm and suffering. The boy had been a mistake. And he had let her convince him, let his love for her swaddle him like a warm blanket, smothering all doubt.

But Mary was gone now. Princess was gone. That's how it worked. And, he had destroyed her eggs in the grill, burnt them, and buried the putrid ashes in the ground. He told himself it wasn't possible. He told himself it could be some other kind of rash. Then, an exchange he'd had with Sam tapped at the back of his mind. The boy had asked about creatures being able to communicate. Something about preferring animals over people because people didn't always mean what they said. And Ben had answered that if creatures could talk there might be the same problem. Could it be Mary had lied to him? No, but Princess may have lied to her. Maybe the connection wasn't complete. Maybe the creature half of it could survive beyond its host.

That didn't completely solve the mystery of what had happened to Tyler's neck, though. Princess was strong, voracious when she fed. If Princess had been responsible for the injury, the boy, with all his pent-up rage, thanks to his father's actions, would be gone.

Ben sat across from Tyler and sipped his tea, thoughts tearing through his brain like Formula-1 cars.

"Tell you what," he said, pausing until Tyler looked up and made eye contact. "You finish up your hot cocoa and the cookie you're working on, then you can head home. I already did most of what I needed done today. Had a burst of energy earlier. I'll have to go buy materials before we can do much more."

"Are you sure you don't need me to do anything? Mom'll get mad if I go home without helping."

"Don't you worry about your mom. I'll shoot her a text to let her know. And I'll throw in a baggie of M&Ms that I saw in the pantry. Probably left over from those M&M cookies Mrs. Thomas used to make me. I'm not allowed to eat too much sugar anymore, you know. You'd be doing me a bigger favor than yard work getting them out of here, eliminating temptation."

He stood and placed his mug in the sink, biting his lip when his back was turned to the boy.

"If you're sure it's okay," said Tyler, popping the last bit of cookie into his mouth and gathering his plate and mug.

Ben went to the pantry and pulled out the bag of chocolate candies. He exchanged them for the dirty dishes, which he set in the sink. Then, they walked to the front door together, Tyler with sleepy eyes and a spacey grin, Ben trying not to decimate the inside of his bottom lip.

"Thanks, Mr. Thomas," the boy called back as he descended the front steps.

"Thank you, Tyler," answered Ben before pushing the door shut.

The moment the latch clicked, Ben took off down the hall to the door leading to the garage. He opened it and reached in to flip the light switch. Then, he rushed across the two-car garage to a smaller door—the one that lead to the third garage where they kept the camper. He pulled out his keychain and fumbled through the keys until he had the correct one gripped between his index finger and thumb, then unlocked the door. That side of the garage had no switch. Instead, a string hung down from a chain, which was attached to a socket on the ceiling fitted with a 25-watt bulb just a few steps into the space.

He reached up and pulled the string, spilling light into the room and illuminating Ginnie, the pop top, whose slider was ajar, just as it had been when he showed her to Sam. He hesitated, the hairs on the back of his neck rising on a sea of goose flesh. A couple deep breaths later, he was able to convince his legs to carry him forward. Grasping the handle of the long side door, he slid it until it clicked into the mechanism that would keep it from sliding back. Stale, musty air floated out to greet him, searing his nostrils when he inhaled. Mixed into the inevitable smells of age and disuse were scents that triggered memories of Mary and their trips, and darker, more insidious odors that summoned images of Princess.

The camper had not been fully unpacked from the last trip they took together. They'd meant to get to it the day after their last trip, but Mary had an appointment with her internist. And they forgot. Then, Ben was going to do it before the appointment with the oncologist, but Mary wasn't feeling so well and all of his attention shifted to helping her.

Pots and pans were stacked in the sink, tidied but waiting to be gathered for their usual deep cleaning at home. The fridge was cleared out and propped open, thank goodness, or the smell would have been even worse than it already was. The sleeping bags they used as a mattress topper and duvet sat on the back seat bench, pillows rolled into them. A stack of maps lay ready to be sorted back into the library in the office at home. Ben reached over and picked up the map on the very top. St. Louis, Missouri.

He closed his eyes and forced the trip back to mind. It had been the last fruitful trip for them. And, though Princess had been satiated and spent the entire ride home in her resting phase, Mary had seemed off. Sure, with hindsight being 20/20 and all, he now knew why. But, at the time he just remembered how quiet she was, how out of sorts. He remembered revisiting for the millionth time coming up with a way to free her, in his head. Only once had he ever voiced even the shred of an idea leaning toward her *freedom* out loud to her. And he had regretted it. From then on, he would muse about possible plans in his mind now and then, careful not to allow any of those thoughts to be reflected in his expressions or mannerisms.

Ben reached back and massaged the base of his neck.

And he was always careful not to let these thoughts rile him up or seep in so deeply as to charge his emotions. Princess could sense those changes, resting or not. Though she did seem slower to get there after a satisfying meal. Besides, he had known what he was getting into when he proposed to Mary, dedicated his life to her. Mary had done everything in her power to make sure of that.

Memories of the day she had chased him away ran through his mind vivid in color and focus, like a movie on a flat-screen TV.

"The heaviest burdens must be properly pondered," she had insisted.

Try as he might, he could never imagine any part of her as a burden, but he had complied. If that was what it would take to convince her of his dedication, then that was what he would do.

"I will write to you every day," he'd said.

"If I receive even one letter in the next three months, then you are not to bother returning. Your time away must be entirely spent away, mind and body. If you so wish, you may contact me by means of a letter in three months' time, not a day earlier. And I will check the postmark."

"But..." She'd pressed two fingers to his lips and trapped his gaze, holding it with her own.

"My sweet, gentle Ben." Her voice was sensuous, though she made no obvious effort to render it so. Perhaps it was her raw and earnest candor that he found seductive, delivered in a tone that was both innocent and sage at the same time.

Ben had reached his hand out and gently brushed a few stray hairs away from her eyes with the backs of his fingers. When he smoothed them back, he noticed a few specks of blood high up on her forehead. He brought his fingertips to the offending stains, applying some pressure when he passed over them. Mary took his hand in hers and brought it to her lips. She kissed it, then took a step back.

"I'm going to clean up now. Princess will take care of the rest."

A shudder scuttled through him when he realized the rest to which she was referring. A melancholy smile graced Mary's lips. She released his hand

A thought occurred to him, like a puppy scratching at the door to be let in. He scanned the inside of the camper van once more, through the filter of a realization. St. Louis had been messy. Messier than they'd hoped it would be. When they wandered into one of the most dangerous cities in the country, they expected it to be an easy mark for their purposes. What they didn't expect was the speed at which the first hit occurred.

They had stopped for gas and then pulled to the parking lot for some prep talk when the men slid open the door. It was Ben's fault for not remembering to latch the door after climbing in to sit at the little swivel table to examine the map. Mary was seated on the small, cushioned storage box between the driver's and passenger's seats. He remembered she looked tired, pale even, but had chalked it up to the long trip and the amount of time that had passed between trips. Diets of raw meat, squirrels, and rabbits gave sustenance but lacked that extra little something that offered true energy.

Yes, St. Louis had been messy. The camper should be in a worse state than it currently was. Not much time had passed between their arrival home, the appointments that followed, and Mary's passing. The cancer had been "aggressive," her team of doctors had said. They were surprised at the fact that she hadn't come in sooner, hadn't felt the pain earlier. Ben thought maybe it was due to her connection with the creature. Though, he couldn't quite bring himself to be grateful for it.

He set the map down and stepped over to the back bench, lifting the bottom of the blanket draped over the seat to keep it clean and to conceal the storage area beneath. They had converted the door into a kind of doggie door so that Princess could enter and exit her quarters at will. Ben dropped to his knees and pulled the swinging door away from the opening. He could make out only shadows and shapes inside, so he pulled out his phone and pushed the icon that controlled the flashlight, then aimed the beam inside.

It was empty, of course. But something didn't feel right. The dog bed they had put in there for comfort looked used, and not a-long-time-ago used, recently used. A lump formed at the bottom of his throat, pushing its way up like foam insulation. He reached in and picked up a handful of the grasses and leaves littering the bottom. Green blades of grass were mixed in. Green and flexible, not brown and brittle. There was no way they could have been in there since Mary's death. He turned the beam of light to the far side of the storage, and gasped, sitting back hard on the camper floor.

There, in the corner, sat an egg. Identical to the clutch he had pulled from the back of the garage and burnt in the grill, despite his promise to Mary, a promise made solely to comfort. Identical, except for one thing. This egg was missing a piece from the top. It was open, a layer of clear, brittle film glinting against the rays of the flashlight down one side. His thoughts wandered back to Sam's comments about the loggerhead sea turtle.

THIRTY-TWO

The doorbell rang, interrupting the work Ben had begun in the third garage. He set the bucket containing the remnants of the quick-mix cement on the floor, giving the new patch a few pats with a spade. He reluctantly pulled himself away and walked back through to the main garage, closing the door behind him, and reaching into his pocket for the keys. Empty. He must have set them down after unlocking the door. He tried to remember where, but the bell rang again and his head was aching.

I'll go back and lock it later, he thought to himself. *Not like it makes that much of a difference with those holes.*

"I'm coming," Ben called out once he was inside the house. He shut that door and turned the knob lock, as well as the deadbolt above it.

"Almost there," he said just before arriving at the front door. He took a deep breath through his nose and let it escape his lips in a soundless whisper. Then, he opened the door.

Sam stood on the stoop grinning, the manual for Mary's camera tucked under his arm. To say he looked happy would have been an understatement. The boy was practically beaming bliss through his very pores. When he looked up at Ben, his grin transformed into a full smile, revealing a mismatched row of mostly adult teeth, with a baby tooth peppered in here and there.

"Hi, Mr. Thomas," he said. "Guess what? I think I figured out some things with the camera."

He reached his hand over and pulled out the manual from under his armpit, waving it in front of Ben, before stepping past him through the door.

"That's wonderful," said Ben, stepping in behind the boy and following him down the hall. As they walked, he scanned the boy the best he could for marks. Not an easy task with the collared jacket Sam was wearing. He was sure he would be able to see better once the jacket had been removed. He'd noticed that kids nowadays almost exclusively wore short-sleeved t-shirts no matter how chilly it was outside, if left to their own devices. He imagined most moms just didn't have it in them to pick every battle.

Sure enough, Sam slipped out of his jacket and set it on the chair, revealing a short-sleeved t-shirt with a gecko on the front.

"Have a seat," said Ben, giving the boy a pat on the shoulders on his way by. He was relieved to find that nothing felt out of the ordinary. "I'll make you some hot cocoa. Marshmallows?"

"Yes, sir." Sam's voice was giddy, bordering on euphoric.

"Anything exciting happen in school today?" If it had, maybe that would explain the boy's high spirits.

"Not really, but it was a really good day. My friend Sam is going to meet me at the stream this weekend to do some herping." A slight blush brightened his cheeks when he mentioned her name. "And guess what?"

His eyes widened, as he waited a moment for Ben to guess. Ben shrugged and smiled, shaking his head.

"Tyler is leaving me alone. At school, he actually said 'hi' to me without calling me a weirdo. And he might come to the stream with me."

Ben knit his brows, nodding. "Again," he said.

Sam looked confused.

"He might go to the stream with you *again*. Your mom told me you guys were looking for turtles yesterday. How'd that come about?"

Sam looked down at the table and took a quick nibble at his thumb.

"Yeah," he said, quickly stifling a slight quiver in his voice. "I was already there and he just happened to show up. Whatever you said to him, it worked." He took another bite at his thumb. "Do you have any of those cookies with the cinnamon on them? Those were really good."

Ben nodded, turning to get them and the marshmallows from the pantry. On the way by, he lit the burner under the kettle to start it heating.

"Your mom said the same thing," he said while he was gathering up the cookies. "It's strange." He turned now and focused his full attention on Sam. The boy had the side of his thumb pressed against his teeth. "I really didn't say that much. I mean, I was hoping that he would leave you alone for fear of risking his spot on the football team. But, I don't recall saying anything that would have resulted in such a quick turnaround and an actual friendship blossoming."

"Weird," said Sam, his voice wavering.

Ben set the cookies and marshmallows on the table and walked over to get mugs and spoons. The kettle, which had been working extra hard lately, was beginning to rattle, and fingerlings of steam reached up through the spout. He turned off the burner and poured the hot water into two mugs. Then, he threw a tea bag into his and brought them to the table. The canister of chocolate power was still set on the table from his earlier visit with Tyler. He popped off the top and handed Sam a spoon, then sat watching the boy while his tea steeped.

"Sam? Remember that talk we had about creatures talking to people?"

Sam, who was in the process of scooping hot chocolate into his mug, stopped mid-scoop. His eyes rolled up to catch Ben's gaze and his bottom lip slid in between his teeth. He nodded.

"Tyler was here earlier. He was supposed to help me with the yard. He seemed very different, not like himself. And, he had an interesting looking bite on the back of his neck."

Sam's eyes darted down and to the side. He pinched off a grin and squirmed in his chair. His reaction told Ben everything he needed to know. Now, he needed to decide how to approach the subject without scaring the boy off or getting him upset. He thought of interactions with Mary that had flipped her like a switch from cohort and companion to protector of Princess, blocking him out. Maybe it wasn't too late for the boy. He was damn sure going to do everything in his power to figure this out and to stop whatever had started if he could.

"Do you know how that happened? What did that to him? You can be completely honest with me. I do know of a type of creature that is capable of something like that. I won't think you are making things up. I promise." He offered a gentle smile and sat across from the boy, cupping his hands around his mug.

"I don't know what he is, but his name is Whisper," said Sam, his voice hesitant.

He already had a name for it. Ben wondered if the creature knew this, if the boy had told it the name. If he had, even if the creature had not yet fed on him, it would be harder to interfere with their connection.

"Does this mystery creature know its name? Has it been... communicating with you?"

Sam looked down at his hands. He sucked his top lip into his mouth and nibbled on it.

"Sam, this is important. I don't want to frighten you, but if this creature is what I think it is, it is very dangerous. You don't want to mess with it." Ben paused, waiting for the boy to make eye contact.

"He doesn't seem dangerous to me," said Sam, raising his eyes to glance at Ben, and letting his lip slip back out from between his teeth. He furrowed his brows. "He cares about me. He helped me. Why is that dangerous?"

Ben listened, trying his best to show that he was open to what the boy was saying. Every ounce of his being was silently screaming for him to save Sam. Save him from Mary's fate.

"You need to tell him to leave," he said, his voice calm, but firm.

A puff of air rushed from the boy's nose and his face darkened. "Why?" he growled. "He needs me and I need him."

"It's complicated, Sam. I know the creature..."

"Whisper." This time when Sam said the name, Ben heard determination in his voice. He needed to tread carefully.

"Whisper says he needs you, seems to care. And I'm sure he does care, in his own way. But you don't understand the implications. You don't know what that means. It's not your fault; you're too young to understand."

Sam looked down at his shoes with a glare so intense, Ben half expected to see the laces untie and retie themselves. He guessed Sam was tired of people telling him what he did or didn't understand. He was a clever boy, at an age when sometimes it was hard for adults to see that he wasn't a little kid anymore.

Ben, himself, was the youngest of five children. He'd detested the teasing and babying at that age. Mary had been the first to take him seriously, to see him for the man that he was. She had seen him, respected him, loved him, and he now called on her ghost to help him reach this boy.

Sam brushed a hand under his nose to stifle a sniffle. Ben could see he was upset and wanted him to know that he didn't think him a silly child. Quite the contrary. He admired Sam and his wealth of knowledge about the natural world. Now, however, they were dealing with something not quite natural, something that Ben knew to be dangerous.

"Sam?" He softened his tone and slid his hand forward on the table. "I may not fully understand the bond you share with Whisper, but I do know something about it. I've never told anyone this before, but my wife, Mary, had a friend just like yours."

Sam shifted his gaze from his mug up to Ben. His face was the image of confusion, eyebrows scrunched and lips parted. Ben remembered something Mary had told him about her *friend,* Princess. When they'd met, bonded, she thought that Princess was one of a kind, the last of a dying species, alone in the world. It was one of the things that made her feel so special and so protective when they first connected. By the time she'd learned the truth, their connection was impenetrable, their fates tied.

"There's others? Or are you just trying to be... relatable?" As soon as he'd said it, Sam flinched like he was afraid he'd been rude. Ben was not offended in the least.

"I swear on my own life. Mary was younger than you are now when she met her *friend*. She named her Princess. In fact, I am pretty sure Princess was Whisper's mother. Actually, that's not true. I am one hundred percent sure."

"Where's Princess now?" The boy sounded curious, but skeptical. "Can I see her?"

"Princess is gone. She passed when Mary died. But right before that, she laid some eggs."

"A clutch," said Sam, nodding.

"Yes. And she promised Mary that the babies wouldn't stay. Mary told me that most, if not all probably wouldn't even survive, but that Princess needed to lay her eggs before she passed. I didn't trust her. Princess, that is. I didn't trust her, so I got rid of the eggs. But I missed one." Ben cinched his mouth and shook his head. His shoulders slumped under the weight of his regret and a sense of dread slid over him like the rising tide.

"Are there a lot of these creatures?" asked Sam, his voice transitioning from disbelief to excitement. "Where are the others?"

"Where is Whisper?" asked Ben, keeping focused on his mission, his obligation.

Sam's gaze dropped again, his lips pursed and brows furrowed. For a moment, Ben had hoped he might reveal the creature's hiding place. But any hint of cooperation quickly faded to obstinance. He wasn't going to tell, to betray his friend. The bond was evolving.

"Do you want to see a picture of Princess?" This got the boy's attention.

"You have a *picture* of her? She let you take one?"

"Well, I didn't mean to. I was taking a picture of Mary. It was late and we had just moved here. Princess was disoriented. She didn't mean to reveal herself. Come with me and I'll show you."

They stood and went into the family room, over to the bookshelf that contained Ben's treasured shrine to Mary. Sam scanned the photos one by one, his gaze coming to rest on the darkest of them. He reached out his hand, but stopped before touching it, looking over at Ben instead. Ben nodded his permission. Sam lowered the frame from the shelf, bringing it closer, squinting his eyes and scrutinizing the image.

"She's almost invisible, unless you know what you're looking for. It's quite fascinating, really," said Ben, his voice matter-of-fact. He waved an arm to usher Sam back into the kitchen.

The boy nodded, continuing to examine the photograph.

"You can bring it with you," said Ben, gently guiding the boy with a hand on the nape of his neck.

Sam walked to the kitchen, his gaze fixed on the image. He ran a finger over the shadow that was Princess, as if to caress her head. Then he paused and looked back at Ben.

"Mrs. Thomas looks like she was happy."

Ben suspected he knew where the boy was going with this. "We were happy, Sam. But there were prices to pay for that happiness, steep unimaginable prices. Her life was very different from yours when she was a child. You have people who love you, people who care about you. They can help you when things are difficult. *I* can help you."

"But, Mrs. Thomas had you."

"We didn't meet until she was older, Sam. When we met, Princess was already a part of her life, a part of her. She owed Princess by then, and that debt was a bottomless pit. The more she repaid, the more Princess wanted."

"Whisper just needs a friend. He needs me." The boy's voice drifted, the last words a distant thread.

"He needs so much more. And he'll take so much more," said Ben, pulling him back. "There are places where he can get what he needs, but not with you. He just doesn't understand. And now he's had a taste of anger here in our little town, a taste of Tyler. Since Tyler's dad left his family, he's been so angry. Angry not only at his dad, but at the world. At kids like you who have what he doesn't anymore. That kind of anger is a trap, and people who feel trapped can become desperate. People make bad decisions when they are desperate. Creatures like Princess... and Whisper... they can sense that kind of anger and desperation."

Sam blinked, his gaze sharpening, shifting from the photograph to Ben. "Was Mrs. Thomas angry when she was a kid?"

"Yes, and afraid. Mary was trapped. She didn't have people around her who cared for her, about her. All she had was pain and fear. Princess freed her from all of that, and for that, I will always be grateful, but she left behind a trail of..."

Ben wasn't sure how graphic he should be. Sam was still a child, after all. But so much depended on his ability to reach the boy, to convince him. "She left behind a trail of blood, of horror. Mary had to run away more than once, until we met, and then after we met. Then, I went with her. She was happy and I was happy because we had each other. Princess was a price we had to pay for our happiness."

"Whisper didn't really hurt Tyler. I didn't let him. Tyler doesn't even remember what happened. And he's actually nice to me now."

This would be harder to explain. He placed a hand on each of the boy's shoulders and leaned down to his level.

"Sam, Tyler was lucky. Some people have anger stuck inside them like a splinter. It's close to the surface, easy to remove. Tyler may be mean at times, but he has his mother and her family, people who love and support him. He has a lot of fears, just like you. He tries to hide his by acting tough."

Sam's lips pursed again and a vein in his forehead poked forward.

"I'm not saying that's okay. It's not. The way he treated you was wrong, and we will deal with that. But it would also be wrong not to give him a chance to be a better person... on his own. It would be wrong not to give the people who love him the chance to help him learn. You may think that you had some control, but Whisper is young and not very strong, yet. Not fully connected. He stopped where the anger ended. Once the splinter was out, he was done."

"So, he helped Tyler. He can help other people, too. *We* can help them together."

"That's not how it works, Sam. There are people who have anger in them, not like a splinter, but as a part of their very being. Maybe they were treated badly for so long that they know nothing else. Or maybe they have let it build to a point that they just can't shake it. When Whisper meets one of them... If you become fully bonded and someone like that crosses your path, he won't stop. He will pull you in with him, and you won't be able to make him stop. The stronger he gets, the more he will need."

"You mean bad people?"

"It is not our place to decide who is bad and who is good. It is not our place to decide who is lost and who can be redeemed. Mary and I have blood on our hands because of Princess. Those people will never have a chance to change their ways."

Sam looked back at the picture of Princess, his face ashen and somber. He brought his free hand to his mouth and chewed his thumbnail, then handed the frame to Ben and nodded.

"I think I understand, sir. Whisper is an invasive species, like an anaconda in the Florida Everglades. He doesn't belong here. It's dangerous for him and all the native species here."

Ben nodded. Of course, Sam would fall back on his knowledge of nature.

At that moment, insistent scraping drew their attention to the door leading to the garage. Ben instinctively stepped between the door and the boy. Another sound, barely audible, came from inside the garage. Vibrations shimmered through Ben's bones to the marrow, and bile scalded his tongue. A soft thump. He turned back to the boy, now prone on the floor, twisting with convulsions.

"Sam. Sam, can you hear me?" Ben knelt beside the boy, gently placing a hand on each of his shoulders. "Sam," he said, jostling the boy, whose eyes were rolled back into their sockets. A thin line of spittle made its way from the corner of his mouth and across his pale cheek.

"What the fuck did you do to that kid?"

For a moment, Ben thought he had imagined the coarse

voice hissing just above a whisper behind him. But a raspy cough convinced him otherwise and he turned his head to find himself inches away from the business end of a Glock G19. He shifted his gaze up from the barrel and stared into the icy-blue eyes of the man holding the weapon.

THIRTY-THREE

On their walk that morning, Alvis was edgier than usual. Sarah didn't even think she could count the walk in her exercise log; given that they'd had to stop so often, her heart was never able to get into exercise mode. Every leaf that blew by, every brake sound or door closing, and of course, every storm drain ground them to a complete halt until Sarah could calm the dog once more and coax him forward.

By the time they crossed paths with the young man with the striking blue eyes, Sarah was ready to give up on reaching her four miles and call it a day at half that. She figured she could count her resulting stress and frustration as exercise, anyway, given the way it increased her heart rate each time.

"I am so sorry," she called out, in an attempt to make herself heard over the barrage of deep throaty barks Alvis was hurling himself at the stranger. "Sit! Come on, Alvis. Sit."

The man waved it all off, a charming smile gracing his lips despite his current status of audience for Alvis's Cujo act. He was moving his lips, to accompany his body language, but

Sarah was only able to catch a word here and there through the barks.

"Lawn... older... help... company..."

She shook her head and hunched her shoulders. She would have touched an ear to drive home the message that she really could not make out what he was saying, but was afraid to release any tension on the leash. The young man tossed his hands up in the air in comic fashion and flashed a grin of surrender. He then put his hands together under his chin, gave a little bow, and waved.

Sarah kept Alvis sitting in place until the man was out of sight. She decided to continue their stuttering walk just a little longer to give him time to get way ahead of them before turning around to head home, which happened to be the direction the stranger was walking.

"Alvis, what the hell?"

The dog looked up at her, ears flapping in the breeze. His sudden transformations from adorable puppy to rabid beast and back never ceased to amaze her. He tilted his head and reached his muzzle up to kiss her hand.

"You are so infuriating sometimes, buddy." Sarah sighed and gave him a few scratches in his favorite spot, just behind his ears. "I suppose, in the end, I should thank you. He was probably selling something anyway. He did have that salesman look about him."

At around three o'clock in the afternoon, Sarah's eyes wandered up from her laptop and she looked out her office window. Sam and Tyler were walking from the bus stop together. She stood up and walked to the window for a better look, brows bunched to accommodate her squint.

The boys were chatting and showing each other things on

their cell phones as if they had been best buddies forever. Of course, she was happy to see that Sam was happy. And what she was witnessing between them now was far better than the results she had seen of previous interactions. Still, something seemed off.

When the boys reached Ben's house, Tyler turned onto his walkway. He waved to Sam and walked to the front door. Sarah watched him ring the doorbell, wait, then ring it again. Then the front door of her own house opened and slammed shut.

"Hey, maybe don't slam the door?" Sarah said, walking over to greet her son. He shrugged off his backpack and smiled.

"Sorry, Mom."

"How was school?"

"Okay."

"What did you learn today?"

"I don't know."

Sarah rolled her eyes. Gone were the days of her chatty little elementary school boy who would tell her about every second of the school day, from arrival to departure, the moment he stepped through the door. Back in the day, it was a little overwhelming. Now, she missed it dearly.

"I'm gonna run down to the stream for a few minutes, okay?" Sam said, reaching for the door.

"Any homework?"

He sighed, his grin fading. "Yeah. I have to make a poster for science class."

"Homework first. Then stream."

"Do we have any poster board?"

By his tone, Sarah presumed he was hoping she'd have to go buy some so he could slip off to the stream while she was gone. Sadly, for him, she'd opted for a five-pack not too long ago when Christina needed one for a class project.

"Yes, sir. We happen to have poster board *and* backup poster board, in case you make a mistake. Still, I would suggest drawing out what you want to do on plain paper and arranging things on the board *before* you do any gluing."

Sam grabbed the strap on the top of his bag, picked it up, and trudged down the hall.

"Hey, Sam?" He turned and let the bag rest on the floor. Sarah glanced at the backpack, once again marveling that kids could lug those things around all day. She didn't remember hers ever being that bloated and heavy. She turned her attention to Sam. "How are things going with Tyler?"

A confident smile appeared. "Good. He and Sam are probably going to meet me at the stream this weekend. They're cousins, you know."

Sarah rested her thumb under her chin, letting her middle three fingers run back and forth along her top lip while she listened.

She shook her head. "No, I did not know that. Looks like you guys are going to be the Three Musketeers."

"Like the candy bar," said Sam, causing Sarah to bring her palm to her forehead. How could this child be the son of a writer? Where had she gone wrong? Sam burst into giggles. "Gotcha! I know who the Three Musketeers are, Mom. Duh... Grandpa read it to me a million times. Remember? We used to do sword fights?"

She smiled at the memory of Sam and her father-in-law prancing through the yard, fencing with pool noodles. Then nodded, melancholy setting in.

"I remember. You and Grandpa were the Two Muske-teers. I miss that."

"I miss it, too." Sam's face took on a dreamy look, like he was trying to corral memories in the air around him, to secure them so they wouldn't escape.

"Are you mad that we moved, honey?"

He screwed up his mouth and let his gaze wander for a moment. "I was mad. But now I think it's going to be okay," he said, nodding and lifting his bag. "I'd better start on the poster, Mom." He walked down the hallway to the kitchen.

Sarah went back to the office, sat, and stared at her screen. After a few minutes of contemplation, she decided that she needed a cup of coffee to get the words flowing again. She stood and stretched, cracking her neck, moving it from side to side. A soft thumping sounded somewhere inside her head. Of course, her tinnitus would choose now to act up; she wasn't even halfway done with the first draft of the article she needed to submit by midnight: "Ten Surefire Ways to Detect a Lie." Like she knew even one surefire way to detect a lie. Wouldn't that have come in handy a few years back?

She closed her eyes and focused on her breathing, her go-to method for packing devastation back into its box in her mind. It was getting a little easier as time passed. Her memory flare-ups, as she liked to call them, felt less like devastation and more like soft rage now. Wouldn't it be lovely if years from now, the feelings would simply disappear? Somehow, she doubted that would ever be the case.

The thumping was a little quicker now, almost like the purr of a cat. Time to get some meds into her before she faced a full-on migraine. Sarah hurried down the hall into the kitchen, where Sam was working on the design for his poster.

The board occupied most of the surface of the table, and Sam was setting pictures down here and there, moving them around, and assessing his work.

"Don't rush," she said, stepping past him to get to the medicine cabinet over the refrigerator.

"I'm not, Mom. Don't worry. Science is my favorite class. I want to get a good grade on this." He shook his head and rolled his eyes.

Sarah took out some tablets and got herself some water from the front of the fridge. Then, she looked over at the poster board to see what he was doing. The theme was *Crustaceans*.

"I already printed the pictures and information I need to include at school. So, I just have to arrange them and maybe add some more facts by hand."

Sarah nodded, impressed. After taking her medicine, she set the glass on the counter and picked up a book that was next to the sink. She waved the book toward Sam to get his attention.

"Not a good place for Mr. Thomas's camera manual, bud."

"Sorry," said Sam.

"Have you been looking through this to see how it works?" She ran a thumb along the front of the pages, feathering them.

"Actually, yeah." Sam set a picture of a lobster down on the board and reached for the book. Sarah handed it to him and watched him flip through to a page he had marked with a yellow sticky note. "Check this out." He held the page up so she could see. "You can take pictures with *water painting effect*. Isn't that cool?" She nodded. "It has like ten filters you can use. And..." He flipped back a few pages. "It is really good at taking close-ups, so Mr. Thomas and I will be able to get some awesome shots at the stream."

"Okay. I guess you *have* been reading it." She met his smile with one of her own, took the manual back, and walked over to set it on the little desk in the corner of the kitchen. "Still, not the best idea to leave it near the sink." She winked at him, making a clicking noise with her mouth at the same time. "Maybe you should swing by Mr. Thomas's house after you finish your homework. You can tell him what you found out and *then* go to the stream."

Sam nodded and uttered an "uh-huh." His attention was already back on arranging pictures on the poster board for school.

Sarah smiled to herself, giving him a pat on the back on her way to the coffeemaker. She flipped it on, prepping the coffee in the filter to make a fresh pot when the water was hot enough. Then she slipped down the hall to the office to avoid breaking his concentration, marveling to herself at how quickly he was growing, both physically and in maturity. When she sat at the desk, she glanced at her watch, concerned for a moment that Christina wasn't home before remembering that she had play rehearsal. Sighing, she set to the painstaking work of dragging words past the purring in her head and arranging them so they made some kind of sense on her screen.

A little over an hour later, a triumphant voice sounded from the kitchen.

"Finished!"

Sarah looked at her computer screen. Somehow she'd managed to tap out a fairly intelligible account of tactics one could use to spot a lie, though she herself wasn't confident they worked. Fluff wasn't generally judged by accuracy, after all. It was a matter of opinion and a flare for the written word, at least where she was currently working. After reading through her work once more, she closed the screen. She could give it another edit before bed and still get it in on time. Another upside of fluff, she could write it with her eyes closed, or in this case, through a headache. After a deep and airy sigh, she stood and walked to the kitchen to check Sam's work.

On the way down the hall, she thought about taking another shot at the book she'd been working on since college. The one she'd first set aside after Christina was born and they were struggling to make ends meet, and again when Sam and a coveted promotion had arrived one after the other and she'd felt the need to prove she deserved both. And again, when more recent life events had unleashed in her an overwhelming urge to kill off each and every character she'd worked so hard to flesh out in her mind. Not the best impulse if one wished to author a viable children's book. She pinched her lips, shrugging off the idea for now. She would revisit later when she was in a better state of mind.

In the kitchen, Sam was holding his poster up in front of him, tipped slightly back in case the glue wasn't quite finished drying, he explained. Sarah inspected his work. The kid sure knew a lot about creepy crawlies, no matter what category they happened to fall under. She read the factoids aloud, making sure to exaggerate her looks of surprise and interest at each. It wasn't hard. Most of them were damned interesting and surprising.

"You didn't know that lobsters have blue blood, Mom?"

"No, I did not."

"Well, actually, their blood is colorless until it comes in contact with oxygen."

"Impressive," said Sarah, brows raised, bunching the skin

on her forehead like ripples on a stream bed. "Good job, Sam. It's an A-plus for sure."

He smiled, even blushed a little, his pride in his work obvious.

"Can I go out now? To the stream? I mean, after I stop by Mr. Thomas's house," he corrected when she sighed.

"Sure. And make sure you tell him I said 'hello.' Oh, and ask him when he can come over for dinner again and if he has any favorite dishes."

"Will do!" Sam rushed to the door leading to the garage, then spun on one heel back to the kitchen to retrieve the camera manual. "Almost forgot this," he said, waving it in the air. Then he spun back to and out the door.

He had already grabbed his waders and was most of the way across the street when Sarah leaned out to remind him to get a baggie for his phone before going to the stream. She shook her head, smirking. No need to yell. She could text Ben, ask him to remind Sam.

She ducked back into the kitchen and opened one of the cabinets next to the stove, revealing shelves of mugs, teacups, and cute, colorful espresso cups. She reached up to the shelf dedicated to photo mugs and ran the tips of her fingers across the cool porcelain bases along the front row, pausing at each to remember the moment captured on its surface: family vacations, smiling, toddling toddlers, the kids on either side of Alvis when they'd first brought him home. Then, she pushed the mug in the center to the side and gazed at the shadowed forms of the mugs in the inner three rows. Deciding to choose randomly, she looked down at the countertop in front of her, pushed up onto the balls of her feet, and reached deep into the cabinet until she settled on a handle and wrapped her fingers around it.

Reaching her other hand up to steady the mugs around it, she snaked the chosen one from the back of the shelf, examining it once she'd set it down on the counter. This one was made pre-children. She had gifted it to Greg. Sarah squeezed her eyes shut for a moment, trying to pull up the name of the friend who had snapped the picture gracing the mug but could not. They had fallen out of touch before even finishing college.

"Red hair," she said, looking down at Alvis, who had, of course, followed her to the kitchen. He cocked his head. "She had red hair. Kathy or Katie... Caroline?" she mumbled, examining the picture of her arm-in-arm with Greg on the Quad.

They'd just started dating when her friend snapped the picture and later gave her a copy. She'd had the mug made to mark a year of being together, back when it actually took some effort, before you could just snap a pic on your phone and upload it to some website. She poured hot coffee into it, added a teaspoon of sugar, and gave it a quick stir. All while never taking her eyes off the picture.

They were happy, right? She was holding the proof in her hand. She stared at their easy, carefree smiles and sparkling eyes. She didn't bother trying to pinpoint the moment or reason he'd stopped being happy. She'd already tried and failed. He said he was happy, that that wasn't the reason. She would never understand. The best she could do was to acknowledge that he was trying to make amends, and try to forgive.

She took a sip from the mug, her mind drowning in memories and second guesses. The purring in her head, which had settled into the back of her mind like a soundtrack to her stream of thought, suddenly became louder. Vibrations rattled inside her head, working their way through her body until it seemed they were flowing through her feet into the floor. Or maybe they were entering her feet through the floor. It was hard to tell.

She set her mug down and grasped the edge of the counter with both hands. The oscillations grew stronger, nothing like her usual inner sounds. Was this an earthquake? She'd never experienced an earthquake before and had no idea if they were *a thing* here. Stuff wasn't falling off shelves and the pendant lamp over the kitchen table showed no signs of movement. Maybe these were the tremors that came before an earthquake. Maybe her inner ear condition allowed her to hear the vibrations early, like she'd read that some animals could.

Alvis whimpered and nudged her with his muzzle.

"You hear it, too. Don't you?" Sarah set a hand on the dog's head. "It's okay, Alvis. I think."

If this was an earthquake, certainly the school would have some kind of protocol to follow. She pulled out her phone and stared at the screen, trying to decide whether or not to text Christina. Besides, she didn't know for a fact that there was an earthquake on the way. Schools were often used as shelters for all kinds of emergencies. Christina should be fine in either case. Greg was still at work in the city. He could take care of himself.

"Sam," she said to the dog, who stood by her side at attention. "We need to go make sure Sam and Mr. Thomas are okay." She gave him a quick scratch behind the ears. "I hate to say it, buddy, but I think you would be safer staying here while I run over there."

Alvis whimpered again, as if he'd understood her intentions and was voicing his disapproval.

"Sorry, but if a simple storm drain frightens you, I don't even want to imagine what you'll do if the ground begins to shake. You'll have to stay here. I'll be right back."

Sarah ran to the front door, opened it just enough to slip through, and pulled it shut before Alvis could follow.

She climbed the steps to the front door of Ben's house, grabbing the railing to steady herself near the top. The purring could no longer be described as such, unless one imagined it to be coming from some kind of gigantic saber-toothed creature. A noise, high and shrill, somewhere between a whistle and a scream, shot past the purr, penetrating her head like an arrow. This was no earthquake.

THIRTY-FOUR

Ben turned and shifted his body to shield Sam as best he could from the stranger. He raised one of his hands, palms out, keeping the other firmly on the boy behind him.

"Can I help you?" His voice was shaky but soft. His life with Mary and everything it entailed had made him a master at tucking away fear and horror, hiding them behind a wall of calm.

"What the fuck did you do to that kid, you sick old bastard?" With both hands clasped around the grip of the Glock, the man tipped his head to the side to get a better look at the boy laying prone on the floor.

The convulsions had stopped. And the slow rise and fall of Sam's chest under his hand assured Ben that the boy was breathing. He recalled Mary's description of her initial connections with Princess when they had first bonded. Until the body grew accustomed to the invasive process that melded creature and host, it was both painful and confusing. His guess was that the creature, Whisper, was attempting to incapacitate

Sam until he could reach the boy to feed, finalizing their connection.

Over my dead body, thought Ben, his mouth pinching and features hardening. He took a deep breath and brought his other hand around, making sure to take his time and to keep his palm out so the intruder could see that he was not armed.

"The boy is having a seizure. I need to call an ambulance. I have some money I can give you. Just let me call an ambulance." His hope was that the man was looking for some quick cash. The fact that the stranger showed some concern for Sam was a good sign, a sign of empathy.

"I don't want your money," said the man, shaking his head. He shifted his gaze from the boy to Ben, hardening it into a glare, and curled his lips in disgust. "You killed my brother. I'm here because you and that bitch wife of yours killed my brother with whatever that thing was you keep as a pet. Remember me?"

Ben's jaw slacked, pulling his mouth open. He squinted, scanning the man for clues as to who he was. Nobody had ever seen Princess... well, at least no one who could talk about it after the fact. The stranger continued to stare, drilling into Ben's soul with those icy blue eyes. Those eyes. Something stirred in Ben's mind, and a thought tapped to enter like a dog locked out in the rain.

Now, he was staring back at the man in front of him with the gun, but the image of a young boy around Sam's age floated forth from the place he had banished it to in his memories. His breath caught in his throat and the walls of his chest pressed in against his heart, a steady *thump thump thump* rushing up to his ears. The boy, the one with the icy blue eyes, was on the ground. Princess was on top of him and had gained access to him through a wound under his rib. The eyes Ben was looking into now, in this room, burned with hate. The eyes of the boy within were a twisted mix of anger, fear, and loss.

Yes, he remembered this boy. He remembered the boy and he remembered Mary's expression... or the complete lack of Mary in her expression. He knew she was all but gone then, at least subconsciously. He knew, but his heart would not let him leave her. Because during the in-between times, as much as they were diminishing, during those times he had Mary mostly to himself. He took solace in the fact that their hunts were limited to those with harmful intentions, though he and Mary had searched them out, even provoked them with their presence in places they did not belong. Places they could easily have avoided.

The boy was not an intended victim and Ben could not bear to label him *collateral damage*, not when he could do something to stop it. He knew that letting the kid go would have its own risks, but had rationalized that nobody would believe him if he talked about monsters. And he was right. The papers said that the boy and his brother were attacked by a mountain lion. They speculated that perhaps there had been cubs nearby.

Now that he was trying to save another boy, it seemed his sins had caught up with him.

"I do remember you," said Ben, keeping his voice as soft and soothing as he could manage against his rising panic.

THIRTY-FIVE

Jacob was going to break into the house, find the creature, kill it, and get the hell out of town, state, maybe even country if he could find enough cash or sellable items to manage it. He hadn't decided on the fate of the old man, yet. He figured he would just go with his gut on that one.

Finding the house was easy. Most people had no clue how much personal information was available online with minimal digging, and did nothing to protect themselves. When it came to old people, finding them and scamming them was like dropping a line into a freshly stocked pond.

When he arrived at his destination, Jacob scoped out the area, opting to leave the car in a small lot next to a park blocks away from his intended target. Then, he popped some courage into his mouth, in the form of a little pill he pulled from the supply he'd picked up in the underbelly of this quaint little town, and walked the neighborhood dressed like a respectable, average, nondescript salesman. He had even purchased a clipboard at a nearby office surplus store and clipped a pen and some graph paper to it, to complete the illusion. He didn't want anyone looking twice when they saw him walking up the old man's driveway. In his experience, apart from his eyes, which were the striking color of moonstones and the perfect lure for scoring company of the female persuasion, it was easy for him to render himself unremarkable and to blend in.

Aside from the psycho-looking mutt that had decided it wanted to murder him, but was, fortunately for him, attached to a nice strong leash, he walked the sidewalks unnoticed. Even then, the woman holding the leash seemed unfazed by his presence there, apologizing profusely for her dog and going on her way without a second look. After she passed, he did another lap around the block to make sure he was out of sight before approaching the Thomas house.

Getting into the house was easy. People just didn't lock their doors during the day as much in quaint little neighborhoods in suburbia. He was prepared to ring the doorbell and force his way in if necessary, of course. He hadn't come all this way for nothing. But his preference was to slip into the home and to take Mr. Ben Thomas by surprise. So, he sauntered up the steps, pretended to ring the bell, waited a moment, then gave a wave and carefully pulled the storm door open while reaching in to open the main door, which was, in fact, unlocked. He was counting on the reflection from the storm door to impair the view of anyone who might be looking out a window in one of the neighboring homes, so they would assume that he had been invited in.

Once inside, Jacob closed the door, making sure to turn the knob when he pushed it into place to keep the latch bolt from clicking when it slid past the outer lip of the strike plate into the hole. Voices floated over from a room at the end of the hall-way, off the foyer. Jacob froze for a moment, closing his eyes, slowing his breathing, and straining to hear any indications that the occupants might be aware of his presence. The voices continued back and forth, seemingly ignorant of the fact they were no longer alone.

Jacob cocked his head. One of the voices sounded young. Maybe they'd had a kid. This might be a grandkid. The idea of leaving flitted through his head, fizzling like a shooting star at the end of its path. No, he was here now. He would figure it out. He *needed* to kill that thing, to avenge his brother. And he needed to prove, if only to himself, that he wasn't crazy.

He reached around and slid his gun from its nest, tucked between his waistband and lower back, and used his sleeve to brush sweat off the barrel. Then, he steadied himself with a deep breath, forced a hard swallow to push down the lump of acid occupying his throat, and crept toward the voices.

When Jacob neared the end of the hallway, he edged closer to the wall, focusing on the voices around the corner. His heart was thumping too loudly, a frantic pounding ricocheting about in his head, for him to make out what they were saying. Not that it mattered. At the edge of the room—a kitchen he guessed by the hutch on the wall in front of him, he brought the Glock up to his chest, holding it steady with both hands.

His mind raced back to the rest area where Jimmy had died... was murdered. Jacob had been too far away to see the moment Jimmy was attacked by the monster that killed him. But he knew it had to have been lightning fast to get one over on his brother. How many times had Jimmy taken him out to the field behind the salvage yard to practice shooting? How many times had Jacob witnessed his brother's amazing quick-draw and watched cans explode off the wall like popcorn kernels over a fire? Of course, Jimmy had been distracted by the old couple. In any case, Jacob knew what he might be facing around the corner in the Thomas house. He was prepared.

"I think I understand, sir," said the child's voice around the corner.

Then, the scar under Jacob's rib began to sear like it was on fire, like waves of lava were pulsating through it and into his blood. He doubled over, pressed an arm against his shirt, somehow managing to hold onto the Glock. Scratching noises filled the air around and inside his head. He brought a hand up and pressed it against his forehead, willing it to stop.

The pills. He had the baggie in his front right pocket. He gripped the gun in his left hand and willed his right hand to make the seemingly impossible journey down into his pocket. Leaning against the wall behind him for support, he reached his index finger into the bag, moving it frantically until he was able to trap one of the chalky little pills. Fish it out and into his mouth, biting down hard and crushing it to speed up its effects.

When he was back in control of his pain, Jacob turned the corner into the kitchen, gun first. There was, in fact, a kid. He was laying on the floor, eyes rolled, back arched. His body twitched, contorting from one unnatural position to another, while a thin line of drool streamed from the corner of his mouth.

Jacob gasped, then remembering the rest area, gave the room a quick scan before saying, "What the fuck did you do to that kid?"

The old man turned, tried to tell him the kid was having some kind of seizure. He wanted to call an ambulance. Jacob didn't falter. Maybe the kid was having some kind of seizure, or maybe this sick old bastard was getting him ready to feed to his pet. The latter seemed more likely to Jacob. In any case, any distractions could mean the end for him. He needed to stay focused.

When he stated his reason for being there, the old man seemed thrown. His mouth opened and shut, and for a moment he looked like a fish pulled from the water. Then his eyes sharpened and his brows climbed. And Jacob saw recognition in his expression.

"I do remember you," he said. The old man was doing his best to seem calm, but Jacob could see he was terrified. Or maybe he was upset that he'd been interrupted.

Jacob raised the gun to the level of the man's head, his finger steady beside the trigger. "Then you must remember my brother, Jimmy," he said, drops of spittle flying from his lips, propelled by a level of hate that countered the pain in his scar, threatening to consume him. "Where is that thing, the creature that killed him?"

The boy lay still now, his body relaxed, rising and falling with the shallow breaths that puffed through his open mouth. His eyes were closed. It looked like he was sleeping. Jacob's gaze floated back and forth between the two. He fought back memories of the dark slimy body sliding up on top of him, the sensation of the creature's probing tongue, the numbness then the darkness that overcame him.

"It's dead," said the old man, his arms out to his sides, palms forward. "It died when my wife died last year."

"Mary," muttered Jacob, disdain powering his voice.

"Yes, Mary. Cancer took her last year. The creature couldn't survive without her and it died."

The door to the garage shuddered, vibrating as something behind it scraped and clawed from top to bottom.

"Bullshit!" yelled Jacob, motioning to the door with his gun. "You sick bastard. You were going to feed this kid to it!"

"No!" the old man said, his voice jolting away from the calm it had portrayed until now. "The creature that attacked you is dead. It laid eggs before it died. I tried to destroy them, but I missed one."

Jacob shook his head. His torso was throbbing and he was tired of this bullshit.

"I swear," the old man continued. "The one behind that door is trying to bond with the boy, Sam." He pointed to the kid.

Jacob looked from the old man to the boy to the door, and back to the old man. The kid's body was shivering along with the scratching now. Something slammed against the other side of the door, bowing it out and producing a noticeable crack in the frame where the hinges were. The old man turned, took hold of the boy's shirt, and pulled him further from the door.

The boy moaned and rolled his head toward Jacob. He reached his hands up and rubbed his eyes. When the boy pulled back his hands, his eyes were open. Jacob stumbled away at the sight of them, the same eyes he'd seen when he was a child, when he'd looked at the woman, Mary. He pointed the gun at the boy. The old man sprang forward and pushed his arm before he could get off the shot. He recovered his balance quickly, but the old man grabbed ahold of the top of the gun.

"Don't shoot him. It won't kill the creature, just the boy."

"You said the one that attacked me died when your wife died. So, this one will die if I kill the kid."

"Please." The old man was standing in front of the muzzle

now, his eyes pleading. "Don't shoot the boy. They haven't finished bonding. You won't kill the creature that way, just the boy. Please. This is my fault. I thought I destroyed them all. This is my fault. I'll help you kill the creature and then you can kill me if you want. But please don't hurt the boy."

He was babbling now, and Jacob felt a twinge of sympathy despite himself. Maybe the old guy was telling the truth. And Jacob was an asshole, for sure, but not the kind of asshole who went around shooting little kids for kicks. When he came here, he knew he would probably have to kill the old man, and he was fine with that. But, if what the old man was saying was true, the kid was as much a victim in this as he'd been back in the rest area. He lowered the gun.

"How do we kill it?"

THIRTY-SIX

Sarah steadied herself and rang the doorbell, gripping the railing with both hands while she waited. No answer. She opened the storm door and gave three hard knocks. Still nothing. Slipping between the two doors, she cracked open the main door and leaned her head inside.

"Ben? Sam? Are you guys in there?"

No answer. Though the piercing shriek had all but disappeared, her ears rang with the steady assault of vibrations that continued to push through her, flowing, she now realized, from inside the house like ripples on a windblown pond.

"Is everything okay?" Panic squeezed her chest like a boa constrictor. She was done waiting.

"I'm coming in," she called, and took a step into the foyer, listening for clues as to where they might be.

"Sarah," Ben called from the kitchen. "Sorry, we didn't hear you. Everything's fine. I'll get Sam home to you as soon as we're done fiddling with the camera."

Sarah pinched her brows together, tilting her head. She didn't need to read any fluff article to pick up on the glaring deception in Ben's voice. She hurried down the hall, her mind racing. Why would he be lying to her? Why didn't she hear Sam's voice?

When she turned the corner into the kitchen, Sam was seated at the table with his back to her, the camera manual open in front of him. Ben stood by the counter holding the coffee carafe. He was pouring steaming hot java into a mug held by the young salesman Sarah had seen earlier in the day.

The stranger turned his piercing blue eyes toward her and smiled. It was a strained smile. The kind little kids made when you give them candy after they skin a knee. He held out his right hand.

"Nice to meet you. I've heard so much about you and your beautiful family. I'm Brian. I'm here signing up customers for our wonderful lawn service." His smile widened, revealing a set of pearly whites and creasing the corners of his eyes.

Sarah caught a furtive glance from Ben to the stranger, Brian, in her peripheral. Man, this guy was a salesman for sure. The kind of guy you don't want to run into at a used car lot. She donned a cautious smile and took his hand, the reporter in her tugging at the shirt tails of her mind.

"Would you like me to take a look at your lawn? We might have some products for you. Which one is yours?" He led her toward the hallway. "I mean, if you promise your dog won't eat me." He laughed.

It sounded a little forced, but he had such a smooth and natural charm about him.

"We have an irrigation pump running in the back of Mr. Thomas's yard that could do wonders for yours, too," he continued, waving a hand toward the back of the house.

A pump. Maybe that was what was playing havoc with her inner ears. She nodded.

"Sam, come on home when you're done... maybe in another fifteen minutes or so. It's your turn to set the table for dinner."

"Great kid," Brian declared.

Then Sarah noticed something that she never would have if her grandfather had been the sweet old man she'd wished for when she was younger. If he'd been the kind of grandfather that gave out candy and compliments instead of who he was—a conspiracy-addled, paranoid, weapon-hoarding, abuser—she never would have understood what the thickness at the base of Brian's shirt represented. And, she might not have second-guessed the fact that he hadn't given Sam a chance to answer her.

When they reached the front door, Sarah smiled and held her hand out to him.

"Nice to meet you, Brian. I might just take you up on that offer to take a look at our yard. We've been having a terrible time with weeds invading the lawn."

As soon as he took her hand to shake it, she braced her feet and pulled him off balance, reaching around to the back of his waistband with her free hand to grab the gun that was hidden there.

"Dangerous work, landscaping," said Sarah, taking a step back and training the firearm on him. "Ben? Sam? Everything okay in there?"

Ben walked out of the kitchen, shock and amusement jockeying for position on his face when he saw them.

"Ma'am, I always bring protection when I walk new neighborhoods," the young man at the wrong end of the gun said. He took a step toward her, hands held high.

"Do not get any closer," said Sarah in her best bad-ass voice, her brows pushing her eyes into a focused squint.

"Drop the act, Jacob," said Ben, the corner of his mouth curled up. "She's got your number."

"Give me the gun, bitch. You probably don't even know how to use it."

"Ah, there you are," she said, as if she'd just caught a roach in the pantry. "Jacob, is it? Want to find out?"

Her pulse quickened. Why hadn't Sam come in with Ben?

"Ben, is Sam okay?" The trepidation in her voice contradicted the resolve reflected in her eyes.

Sarah rushed toward the kitchen, motioning Jacob back with the gun as she passed him. When she reached the table, she set a hand on her son's shoulder, keeping her eyes on the intruder the entire time. He had followed her in but didn't attempt to approach. She had apparently convinced him that she knew full well how to use the weapon she now brandished.

"Sam, are you okay?" His muscles tensed under her hand, but he didn't answer. She took one more step back so that she could see his face while keeping an eye on Jacob.

"Sam?" Her eyes drifted, pulling her gaze from Jacob to her son. "Sam!"

He was staring straight ahead, at a door on the far wall. She could see that his breathing was calm and regular and he had no apparent injuries. But... her face contorted, confusion and terror sculpting it like clay. Those eyes were not his. They weren't the same beautiful hazel eyes that had strangers declaring he'd be "a heartbreaker" since he'd entered the world. The eyes she was looking into now held no hint of humanity in either color or shape.

The door Sam was staring at creaked, and rhythmic scratching began to rise up from behind it. She jumped back, the gun in her hand swaying from Jacob to the door—which she now recognized as the source of the vibrations that rippled through her skull, as well—and back to Jacob.

"What the hell is going on?" she asked. Though the question was clearly directed at Ben, Sarah's eyes flickered about like the ball in a pinball machine, throwing her gaze between the other occupants of the room.

THIRTY-SEVEN

When the doorbell rang, Jacob raised his gun again, his hand visibly trembling.

"Who the fuck is that? Are you expecting someone?"

Ben pushed his outstretched palms downward, motioning for him to lower the weapon. His eyes pleaded, and his mouth was pinched and strained.

"Please, just lower the gun. It's probably the boy's mother. I can get rid of her. Please."

Jacob shook his head. His mind was racing, and though he felt lucid thanks to several bursts of adrenaline his body had served up since breaching the Thomas home, the pills he'd taken early were lingering, threatening like storm clouds creeping in on a sunny day.

"What if she comes in here? She's gonna see her kid on the floor and start screaming or something." In his head, he continued the thought. *If some bitch starts screaming on top of that scratching, I'm gonna lose my shit and kill them all.*

Ben closed his eyes for a moment, his face chiseled into the image of concentration. Then, his eyes flew open and he waved a hand for Jacob to approach.

"Help me get him into the chair. If he's sitting facing away from her, we might be able to distract her, create the illusion that he's fine."

Jacob puffed air through his nose. It was a stupid idea. The kid would probably slump the moment they set him in the chair. But, whatever. It wasn't like he was coming up with any brilliant ideas, himself. Besides, he had the gun. And that meant he was in control. If the situation got out of hand, he would handle it in whatever way he needed to. He slid the gun into the back of his waistband, making sure to position himself in a way that denied access to the old man. He wasn't overly concerned. He knew that if it came to it, he could overpower Ben. And he was sure the old man knew it. He wouldn't dare risk the kid's life attempting something stupid.

They hooked a hand under each of Sam's armpits and pulled him up onto the chair. The old man whispered to the boy the entire time, telling him everything was going to be okay and explaining what they were going to do step by step while they moved him... as if the kid had any idea of what was going on. He was staring straight on, like a freaking zombie. Jacob made a point of trying to stay out of the boy's line of vision. Eerie sensations that something else was watching through those eyes slithered through him like eels.

Once he was seated, Jacob was surprised at how normal the kid looked from the back. His torso was upright, but not overly stiff. And, from behind, it really did look like he was just sitting there shooting the breeze. From behind, where you couldn't see those cold, reptilian eyes.

Ben walked over and grabbed some kind of paperback

284 ELIZABETH S. DEVECCHI

manual that sat open on the far end of the table. He slid it in front of the boy and stepped back.

"See? It looks like he's reading," he whispered, meeting Jacob's gaze and nodding.

Jacob shrugged and gave a nod. He reached around to retrieve his gun.

"You won't need that," said the old man, motioning for him to leave it where it was. "And, if that is Sam's mom, what do you think she'll think if she sees you standing in my home holding a gun?"

He had a point. Jacob slid the gun back down, took a deep breath, and the two men listened in silence, hoping whoever rang the bell would give up and go away. The front door creaked open. The men looked at each other and then at the boy, synchronized like line dancers.

"Ben? Sam? Are you guys in there?" a woman called out.

Jacob rubbed a hand across his chin, still smooth from his midmorning shave, fighting the instinct to grab his gun. He took a deep breath through his nose, silently released it from his lips, and smiled, transforming himself into the charming, sweet-talking young man that had gotten him out of many a sticky situation. Maybe he wasn't as classically handsome as Jimmy had been, but when he was cleaned up like now, his impish good looks gave him the appearance of a young, ambitious go-getter. A little awkward due to youth and inexperience, but not at all dangerous. The kind of young man you want to give a hand as he makes his way in the world, works his way up the ladder.

And it was working. He almost had her back out the door and on her way home, until the bitch made the Glock tucked into the back of his pants. Not only that, but she'd managed to do it without him noticing. And worse, the bitch had disarmed him. He was seething. Not enough to risk getting shot once it was obvious she knew her way around a firearm, but more than enough to imagine at least a dozen satisfying ways he could make her pay for his humiliation when he regained the advantage... which he was sure he would.

He was imagining her on her knees, begging for her life and that of her child, telling him she'd do anything he asked, when the boy seated at the table turned his head and swept the room with his reptilian glare, pausing first on his mother, then Ben, then Jacob, before continuing back to the door.

"Ben, please tell me what is going on. Is Sam okay?" asked the woman. She went to the boy's side and knelt down next to him.

A sneer snuck onto Jacob's face, prompted by the similarity of her position in his recent daydream. It disappeared when the door rattled and a crack snaked along the frame holding it closed.

Ben placed a hand on the woman's shoulder and motioned for her to stand. Jacob saw that the motion wasn't necessary. She had begun to rise with the sound, gripping the Glock in both hands and training it on the door. He thought about grabbing for it, but it only took one step to realize that her fear of whatever was behind the door was not enough to distract her from keeping an eye on him.

"Get the fuck back," she said, shooting an apologetic glance toward Ben and her son.

Like dropping an F-bomb was the thing that was going to shock them right now. Stupid bitch. Jacob growled.

"There's no time to explain," said Ben.

"Give me the short version," she insisted.

"The creature behind that door is trying to complete a connection with Sam. It must have found him at the stream, in the tunnel down there. Started a bond. It needs to connect to someone to survive and to thrive. It needs someone to bring it food or bring it *to* food. We have to stop it."

She looked from Ben to Jacob, brows furrowed, head shaking. Her inner conflict was etched onto her face for all to see. Jacob had seen that look of concern and fierce protective instinct on his own mother's face when he was young, but it was never displayed for him. Jimmy was the son she'd wanted, the one she would have died to protect. And, if he'd once thought that motherly instinct would transfer to him when he was her only remaining child, he had quickly learned that was not the case.

"What is this *creature*? How do you know so much about it?"

This was a question to which Jacob, too, was dying for an answer. He shifted his weight and turned to face Ben, giving up on disarming the woman for now.

Ben looked down at his feet, shoulders slumped.

"Mary. My Mary was connected with one, bonded to it." His voice was barely audible over the persistent scratching now shaking the door and widening the crack in the frame. The woman stared, open-mouthed, her eyes prodding him to continue his reluctant confession. "It found her when she was a child, before I met her. Before I fell in love with her. By the time I came into the picture, they were a package deal and there was nothing I could do."

The woman looked at the door. She seemed to be processing the information pretty well for someone who had it dropped on her like a rock on a bug. Sure, he was still fuming at the fact that a woman... a little suburban soccer-mom-house-wife... had bested and disarmed him, but the tiniest hint of respect for this badass chick simmered inside him.

"What is it? How do we kill it?"

We, thought Jacob. *I guess we're a team for now.* He tried to stifle a chortle, casting his gaze to the floor when she side-eyed him.

"I only know what Mary told me over the years... when she was truly Mary." The woman squinted at this. "I would call it a kind of parasite, though Mary never did. A species that has been a clandestine, predatory companion to mankind from its beginnings, though mostly in times and places of extreme conflict. Places like where Mary grew up. Where hate and evil acts thrive almost unnoticed. It can survive on small creatures—mammals, reptiles, pretty much anything—but only truly thrives on people. There are cultures of people who believe that the adrenaline from fear tenderizes meat during the slaughter. These creatures prefer their meals tenderized with rage and hatred. And it consumes them from the inside out."

He passed a hand across the stubble on his chin, then through his thinning hair. "After the creature feeds to satisfaction, it goes through a dormant time." Ben bit his lip and shook his head. "Not really dormant, just slower and weaker. That's when Mary was mostly just my Mary."

"Grandpa's sewer dogs," whispered the boy's mother.

"What?" asked Ben, head tilted.

"Nothing," she said, shaking her head.

"Great," Jacob said, remembering how quickly the creature had overtaken first his brother, then him. He laughed and pointed to the door. "Any offers to be the *satisfying meal* that slows that thing down so I can kill it? I say we feed it the old man and shoot the fucker while it's eating."

The woman cast a disparaging look at him and turned her attention back to Ben.

"It eats... people? The *insides* of people?" she asked, but it was less of a question and more of a horrifying affirmation.

Jacob cleared his throat to get her attention and pulled up the front of his shirt, revealing the angry red scar. She gasped and looked back at Ben, her eyes wide.

"And I was lucky," he said, letting his shirt drop. "One of those things tore my brother to shreds."

"Your brother was going to rob us. He pulled a gun on Mary."

Jacob snarled at the old man, starting toward him, then backing off when the woman once again pointed the gun at him. No worries, he could settle all scores once they killed the thing behind the door. He'd waited this long.

THIRTY-EIGHT

Sam listened to them talk, trapped inside himself, seeing for two, a vessel for the goals of one. He was a host, like in the nature books he read, a means to an end. When Mr. Thomas, Mom, and the stranger argued, fought, he salivated unintentionally, and excitement shivered through his body. He felt sick and famished at the same time, trapped and desired.

They were plotting. Sam was torn. He opened his mouth to speak, to tell them he was okay. To ask them to take him away from here.

Sam. Sam, my friend. The voice interrupted before he could speak.

Sam, I need you.

Whisper, go away. You don't belong here. I want you to go away. I don't want to hurt anybody. He was thinking of what Mr. Thomas had told him, sharing his thoughts and change of heart with the creature.

Sam, I won't hurt anyone. I promise. I love you. I only want to help you. You gave me my name. I only want to be your friend.

The words caressed his nerves, calmed his fears. Images of Tyler floated through his mind. Sterilized pictures of his bully's encounter with Whisper, almost cartoonish, followed by the two boys walking home together, then Tyler talking to him at school. Sam's lips curled up into a smile. He was going to meet up with Tyler and Samantha at the stream this weekend, with his friends, his first real friends in his new town. Whisper had made that possible.

Sam, open the door. Please. I need you.

Sam eased out of the chair and walked to the door. From deep inside, his rational self begged for him not to open the door. But that small, nagging portion of him diminished with each step. Whisper needed him. As he walked, the creature continued to reassure him, promised not to hurt anyone.

He reached both hands out, flipping the lights off with one while the other unlocked the door, turned the knob, and pulled. For a moment the room fell silent, then a rush of air and a scaly, slippery weight on his chest as Whisper nestled against him in his arms, his long, sleek, tubular tongue sliding around to the back of his neck. And, a scream.

THIRTY-NINE

They huddled as close as Sarah would allow, for fear of Jacob seeking to grab the gun, she explained. Keeping their backs to Sam so that the creature would have no access through the boy, they devised a plan of action.

Ben told Sarah she needed to physically distance Sam from the creature to break the still-fragile bond. He and Jacob would lift the boy onto her back, to facilitate that. Then the two men would rush the door and go after the creature.

"I'm gonna need the gun," Jacob said, matter-of-fact.

Sarah scoffed. "There is no way on God's green earth I am giving you the gun."

Ben, a physical buffer between them, spread his hands on either side of him, widening the distance. He sighed. "The gun won't be of much use. These creatures are fast. It would be more prudent to arm ourselves with something we can use up close."

"My Glock offers pretty good *up-close* protection," Jacob protested.

"Something that limits *accidentally* killing one of us," added Ben, ignoring the scoff that followed.

Ben edged slowly over to a drawer near the refrigerator and slid it open. He pointed inside and mouthed the word "take a knife" to the other two. He wasn't that thrilled about Jacob having a knife, either, but he supposed the young man had a right to protect himself. Besides, he seemed to understand that they all needed each other, for now. They were reaching in to retrieve knives when the lights went out, casting the room into shadows backlit by the fading sunlight filtering in through the shade over a small window above the kitchen sink.

Sarah screamed, raising the Glock with her right hand while brandishing a seven-inch boning knife with the other.

Ben gasped. He turned to see the creature—whose name he refused to even think, as if doing so would reinforce the link it had with the boy—cradled in Sam's arms. Its tongue was snaking around to the back of his neck.

Jacob stood frozen, the handle of an impressive utility knife grasped in his fist. His piercing blue eyes were wide and fixed and in the cool hues granted by the filtered light, he almost looked like a marble statue. Almost, since Ben could see his bottom lip quivering uncontrollably. And, for a moment, Ben was looking at the boy from the rest area, not the man that had broken into his house.

"Jacob!" he yelled, flipping the closest switch, illuminating the hallway behind them.

He pointed to Sarah, who was on her way to her son, frantically searching for a clear shot at the dark, scaly creature. Its skin glistened bright against the light from the hall, taking on an odd bluish hue where it was instead caressed by the shadows. The young man blinked hard, shook his head, and met Ben's gaze.

"Get off of him," Sarah screamed, kicking at the mass against her son's chest and knocking them both back.

"Shoot the fucking thing," yelled Jacob. "Kill it!"

Ben could see that there was no way she could shoot the creature without risking hitting Sam. She ignored Jacob and kicked again, this time gasping in pain. She'd managed to knock Sam off balance but at the cost of a clean swipe of the creature's claws across her leg. Red stripes flowered across her jeans, meeting and blending together.

"Get the fuck off of him," she shouted, face marked with pain and anger. She delivered another kick.

"Watch out, Sarah!" Ben pointed to Sam's neck. The creature's tongue flicked away from the boy and shot out toward his mother. She stumbled back, sweeping the hand grasping the knife in a wide arc in front of her.

"Damn!" yelled Jacob, who was now moving toward the melee. He paused to watch the midsection of the creature's tongue explode, drops of liquid the color of oil spraying out from the piece still attached, while the sharpened end flopped to the ground.

Sam opened his mouth. An airy screech rushed through his lips, building in volume and combining with a penetrating sound/vibration coming from the creature until it felt like they were all in the center of a hurricane, its howling winds whirling around them. The creature pushed off from the boy's body and skittered back through the door into the garage, with a gargling hiss. Without hesitation, Ben ran over and shoved the door shut with his back, and the room fell silent except for the collective panting of the three adults.

Sam lay still, arms and legs splayed, looking like a discarded puppet. Sarah rushed over and knelt beside him, her injured leg outstretched. She looped a hand under each arm and pulled him up onto her lap as far as she could, sliding his arms and legs into more natural positions as she pulled.

"Shit. You really fucked that thing's tongue up," declared Jacob, approaching mother and son. He stopped just short of them and showed his palms when Sarah glared up at him, Glock still clenched in one hand. "Whoa, don't shoot. I apologize for ever doubting your skills."

"Sarah," said Ben, walking over to stand by Jacob's side. "I have to go after it. It's trapped in the garage, for now. I patched up some holes to the outside earlier, but the concrete hasn't had time to properly cure, so I'm not sure how long it will hold. You need to get Sam out of here."

She looked up at him and nodded, her fierce mother-bear expression melting into one of fear and understanding. She handed Ben the gun. He lodged it into the back of his belt.

"I don't know if I can carry him," she said, looking down at Sam and gently brushing his hair back from his forehead.

She set the boy down on the floor and pulled herself up. The front of her right pant leg was stained red from just below the knee down to the hem. She limped forward a few steps, then back again.

Jacob looked from Sam to Sarah, then directed his attention to Ben. "Can you wait a minute before charging in there? I'll get them out to the front stoop and come right back. I owe that little fucker and its family some payback."

He shifted his gaze to Sarah, who nodded permission. Then he reached down to gather up the boy and they rushed down the hall to the door.

FORTY

Sarah and Sam stood for a moment staring at the Thomas house from the bottom of the front steps. There was no way to describe the relief that Sarah had felt when her son reached out to grab her arm just moments ago on Ben's front stoop and she'd turned to see that his eyes were once again their natural color.

"Who are you?" he'd asked Jacob, squirming to be let down. "Mom, what happened?"

Jacob set him down and took a step back with his hands up. "Okay. Okay, little man. You're down. Now, you and your mom need to get the hell out of here."

Sarah pulled her son into a tight hug, kissed his forehead, and smoothed his hair. Then she looked up at Jacob.

"Thanks for getting him out," she said, giving Sam another squeeze. "We'll be waiting in our house for you guys. Please make sure Ben is okay... that he doesn't do anything stupid."

She had sensed the guilt he carried in his words, seen it in his posture.

Sarah bit her bottom lip, then added, "You be careful, too."

Jacob shrugged and allowed an impish grin to light up his face for a moment.

"You're gonna wanna disinfect that." He nodded toward her leg. Then, without another word, he turned and ran back into the house.

"Where's Mr. Thomas?" asked Sam, rubbing his eyes with his fists and looking around.

"He's taking care of something. He'll come over to the house with"—she paused for a moment, realizing she didn't know Jacob's last name. "With Mr. Jacob, the man who helped me bring you out here when you got dizzy."

He steered a confused gaze to the bottom half of her jeans. "Mom, what happened to your leg?"

"It's nothing." She smiled and shook her head. "I scratched it on something. I'm going to wash it off and put a nice bandage on it when we get home."

No use explaining anything right now. When they were all safe, and when that *thing* was dead, she could worry about what he did or didn't remember. Right now, she needed to get him as far away from this house as possible.

They crossed the street together, Sarah limping and coaxing Sam along. He looked down while he walked, dragging his feet. The poor kid was visibly exhausted.

"Come on, buddy. Let's get you home and to bed." She reached over and gave him a gentle pat on the back of the neck.

He flinched and ducked away, and when Sarah pulled her hand back, there was blood on her palm. Sam looked at her hand, then reached around and felt the nape of his neck. He rested his hand there, squinting so hard his eyes were nearly closed, as if he were trying to force his eyes inward to see some-thing inside his head.

"Whisper," he said so faintly she almost missed it. He looked up at her. "Whisper." This time louder. "I have to go back there. Whisper will hurt them."

"No," said Sarah, taking hold of his wrist and moving his hand so that she could get a look at his neck. She exhaled and mouthed the words "thank you" to the sky when she saw what looked like a cat scratch. Yes, it was bleeding, but a quick rub with the collar of his shirt verified that it was just a flesh wound.

"Mom, you don't understand. He *wants* to hurt them. He showed me. Mr. Thomas killed his brothers and sisters." He looked up at her, brows furrowed. "Don't worry. I know he had to do it. But, if Whisper hurts him, it will be my fault." His eyes glistened with tears that fought to be released.

Sarah leaned down to eye level and put a hand on each of his shoulders.

"None of this is your fault." He shook his head. She caressed his cheek and leaned in closer. "Sam. None of this is your fault. Mr. Thomas knows what to do. He said you need to be away from that thing so he can take care of it. And I agree."

Sam looked down at the grass. He brought the side of his thumb to his mouth, pressing it against his teeth, then pulled it away, letting his shoulders slump.

"Mom?"

Sarah pulled in a breath. His hesitant tone spooked her.

"What is it, sweetie?" she said, forcing calm into her own voice.

"I think Whisper was trying to hide something from me." He brought his hand to his forehead, pressing his thumb to his temple, while the rest of his fingers rubbed the skin above his eyebrows. "I think it was something important. Something I need to tell Mr. Thomas. But it's like there's a wall in my mind or a locked door..."

A shot sounded from the direction of the garage, causing both of them to jump.

FORTY-ONE

The moment he was alone, Ben walked to the back of the kitchen and rifled through a drawer next to the stovetop, the one Mary liked to call their *everything drawer*. He pulled out the long flexible lighter he used to light his grill. On his way to the garage door, Jacob joined him.

"The kid woke up when we got outside. He and the bit-... his mom... are heading to their house. She wants us to go over there when we're done."

Ben nodded, lips pinched, eyes focused on the door to the garage.

"Why don't you wait here? When you hear me yell 'run,' get the hell out of here and get the hell out of town. Leave Sarah and her family alone."

Jacob's brows climbed, then furrowed. He shifted his gaze down to the lighter clasped in Ben's right hand.

"What the fuck are you going to do with that?" he asked, waving a hand toward the lighter, then locking eyes with Ben. "You gonna blow the place up?"

"I think I know where it's hiding," said Ben. "It's too fast to shoot. But maybe I can trap it in there, burn it in its nest. Burn down the whole place if necessary".

"I need to know that thing is dead and gone. I need to *see* it. Give me the gun. Tell me where it is," said Jacob, extending a hand.

Ben took a step back and passed a hand across his chin, his gaze locked on Jacob's eyes. He owed the kid, the one he'd abandoned in the rest area lot in favor of getting Mary out of there. Sure, he'd called for help, but the time it had taken him to get his wife back into the van, to drive to the first pay phone, that time could have cost the boy his life. Still, he didn't trust Jacob to leave Sarah alone. He'd seen the rage in those frosty blue eyes when she disarmed him.

Jacob seemed to sense the problem. "I'm not gonna go after her," he said, waving a hand behind him toward the front hall. "For all I know, she'll be calling the cops as soon as she sees me leave the house, with or without you. Let's go kill that thing. Then I'll maybe load up on some stuff as payment for helping you deal with your little pet. Old people have the best meds... and don't you still hide money and jewels and shit like that in mattresses?"

Ben let out a short laugh, despite himself. He took a deep breath, pulled the gun from his belt, and reluctantly handed it to Jacob, who set down the knife he was holding in favor of his trusted gun. Once he had the Glock, Jacob slid his finger along the LCI, the loaded chamber reassuring him as much as any pacifier ever had a crying infant.

"Let's go," said Jacob, grabbing the door handle.

"Wait," Ben said, going back to the everything drawer. He pulled out another lighter and handed it to Jacob. "If it gets ahold of me, light up the garage. It's packed with boxes and there are propane and gas tanks inside, so it'll go up pretty quickly. Light it and get the hell out."

Jacob nodded, pushing the lighter into his pocket. Then he licked his lips and let them curl into a devilish grin. Gripping the Glock with both hands, he motioned for Ben to open the door.

When the door opened, silence greeted them from the garage. Ben entered first, slipping to the side and flipping the light switch. He cursed himself for not having replaced the dim bulbs yet.

"What's up with the lights?" whispered Jacob. "Isn't there another switch you can flip? I can barely see in here."

"We kept the light low for Princess. They aren't fans of bright lights. I think it's been taking advantage of the storm sewers to get around outside during the day, but I found a nest in here. I was going to change the lightbulbs, then other stuff came up."

"Hmmm," said Jacob, the sound coming out like a guttural growl. "That would have been helpful."

Ben shrugged and pointed to the far wall. "The door over there leads to the small garage. There's another light in there. It's closed, but I think there's at least one hole somewhere in the drywall connecting the two areas. I sealed the holes I found in the outer walls. Hopefully, there aren't any I missed, but I can't be sure."

"Fantastic," mumbled Jacob. "Where's this nest you found?" He took a couple steps forward, training the gun on every creak and rustle, real and imagined.

"In a camper van parked in the small garage." Ben looked down at his feet and shook his head in an attempt to ward off memories. He needed to be firmly in the present for this. "We had a compartment for Princess in there. I found fresh signs of use and the door wasn't secured."

"Let's go, then." Jacob motioned with the gun for Ben to proceed to the door.

The memory of Jacob's brother holding what was maybe even the very same gun to Mary's head coursed through Ben's mind. He bit his bottom lip hard to refocus.

I need to stay in the present. I need to finish this, to protect Sam.

They walked to the door, careful to scan the area around them as they went. Ben told Jacob to stay a few strides behind so that he would have more time to react if something happened. He included instructions *not* to worry about hitting him if he had a shot at the creature.

"And burn the camper, please. No matter what. The fire station isn't far from here. I trust they'll have anything we start out before it gets too far into the house or threatens neighboring homes."

Jacob nodded, his face serious and somber. Not what Ben would have expected a mere few hours ago when he seemed eager to end Ben's life to avenge his brother.

When they reached the small door on the far wall, Ben took hold of the knob and waved Jacob around to the business side of the door. Once he was in place, Jacob gave a nod and raised the Glock, gripping the gun with both hands. Ben nodded, revealing the knife he had taken from the drawer, a silver carving knife with a dark handle he was now gripping so tightly his knuckles practically glowed in the dim light.

Ben took a deep breath, turned the knob, and pulled the door open. When nothing came at them, both men released their breath in an audible, synchronized rush of air. They stepped into the smaller garage one behind the other, not bothering to close it. If the creature was in here, it had to have come through its own entrance. Closing the door would only make it harder for them to get out quickly if so needed. Though Ben had no intention of leaving.

Ben reached up and pulled the string dangling down just inside the garage, bathing everything in a soft yellow glow. This side of the garage was slightly more illuminated, due to the small size of the room and the reflective nature of the orange paint on the camper van parked inside. But, that very camper and the piles of boxes set around it also offered endless places to hide.

As expected, the door to the camper was not secure. It sat ajar, just as Ben had left it the last time he'd been to the camper to investigate. He wasn't sure why he hadn't just closed it. Perhaps this was due to the nagging feeling that he had closed the door when he and Mary parked it here for the last time. Finding it open yet again, after knowing for sure he'd closed it, would have had implications, allowed for possibilities that he hadn't been prepared to accept.

Before getting any closer to the vehicle, Jacob got down on all fours and looked underneath.

"You got your phone, old man?"

Ben nodded and produced a cell phone from his pocket.

"Put on the flashlight and shine it under the van."

Ben powered up the phone and put it into flashlight mode, thinking to himself that this young man was pretty sharp. Too bad he'd gone down the road he had. Ben frowned, wondering how many of those bad decisions had been results of the trauma he'd been through as a child. Then he reminded himself of the role model that child was with at the rest area.

"All clear," said Jacob, standing and brushing off his knees.

Ben stepped up to the camper, put his knife in the hand with the phone, and grabbed onto the sliding door handle. He gave Jacob a here-goes-nothing tilt of his head, complete with a brow lift, and pulled the door open.

A box fell out and both men jumped back. Ben trained the beam of light on it, sending shadows scurrying across the floor. Jacob reached a foot out and kicked it. The box slid across the floor, spilling out its contents.

"Almost wasted a shot on a fucking box," Jacob whispered, shaking his head.

"I don't remember that being there," said Ben, illuminating the container and the items now strewn out next to it. "I was out here earlier, and I don't remember that being here."

He leaned closer. The box was worn, and flecks of dirt caked its surface. Something was written near the open side. Though it was almost completely covered by the top flap of cardboard bent back on that side, he could see that it was scribbled out in Mary's pointed handwriting. He lifted the flap and directed the light onto the words "Princess's things."

"Impossible," he whispered. He had buried that box out in the garden when Mary had taken a turn for the worse, afraid that a visiting nurse might happen upon it. Had she gone out to retrieve it before she died?

"What is it?" asked Jacob, craning his neck to get a look. He gave the box another nudge, spilling out more of its contents, and gasped.

Spread out before them was an array of watches, chains, rings, and other jewelry. With his gun stretched in front of him, and his eyes scanning the space around them, Jacob shot a quick glance at the pile of valuables and reached down to pick up a thick silver ring with a green stone.

"Shine the light here," he said, elbowing Ben.

Ben did as instructed. Both men looked at the inside of the ring, at the inscription *Jimmy #25*. Ben turned to Jacob. Some of the ballsy spunk had melted away from his expression, and he thought he saw the glimmer of a tear in the young man's eye, though it was hard to tell in the dim-lit room. His rage, however, was glaring. From the turn of his lips to the angle of his brows, diving toward each other as if to brawl, the anger that consumed him was on full display.

Ben cinched his brows. He took the knife back into a shaky right hand and did a sweep of the floor around them with the flashlight, brandishing the blade at an awkward angle.

"What?" asked Jacob, clutching the ring and looking around nervously.

"I thought I saw something."

"Shit!" yelled Jacob, doubling over. Jimmy's ring slid from his hand, bouncing on the cement with a sharp *ping*.

Ben dropped his phone, plunging them back into the pale yellow light. He lay a hand on Jacob's shoulder.

"Are you alright? What happened?"

Jacob clutched at his gut. He straightened himself as best he could, moaning with the effort, then swallowed hard and lifted the front of his shirt, his eyes gray and spent.

"You're injured," hissed Ben, when the skin under Jacob's shirt was revealed.

The scar was pulsating, and at its mid-point the flesh had opened up into an almost perfect circle. Blood and puss oozed from it.

"Did it bite you just now?" asked Ben, his hesitant voice

reflecting his confusion. He thought he'd seen a dark shadow skitter by, but nowhere near where Jacob was standing.

"No," said Jacob, a bitter edge in his tone. "This is what *your* pet did to me. *Princess.*"

Ben stared at the wound. It wasn't possible. If Princess had made that wound all those years ago, it would only react that way in *her* presence. And Princess was dead. She'd bonded with Mary, *completely.* Mary said they were one. Mary swore she couldn't survive without Princess, and Princess couldn't survive without her. Ben was struck with the sudden realization that basing his knowledge on what Mary, more and more a simple vessel for Princess, had told him was like counting on a thief in your home to give you an inventory of what he'd stolen.

Ben stumbled back, reaching down to grab the phone which rested on the floor of the garage, glowing in a halo of its own light. He directed the flashlight beam into the camper, and onto a grotesque face he had last seen the day before his wife died. The hand holding the knife shot toward her, but she was faster. His shock had slowed him, given her time to prepare and to calculate. And she wasn't young and inexperienced like Whisper. She was a polished, professional killer. An expert on the human race, thanks to her time with Mary and their travels. She slipped past him.

Before he could turn, he heard the nauseating slurp he had heard so many times, when Mary was alive. The same sound he'd heard in the rest area years ago, moments after Jacob's brother drew his gun and again when the creature went after young Jacob. A shot rang out and a dark hole opened on the side of the camper where the bullet penetrated its happy orange skin.

The sound of the discharge surged through Ben's head,

setting his ears ringing with a high-pitched hum that had the benevolent side-effect of covering the sound of Princess helping herself to Jacob's insides. Ben spun around. The first thing he saw was the hand that had fired the gun. The hand that still gripped the firearm but was no longer attached to the man that had fired it. Ben willed himself away from regret and fear, to resolve. He had seen horrific scenes like this many times, but seeing it happen to someone for whom he had some sympathy, even if it came from a place of guilt, was different.

By the looks of it, he didn't have much time. He knew attacking the creature directly would only hasten his own death. And though he fully expected to die here, he needed his death to mean something. He needed to atone, to protect Sam and his family, as well as any others who might have the misfortune to encounter Princess or Whisper, or whatever names they may be given. He knew the knife could not penetrate the skin of a fully grown and developed adult, like Princess, and that he had no time to search the garage for her offspring, scratching at the walls somewhere on the other side of the camper.

He placed the knife down just inside the camper and lifted two plastic five-gallon gas containers that sat next to the front tire of the VW. Relief washed over him at the weight of them. He'd set them there, intending to top off the tank before Mary's illness, and was happy to discover that, though they weren't full, they both still contained a fair amount of gas. Careful to make as little noise as possible, he unscrewed the top of each and turned them onto their sides, letting their precious contents flow out across the floor.

He threw a reluctant glance in Princess's direction, not wanting to witness any more than necessary, while making sure she remained distracted. She was still on top of Jacob's now motionless body. Her body stiffened slightly, perhaps at the smell of the gasoline, then relaxed onto her prey, now visibly depleted.

No time to spare. Ben slipped into the camper, ready to finish what he had started. He reached into his pocket for the lighter, his hand brushing against another object on the way. His cellphone. He didn't remember shoving it back into his pocket, but there it was, flashlight still beaming, just visible though the material of his pant leg. He pulled it out and turned it on. After extinguishing the flashlight, he tapped out and sent a quick text, then set the phone on the camper's sink. Then he reached over and opened the stove. He could almost smell Mary's stew cooking over the propane flame, as he turned both knobs to release the gas from the double burners. He took a deep breath in through his nose but smelled nothing.

The safety valve, his mind screamed. *The safety valve is closed!*

For a moment, a feeling of defeat threatened to overwhelm him. He was exhausted, and the valve was on the other side of the camper. Then, he focused his thoughts on Sam. Smart, inquisitive Sam, who was going to be some kind of naturalist. Who still needed to go to school, to make friends, to find love. Sam, who needed to grow up without the burden he and Mary had carried for so many years.

Ben left the knobs turned and slipped out the sliding door. He worked his way around to the other side of the camper to the propane tank tucked underneath and opened the safety valve. The camper swayed. Something had either climbed into it or bumped against it. He leaned down and looked underneath. There was no sign of Princess on the other side.

Ben took a deep breath, steadied himself, and crept back to the front of the camper. He peeked around the corner, where only remnants of the man who had accompanied him into the garage remained. He exhaled with a gasp. Closing his eyes, he concentrated on a scraping sound, barely audible over the ringing in his ears. To his horror, it sounded like it was coming from the direction of the door. He darted around the camper and stood outside its gaping door, fumbling for the lighter in his pocket.

When he held it up to find the trigger, his eyes caught a movement to his right. It was Princess and she was coming for him, slowed considerably by the meal she had consumed, but also strengthened after so many months most likely surviving on rabbits, mice, and squirrels. She purred when she saw that he was looking at her. Purred and fashioned her blood-spattered face into what almost looked like a smile.

Ben slid his finger onto the trigger of the lighter and rolled his thumb across the small rough wheel for maximum flame height. Then, he faced the creature that had taken so much from the love of his life, so much from them both, and looked it in the eyes. A faint odor of rotten eggs tickled Ben's nostrils.

"This is for Mary," he said, pressing the safety and clicking the lighter to life, then turning to thrust the flame into the camper.

FORTY-TWO

The gunshot startled Sarah, but also lifted her hopes. She guided Sam over to the front stoop of their house and hugged him to her, watching for Ben and Jacob to appear in the doorway of the Thomas home.

"I still feel him," whispered Sam, nestling against her.

Sarah shook her head. "Maybe that takes a while to go away," she said, pushing his bangs away from his eyes. "You know, like when you're sick and get better, but still have a cough or stuffy nose."

An explosion shook the Thomas house, sending a jackhammer of shock waves slamming into Sarah and Sam and knocking them over. The smaller of the two garage doors bowed out, causing the panels to separate with the scream of twisting metal. Sam stood up and reached down to help his mother.

"Call 911," she said, pushing him toward their house. "Just tell them there's been an explosion and give them the address. Then stay in the house."

Another, louder explosion blew the windows out on the

side of the garage, and flames licked out and up, hungry for oxygen. Sam stood mesmerized.

"Go!" Sarah yelled.

He fished his cell phone from his pocket and speed-walked toward the house. Sarah took a few cautious steps in the other direction, toward Ben's house. It looked like the damage was all on the garage side. Maybe, if she went to the front door, she could see if they'd made it in there. Maybe they were injured and needed her help.

She crossed the street, hoping they would come out the front door, tell her everything was okay, that the thing was dead. Behind her, she could hear Sam yelling their address over the ringing in her ears. Shadows danced around the house, puppets thrown about by the flickering flames in the dusky light of another passing day. Neighbors were starting to come out of their homes, and Sarah was certain Sam's was not the only call to 911.

When the shadow brushed past her, mingling with fluttering leaves and forms projected by the light cast by a fire that now consumed most of the outside of the garage, she almost missed it. Almost, but for the sharp smell that accompanied it. The putrid scent of burnt flesh and gasoline. It dashed past her, toward her house, toward Sam.

She turned and saw the creature skittering across the street toward her son. Instead of fleeing, he straightened and walked toward it, as if in a trance. And, though she couldn't see from where she stood, Sarah knew his eyes were no longer his own.

"Sam!" she called, in an attempt to break the spell. It was the only thing she could think to do. There was no way she could reach him before the creature did.

Whisper climbed into his arms, nestled against his chest.

When Alvis slammed into them, it took Sarah a minute to understand what had just happened.

"Mom, what's going on?" Christina stood on the front stoop with the door wide open.

The dog must have slipped past her.

Sam lay on the ground, Alvis in front of him, hackles up, growling and gnashing his teeth at the darkness. The dog barked, then took off down the sidewalk, snarling. Sarah ran to Sam's side. Christina took off after Alvis, calling his name.

"Christina! Come back!" Sarah felt a good strong pulse on Sam's wrist, then pushed herself up and went after her daughter.

When she reached her about a block away, fire trucks and police cars whooshed past, sirens blaring, bathing them in hues of red and blue. Christina was standing on the sidewalk holding Alvis's collar. Both were panting.

"Mom, he chased something into the storm drain! Reached his head right in! It looks like he got a piece of it, too. We might need to take him to the vet, though. He has a pretty nasty scratch on his side." Christina doubled over and rested her free hand on her knee, blowing out a rush of air, exchanging it for the fresh supply she sucked in through her nose. "Do you think it was a raccoon?"

Sarah didn't answer. She pulled Christina in for a hug, reaching a hand down to pat the top of Alvis's head at the same time.

"Mom, chill. I'm fine. What happened to Mr. Thomas's house? Is he okay?"

They both looked up the street at the smoke billowing up from the house, reflecting streaks of red and blue. Sounds of excitement and confusion mixed with the rushing of water, clicks, and whirs, and radios filled the air.

"I hope so," was all she could coax from inside.

When they got back to the house, Sam was sitting on the front steps waiting. He motioned for Sarah to lean closer.

"He's gone," he whispered into her ear. "Really gone. I can't feel him anymore."

She instructed the kids to go inside and pulled out her phone to call Greg. He was most likely on his way home from work by now. When the phone lit up, she saw that there was a text from Ben.

Mountain lions. We stopped an attack. Trapped in the garage. Shot sparked. Propane leak. No fluff ;) My best to Sam.

FORTY-THREE

A few weeks later, after Ben's funeral and the conclusion of a variety of investigations, the neighborhood quieted down again. The occasional reporter still poked around trying to get yet another angle on the story that Sarah had so eloquently, if a bit deceitfully, written out for her paper, earning her a ticket out of Fluffsville. Her leg was healing nicely, as was Alvis's side. Hardly anything remained of the scratch on Sam's neck.

Of course, there still was the matter of Ben's friend, who had perished alongside him in the fire. Sarah had given them the first name of the man who had helped save their lives when she and Sam had inadvertently come between a mother mountain lion and her cubs.

"Mom, I didn't see it clearly, but that thing Alvis went after was definitely *not* a mountain lion," Christina had protested.

And in this case, Sarah ultimately decided that she preferred letting both kids in on the lie over lying to either. She was still deciding on whether or not to tell Greg. The children thought it would be better to hold off on that, given how crazy it all sounded. And, this was fine with Sarah. She didn't feel bad about keeping something from someone who was still working to gain back trust after his own dishonesty. All in good time.

Anyhow, she'd told the police the name she'd heard Ben yell in the heat of the moment. But, nobody knew exactly who *Jacob* was. A distant relative, maybe, Evelyn Whistler guessed. Ben wasn't exactly known for being open about his past.

The biggest surprise that came from the incident—monsters aside—was the discovery that Ben had altered his will a mere day before his demise. After a quick note expressing his happiness at "finding his people," after Mary passed, he'd left all his earthly belongings to Sam and Tyler, with a special provision that Sam receive the camera and all its accessories. It wouldn't be a huge amount after the cost of home repairs and probate, but a nice start on a college fund for a young man who, at the ripe old age of eleven, had already decided on a research project for his doctorate. Though, Sarah was not in agreement with the subject, given its dangerous nature.

———

"COME ON, ALVIS," said Sarah, sighing at what seemed like his millionth stop on their morning walk.

Alvis, tail tightly curled, gazed up at her with his dark, soulful eyes before picking up a trot. He walked a dozen steps, then veered before she was able to get him to the crosswalk, a mere five steps away, to cross. Then, he tugged toward the street. Sarah set her feet to keep him out of the quiet neighborhood road. Quiet or not, this was not a habit she wished to encourage.

A car rolled up to the crosswalk and stopped. The driver's side window descended and a woman poked her head out, a friendly smile gracing her lips.

"You guys can cross there if you want," she said, leaning an arm out and giving a slight wave with her hand. "I have a dog just like him at home. Stubborn as all get out."

Sarah smiled back and waved. "Thank you," she said, relaxing the leash and stepping into the road with Alvis.

When they were almost to the other side, the dog veered toward the storm drain, poking his head inside and sniffing about. After his inspection, Alvis lifted his head and hopped up onto the sidewalk, tail wagging. Sarah saw the woman in the car giggle at his antics.

"Yeah," she said, laughing and waving toward the car. "He likes to inspect all the storm drains for monsters. You never can be too careful."

THE CREATURE

The light hits my eyes. I seal them shut. Did anyone see?

I don't think so, but I need to be aware. I need to hear, to feel the vibrations.

The space under the front porch is ample, yet concealed. The porch itself is old, but not decrepit. It is solid. The earthy scents of before, of that which once was, encased and preserved in the settling foundation, fill me. They attach themselves to my skin, a comfortable film that marks me as one of their own. Cast out, I have found the perfect home, my very first.

Not really cast out ... liberated, ripened, and released.

"A fruit cannot stay on the vine forever. Its seeds must seek out fresh terrain." The advice of a mother, a creator. Words loaded with the knowledge that not every seed will take.

I am one of many, spread out into the world. My travels through tunnels have led me here. I will take.

My eyelids slide open, palpebral tertia in place to block any shine. There is no more light to block. No excited cries, no flashlights, I am humbled but unnoticed.

My new home provides me with basic nourishment, but I will need more. I will need connection if I am to survive. And, I will. I feel it deep in my being. She has prepared me. Her show of vicious rage spurred me forward and away, but her intentions did not escape me. I know that she is confident. Our line will continue.

Footsteps pull my attention outward. Dawn begins to melt shadows. I will need to recede, but there is still time. I let the sounds guide my eyes to a pair of feet just beyond the edge of the porch. I am hungry and eager. I assess.

They are small and alone. They are nude, clothed only in the shades of the earth around them. I can see a roll of blue cloth just above the ankles. This is a child. I know from observation, from training, that every choice has its advantages and disadvantages.

I recall the final days before release.

"*A child is a long-term guarantee. I found mine young. We have grown together.*" *A hint of nostalgia in Mother's voice.* "*The young are fresh and trusting, require cultivation. Successful connection proves deep and bountiful, but you must be sure they stay silent and you must not startle them.*"

"*We know. We know.*" *The chorus of inexperienced youth, the next generation. We were impatient.*

A snarl and gnashing. "*You know nothing!*"

I start with a whisper, a suggestion.

"Will you be my friend?"

I know that, if I am successful, these feet will bring me everything I need. I know that, if we connect, I will flourish. We will flourish. I am hungry.

"Will you be my friend?"

The feet move closer to the porch. I retreat deep into the

shadows. This is a critical moment. The feet are joined by hands. Then, a small face. I examine its eyes. There is no fear, no anger, no experience. They are dark and deep. They are brimming with life, with curiosity, tinged with a hint of sorrow. They are perfect.

"Who are you? What are you doing under my porch?" I check a box. It lives here. "Where are you?" It peers into the darkness.

Does it realize it is looking right at me? Can it see me? It must. I feel a connection. Mother told us about this part. It is sublime. My voice turns to silk, reaching out, finessing, cajoling.

"Will you be my friend? I am alone. I am afraid. I am different. You mustn't tell anyone I am here. They will not understand. Will you be my friend?"

The child crawls closer, its fingertips come to rest at the edge of the shadows.

"I think I see you. Don't be afraid. I won't hurt you. I'm new here. I don't have any friends, either."

My heart and my hunger quicken together. I calm myself. Eagerness is an enemy.

"What is your name?" Identity, it is the bridge.

Offer it to me.

"Max. What's yours?"

I receive these words with reverence. I breathe them in. They are a gift.

"I have no name, Max. You may name me if you wish."

We lock eyes. I have drifted forward without realizing. I halt myself. I must not breach the shadows until our initial connection is well established.

"Oh, that's sad." Innocence writhes around each word. It

almost overpowers me, igniting a yearning I have never felt before. I am hungry. "What about Shadow? Do you like that name?"

I approve. We belong to each other.

"Are you hungry, Shadow? I can bring you something from the pantry."

"Yes, very." That which comes from the pantry will not satisfy me, but offerings must be accepted to build trust and will draw in meager sustenance to hold hunger at bay until I can finish what I started.

I peek out from the dark, our gazes lock. Max does not recoil. A smile spreads across the small, dirt-smudged face before me.

"I'm not allowed to have any pets."

"I won't tell anyone." I will be much more loyal than any pet.

"You are way cooler than a dog. What do you eat?"

"I like to feed on anger," I admit, perhaps too soon, omitting methods and means. "Do you know anger?"

Max cringes.

Am I going too far, too fast?

"Max! Where the hell are you? Get your ass back in here!" Max shrinks, not away, but toward me.

"That's my dad. He's always angry."

I sigh. "I would love to meet him, Max."

ACKNOWLEDGMENTS

The initial idea for this book was sparked by an incident that occurred while walking our quirky rescue dog, Dante. But, the distance between that idea and this published book was spanned by sweat, tears and support. The realization of this dream—one I put off for way too long—could not have happened without the encouragement of my family, friends, and fellow writers I have met along the way. I am grateful for each and every one of them and their willingness to give honest opinions, as well as the occasional nudge when necessary.

Thanks to all the teachers and professors, in the US, France, and Italy, who pushed me out of my comfort zone and taught me to keep getting up, dusting myself off, and moving forward even when a goal seemed unreachable. And, a special kind of thank you to anyone who discouraged me, told me I couldn't do something, and ended up lighting a fire in my belly —whether or not they meant to.

Finally, a special thanks to Becky Lawrence and Lauren Daniels who, from opposite sides of the world, kept me writing. And, to Patrick and everyone else at Wicked House Publishing who had a hand in polishing things up so that my work could shine.

Elizabeth S Devecchi spent her formative years in Rhode Island, setting out after high school to travel and gather degrees. She holds a BA in French from Wittenberg University (pursued in part at the Université Paul-Valéry in Montpelier, France), a Law Degree from the Università di Torino in Turin, Italy, and an L.LM in International Law, from The University of Iowa College of Law.

Though she writes in a variety of genres and styles, Elizabeth has had a particular interest in horror since first stumbling into her parents' basement, mechanical room library and getting her hands on such classics as *Jaws*, *The Omen*, *Audrey Rose*, and *The Amityville Horror*.

She currently resides in Colorado with her family, where she plays tennis, frequents book clubs, and makes many focaccias in her free time.

Find out more about her past and future projects at
www.elizabethdevecchi.com.
Follow her on Facebook, Instagram, or LinkedIn.

Made in the USA
Monee, IL
22 September 2024

65697271R00194